CR

DI063822

RIVER CIRCUS

RIVER CIRCUS

WEST LATHROP

Illustrated by Dick Dodge

THE JUNIOR LITERARY GUILD and
RANDOM HOUSE
New York

CONTENTS

1

AN UNEXPECTED MEETING

Sometimes, even in the daylight, it was difficult to see the sky. The trees grew high and black and close together above the narrow paths. Now and then as a path crossed the tote road, there would be an open stretch of tree stumps and here Rush and the wolf-dog Shal would rest and warm themselves in the sun. More often Rush slept, his head pillowed in Shal's heavy ruff while the dog remained awake, listening. . . . The faintest of sounds brought her ears upright, whether it was the scratch of a partridge's foot beneath the pines, squirrels playing in the brush, or the cry of a loon on a nearby lake. The creak of an oxcart's advancing wheels always brought an ominous growl of warning and then the two would remain hidden until the cart had passed. It was a strange shadowy sort of existence —but Rush, for the first time since his father died, felt contented, even happy.

It was now three days since they left Eau Claire, following the Chippewa River westward. The Wisconsin noons were warm but the nights were cold. Crusts of ice still skimmed the ruts of the paths and roads, and patches of snow lay in the hollows. It seemed unsafe to build large fires so they ate their beef and beans scarcely warmed, washed down with spring water, and slept together as close as possible. In a little while Rush believed they would reach the Great River—the Mississippi. As he looked from a distance there was an increasing number of barges and rafts on the Chippewa and hardly an hour passed that he did not hear voices calling and the creak of a sweep-oar as it swung between its tholepins. As always, everyone was eager, hurrying to reach the Mississippi. And as his own distance shortened, it was all Rush could think and talk about.

"My mother went down the Mississippi from Clinton to St. Louis," he told Shal as they rested in an open space during the noon of the third day. "Four hundred miles! Of course it was a long time ago. The boat was named *Adventure*, a big white and gold side-wheel, not like these old scows on the Chippewa. There was a captain and a pilot— what's the matter, Shal? Did you hear something?"

Shal had suddenly risen to her feet, her head lifted and her black nose quivering. Motionless, she waited, brown pine needles still clinging to the heavy fur on her hind legs as she strained to catch some warning sound. And then a low rumble in her throat and a quick glance from her amber-brown eyes back to Rush was sufficient.

"All right—over here, Shal."

Beneath the pines, it was cool and dark. Little shafts of sunlight cut the dense gloom in a few places and a bluejay frightened by their approach rose with a wild screech into the sky above.

"We must be nearer the path than I thought," Rush whispered softly and laid himself flat on the ground beside Shal. "Is it someone walking? I don't hear any wheels—"

Shal, tense and alert, crouched as though ready to spring but made no sound. It was several minutes before Rush was conscious of another person's presence, the head and shoulders of a man carrying a light pack slowly following the trail some three hundred feet away. Because of a thicket which separated them, it was impossible to see more. However, the dip and sway of the shoulders made it evident that the man limped. It was also evident that he wore glasses with steel rims as they flashed in the rays of the sun. The walk and glasses were familiar—strangely familiar—and Rush held his breath as he stared. Could it be Len Slocum, the teacher at Eau Claire? School had finished in early May. It was now June and Len often walked home to see his mother who lived in a little town to the southwest. Perhaps he had made his visit and was returning to Eau Claire. Shal was slowly moving her tail— this was no enemy—it was a friend—Len Slocum.

"Mr. Slocum! Mr. Slocum!"

It was Shal who reached Len Slocum first. Her great

white body cleared the thicket in one leap, and bounding over the rough clearing, she gave little short barks of delight. Startled, Len Slocum had turned and met the dog face on, one hand reaching for the pistol at his belt. When Rush drew near he was petting Shal, his face still showing surprise and bewilderment.

"Rush—Rush Taylor! What are you doing here? If I hadn't heard Shal bark I would have thought she was a wolf! Good girl, Shal. My, I'm glad to see you both! Is Delos with you?"

"No—no, sir. He came a little way. . . . I'm glad to see you, Mr. Slocum. I wanted to say good-bye to you but—"

"To say good-bye? But where are you going, Rush?" and Len straightened his glasses and his brown eyes narrowed as he gazed at the boy and dog before him. "What has happened? You are leaving Eau Claire?"

"Yes, sir. We're going away for the summer. Delos thought I should leave. He may join us later. I hope I can find work on some boat on the Mississippi. You understand, don't you, Mr. Slocum? Things have changed—"

"I know—I know," and there was sudden compassion in Len Slocum's voice and eyes. "It's been hard since your father died. Haven't you any relatives somewhere?"

"No, sir—only my stepuncle, Mr. Burton. And he's no blood relation—"

"For which you can be thankful," interrupted Len quickly.

"It's a long time since I've seen him. He's away most of the time and does his business through his lawyer, Mr. Bissett. I don't like him—"

"Another scamp," and Len shook his head slowly. "Bissett would sell his teeth to make a dollar. Has he been bothering you?"

"Yes, sir—that is—he keeps coming to Delos' cabin to see me. He'd like to make Mr. Burton my guardian. They're after the timberlands my grandfather left me. Are you in a hurry, Mr. Slocum? If I could just talk to you a little—"

"I've always got time for you, Rush. Matter of fact, I was planning to rest when you called. Over there by the trees? You'll never know how surprised I was to see Shal come leaping after me."

"I guess she knew you before I did. Her tail began to wag and when I called, off she went. Sit here, Mr. Slocum. Shal, on guard. Keep watching."

Shal moved away and crouched flat in some brush, her head toward the road. Len gazed after her as he lowered himself to the ground and fixed his lame leg into a comfortable position.

"What a dog! I can see her now, waiting for you in the play yard under the big pine. She was like a clock—always knew when school was out."

"She's smart," and there was a pleased expression on Rush's face. "I don't know what I'd do without her," and then his face sobered. "Someone took a shot at her last week and Delos and I think it was Mr. Bissett. She doesn't like him—barks and growls at him when he comes. That's one of the big reasons why I'm leaving."

"Well!" and Len's brown eyes shone indignantly behind the glasses. "Things have come to a pretty pass! Did he hit her?"

"Nicked her ear. It's all healed now. He told Delos that

some dog has been stealing his chickens and now he's probably saying it's Shal."

"Is that why you're walking and not riding by boat?"

"Yes, sir. Shal attracts attention. There's not another dog like her and she'd be easy to trace. Mr. Bissett might send someone after us. He might even come himself—" and Rush's voice lowered to a whisper, showing the strain he had suffered the past three days. Len Slocum removed his cap and dried his forehead with a handkerchief, concern showing in his lean scholarly face.

"Delos told me of some short cuts," continued Rush. "Perhaps, by now, it might be safe to ask a ride. I've a little money in case there's no work."

"It should be safe enough now."

"And while I'm gone, Mr. Slocum, will you keep an eye on Delos? I don't want him to get into trouble—"

"I'll drop in and see him—often. He's a fine old man. He worked for your father a good many years, didn't he?"

"Before I was born. I've lived with him five years now. It isn't easy to leave him. But he's worried about me. You see, if I was hurt—and died—my stepuncle would be the next of kin and inherit the timberlands. That's the way the law reads. So it seems best for me to disappear—for a while. Judge Adams would help but he's very sick and no one can see him. So Delos is going to say I've gone away and he doesn't know where."

"You've never been on the Mississippi, have you?"

"No, sir. I've been studying boats though, getting ready."

"What will you do on a boat?"

"Anything they'll give me to do. Of course they'll have to take Shal, too. I'm hoping to find a captain who likes dogs—"

"That may not be easy. But of course, you can try," and at the doubtful note in Len's voice, Rush looked up quickly. "You see," continued Len, "the Mississippi draws people from all over the country, good and bad. Be sure—very sure of your captain—that he's a decent man and kind. I heard only yesterday that your stepuncle owns a boat on the river. Make certain you don't pick that one! Also I heard another bit of news. There's a rumor that your uncle is involved in the Rollingstone City swindle. I wouldn't put it beneath him. Do you remember what happened two years ago to the New York people who came to Illinois to farm?"

"They thought they were buying good land, didn't they? And instead it was just prairie waste—"

"That's right, and the poor souls died from exposure the next winter. It was an awful fraud and still somewhat of a mystery. Some people think your stepuncle helped to sell the land. Samuel Burton is as tricky as they come—I only hope the law catches up with him some day."

"I hope so. . . . I guess my father had a hard time growing up with him. They always fought."

"I think you're doing the right thing, Rush—leaving for a while. And if I were you, I wouldn't travel to the mouth of the Chippewa. Get aboard a boat, say tonight or tomorrow, and ride as far as Foxtails Wharf. It's a little place—used to be a trading post and no one there now. I just came through that way. Walk from Foxtails to the Mississippi. You'll come to a wood yard and houses where lumbermen live. I recommend you keep on walking down the river until you reach the next town and take a boat from there. A man named Pod has charge of the wood yard. He's friendly. He might let you stay in one of the cabins for a night, but I'd keep Shal out of sight. What's your middle name—I've forgotten—"

"Jamieson."

"I'd use it in place of Taylor. You look exactly like your father, blue eyes and brown hair. If Burton should see you and hear the name Taylor, your goose would be cooked. You will have to think and act sharp, Rush. Once you get started downstream, it will be easier. But always keep your wits about you because you are dealing with unprincipled men, Burton and Bissett. By the way, those are good-looking boots you have on," and Len stared at Rush's feet. "Buy them in Eau Claire?"

"Delos bought them at Aldens. He gave me these trousers and shirt, too. I'm afraid he's spending his savings on me—and I intend to pay him back someday. My father didn't leave much money—I have just the timberlands."

The boots were of heavy leather and laced high, the trousers and shirt of heavy brown wool. A dark green jacket and light canvas shoulder pack completed the costume. Undoubtedly Delos loved this straight, slim lad, the image of his father Charles Taylor, for whom he had worked so many years.

"I know how you feel about Delos—he's the salt of the earth. I'll see him soon and tell how we met here, along the river. You'll probably be back when I leave in the fall—"

"Leave—in the fall? You aren't going to teach in Eau Claire?" At the dismay and consternation in Rush's voice and face, Len smiled a little.

"It's still a surprise to me, too. You see, there's a fine school down in Galena, Illinois, and they need teachers. Someone recommended me and I've decided to go. It's right on the river—near the lead mines. I've just come from there and stopped off to tell my mother about it."

"Galena, Illinois—lead mines—I'm awful glad for you, Mr. Slocum." Rush tried to smile but the news came like a body blow. "It will be hard to find another teacher like you. Why, it won't seem like the same school! You'll leave —in the fall?"

"September, not before. You'll be back by then, and Judge Adams will be well. Tell me—when did you eat last?" Len began to unbuckle the strap of his shoulder pack which lay beside him.

"We had a good breakfast this morning and you'll be needing what you have, Mr. Slocum. Shal feeds herself— rabbits, squirrels—on the side. I still have beef in my bag. We'll eat again tonight."

"You'll eat this noon, too," insisted Len. "My mother tucked in a lot of food in this bag somewhere." Len turned the entire contents of the pack onto the floor of pine needles. There were a blanket, pads of paper, pencils, bullets, a flannel shirt and extra socks. Three books and a brown-paper parcel completed the load.

"There they are—molasses cookies, mince tarts and corned beef sandwiches," announced Len. "A little flattened by the books maybe but just as good. Help yourself and we'll give Shal something later."

"You study all the time, don't you, Mr. Slocum?" asked Rush, his eyes hungrily scanning the array of food before him. "Do you always plan to teach school?"

"It looks that way. The more I study just such books as these the better teacher I'll be. Don't stop going to school, Rush. Even if you wish to earn money instead. Your father was an educated man; your mother was said to be a gentle-woman. Work summers—but study winters. Aim for college. By that time you'll probably sell your timber and use the money for education. That stepuncle of yours won't always be around because he's headed for jail now, if I'm not mistaken. It won't always be as hard as this. Shal is looking this way. Evidently everything is all right. Shall we give her a sandwich?"

"If you can spare it—"

"Of course I can. I have plenty and there's bacon in my pocket. Call her. . . . Chances are she's tired of rabbits and squirrels and would relish a bit of homemade bread."

It was hard to see Len Slocum leave, his slight figure limping down the rough tote road which led north. At the turn he stopped and waved several times. Even at that distance Rush caught the bright glint of the afternoon sun on the steel-rimmed glasses. And then he was gone—as though he had never come that way at all.

2

ALONG THE
CHIPPEWA

To Rush, the forest after Len Slocum's departure seemed filled with an overwhelming loneliness. Although he walked his usual pace along the path with Shal scouting ahead, his mind traveled with Len—Len, whose sympathetic understanding and kindness had warmed him through and through. The unfamiliar paths ahead now seemed doubly hard to follow alone. Several times he stopped to listen, hoping that Len might call, wishing to tell him something more. Perhaps it was time to seek the river, he told himself. Surely there was more life and sound on the Chippewa than in the gloom of dense woods. Moreover, the sky had turned a leaden gray and birds cried noisily of a coming storm. Yes, it was time to seek the river and a rocky ledge for shelter. Tomorrow he would make his first attempt to hail a boat and ask a ride.

Less than an hour later Rush pushed through a growth of new pine and looked down upon the waters of the Chippewa. The river was not wide at this point, the opposite shore clearly visible with its rolling sea of meadows, flanked against the sky with a ridge of dark woodland. Except for the lap of water against some rocks, there was an utter stillness. Not a bird cried out, not a drop of rain had fallen. . . . It was the lull before the storm.

Uneasy and a bit hesitant, Rush descended a slope and walked along the shore in search of shelter. There seemed little prospect of finding an overhanging ledge and he was about to retrace his steps when Shal growled. Then came the sound of voices, scarcely audible and some distance away.

"People on the river," Rush whispered. "We'll walk along—back of the willows—quiet."

A moment later, screened by a green hedge, Rush was able to look upstream. A flatboat had just rounded the bend and was drifting slowly close to shore. At the bow stood a tall man and a boy.

"Not that way, Jake," the man was saying. "Do it like I told you. Take more rope and knot it twice. Then come back and help with the anchor. I don't want your ma—"
There was a splash on the side and the sound of rope sawing against wood. By now Rush could see the outline of the flatboat with its two shanties and a load of furniture

piled in the center. The boy Jake had been helping his
father to tighten an anchor rope, and it was evident the man
could not do it alone. One arm lay crooked against him,
held fast in a handkerchief sling.

"There, she's steady now." The man heaved a deep
breath of relief. "Now let's get the wood before it rains.
You take the small ax an' trim—"

"No, Pa, I can handle the big one—"

"Rain's comin', son. No time to lose," said the man, and
with his free hand he put over a narrow plank, one end
resting on the shore. "Come, follow me," he ordered, and
down the plank he walked. The boy at his heels was the
replica of the man in blue jeans and plaid shirt. From the
doorway of the larger shanty a yellow-haired woman
peered out worriedly but disappeared at the sound of a
baby's thin cry.

"There's grass over there," called the boy's voice.
"When we finish with the wood, I'll cut some for Milkweed," he promised, and then came the blows of an ax.

Walking closer, Rush crouched behind the trunk of a
large pine, listening to the different sounds in a flood of
homesickness. More than once when Delos was absent from
camp, he had helped his own father the same way. These
people seemed to be kindly, honest—why not ask them for
a ride on their flatboat? The man, apparently ailing, might
even welcome his assistance. He was searching his mind for
a plan of approach when a hen on the boat set up a loud
cackling and a rooster crowed.

" 'Nother egg, Pa. That was Sally."

There was no answer from the man who was breathing
heavily.

"Mebbe you'd best stop, Pa. Let me take a whack at it."

"No, you might cut your foot, Jake. Then the two of us would be laid up." The older voice held a note of fatigue and despair. Maybe this was the moment to go forward. Rush struggled to his feet and had clutched Shal by the collar when a gust of wind blew some dry pine needles into his face, making him sneeze. Immediately the sound of chopping ceased and there was a silence.

"Sounded like somebody sneezin'," the man finally said. "Hello, there—whoever you are, come out into the open."

Both Jake and his father were armed with axes as Rush and Shal walked into the clearing. Their eyes, however, were focused on Shal and there was astonishment in their faces.

"It's a dog, mister," explained Rush. "She's safe and won't hurt you. I'm sorry if I scared you—"

"For the land's sakes," muttered the man taking a deep breath, "where'd you come from?" Young Jake seemed unable to speak, his eyes round and bulging as he stared at Shal.

"I'm just following the tote road and crossed to the river," replied Rush swiftly. "I was hoping I could earn my way downriver on a boat. Do you need help?" If these people had been asked if they had seen a stray boy and dog, they would speak now.

"I need the help all right," the man replied slowly, looking first at Shal and then at Rush, "but there's no room. We're full up. How fur you goin'?"

"Foxtails Wharf. I wouldn't mind where I slept."

"That dog—she got wolf blood in 'er?" piped Jake.

"Can I pet 'er a mite? I jest lost my dog," he said, edging a step or so closer.

"Stay, Shal," commanded Rush.

"You keep away, Jake," warned the father. A large drop of rain splashed on the man's hand and he looked down for an instant. "Rainin'. I'm sorry, young fellar, but my boat's full. Family an' stock. There'll be other boats comin'—"

"Oh, Pa," came from Jake in a wail, "it's rainin' an' that dog won't take much room." As if irresistibly drawn, the boy approached Shal and held out his hand.

"She's trained, sir," explained Rush seeing the concern in the father's face. "She won't move until I tell her. She likes him or she'd growl."

"Can she do tricks?" asked the boy eagerly. "Oh, Pa, let 'em ride a ways—"

The rain was coming faster now, splashing loudly on the nearby leaves.

"I'd be glad to help with the wood anyway," volunteered Rush. Bending swiftly, he filled his arms and without further talk walked up the narrow plank which served as a gangway. With no comment the boy followed him also carrying wood.

"Over by the shed," he directed Rush. "We're tryin' to warm up Gramp. He's always cold. You an' the dog could sleep in the shed with the animals; it's dry there. There's room in the corner—"

"I wouldn't mind where," whispered Rush quickly. "And I could be a help. Your father's sick, I think. Did he break his arm?"

"Jake! Jake!" called a voice, and the light-haired woman

whom Rush had seen in the doorway now came outside and stood looking in surprise at Rush.

"He came out of the woods, Ma," explained Jake breathlessly. "He's got a dog, a big white 'un, an' says he'll help us if we give him a ride. He says he wouldn't mind sleepin' next to Milkweed——"

"Mercy me!" breathed the woman, her eyes noting Rush's clothing and general appearance. Her glance then traveled to the shore and she gave a visible start. "Why, what's that? Your dog?"

Obediently waiting, Shal stood where Rush had left her, a still white statue against a background of pine.

"Yes, Ma'am. She's friendly. Come here, Shal. Shake hands with the lady."

The man paused in his work to watch Shal as she gracefully crossed the plank and extended her right paw to the woman.

"Mercy me!" repeated the woman, greatly impressed. "She's got real manners! You goin' fur, boy?" she asked. Her eyes showed she was thinking fast, as if coming to some decision.

"Foxtails Wharf."

"Well, go back an' help my husband. Keep dry under the trees best you can. You can stay the night with us anyway—I'll manage. There's room for the dog, too. Ezra Tolman, you come in here!" she called to the man shrilly. "The boy's goin' to help do the choppin'. Come in, I say! I don't want you down with a cold!"

With his face drawn in lines of suffering, the man Ezra silently handed the ax to Rush and walked slowly aboard the flatboat. There was a defeated droop to his shoulders but a lighted tenderness shone in the woman's face as she reached out and helped him through the door of the larger shanty.

By the time the wood was chopped and stacked inside the shed by Jake, the storm had broken in full fury. Because of the rocking of the boat, Rush helped the woman with the second anchor, wind and rain tearing at them as they worked.

"Now you come in an' dry off, boy. Sit near the fire an' bring the dog, too. I guess the Lord sent you to us tonight. Ezra got struck with the steer-oar two days ago an' it crippled his arm. He's layin' in the upper bunk. Lor', hear that wind howl!"

By this time Rush felt certain no one had approached the Tolman family, asking of his whereabouts. Surely one of them would have spoken before this, particularly young Jake whose conversation babbled like a brook. There was a feeling of great relief as he and the woman entered the one room of the shanty. Within was a certain sense of security and peace. Fire snapped cheerily in the stove and steam poured from the snout of an iron kettle. Seated as close to the stove as possible was a very old man wearing a black felt hat, and a worsted shawl draped over his shoulders. His pale blue eyes stared curiously at Rush but he made no comment.

"Gramp, this boy's been helpin' Jake get wood for you an' is stayin' the night. There's a nasty storm out. You feelin' better, Ezra?" the woman called to the still figure in the top bunk. There was a faint gurgling sound from a baby, and she smiled a little. "He's got the baby up there against 'im keepin' her warm," she explained to Rush. "We've had cold weather ever since we started. Set here— I'm goin' to warm up some stew. Your dog can have the bone later. Your arm better, Ezra?"

This time the man nodded but did not open his eyes. The woman, satisfied, seized two cloth holders and pulled a large kettle of meat and vegetables from the oven.

Conversation during the supper hour revealed that the migrant family named Tolman were bound for Galena, Illinois, where Ezra Tolman was hopeful of finding work in the lead mine. It was on the tip of Rush's tongue to speak of Len Slocum as the new teacher in the school at Galena. However, knowing that the talk might veer to his own affairs, who he was and where he was going, he decided to remain silent. Meanwhile, Gramp's pale blue eyes regarded him steadily while Jake bombarded him with questions about Shal.

"Where'd she come from?"

"An Indian squaw gave her to me when she was a puppy."

"What kind is she?"

"Mixed breed. A lot of wolf blood, I guess."

"Shal's a funny name. What does it mean?"

"It's part of a Chippewa word for white. The squaw called her Shah—but we found it easier to say Shal."

"How old is she?"

"About four years."

"Are you gonna put her on one of them circus boats on the Mississippi?"

"Why, no. I didn't plan to."

"My uncle saw the show on the Floating Circus Palace.

He says it's wonnerful what the animals can do—I want to see it if it comes to Galena. Pa, can I go an' see the Floating Circus Palace if it comes to Galena?"

"I guess so, son." Mr. Tolman was propped up with pillows feeding himself, and the baby, bundled in blankets, lay asleep at his feet.

"Now, Jake, you've done nothin' but chatter. T'aint polite to ask so many questions," scolded Mrs. Tolman. "Gramp, will I pour you more tea?" Gramp nodded and the woman refilled his cup. "Boy, let me give you more stew. Come to think on't, none of us know your name."

"Jamieson, Ma'am. Rush Jamieson."

It was the first time Rush had given only half his name and the words had a strange unfinished sound. How wise Len Slocum was to prepare him for just such questions! However, no one seemed to hear for a tin cover clattering to the floor drowned out his voice and Mrs. Tolman did not ask again.

"Time for bed," announced Mrs. Tolman an hour later, after Jake had performed on his mouth harp and the baby had been fed and rocked. "The rain's let up. Jake, you show The Boy where to sleep in the shed. I put down an ol' comforter after supper an' it's snug an' warm in there. Take the dog along—there's enough room."

"Why can't I sleep with 'em, Ma? They might get lonesome—"

"Jake Tolman, stop your fuss. You wouldn't sleep a wink—pettin' that dog all night long! Good night, boy. Gramp, you ain't said a word all this evenin'. You've done nothin' but stare at the lad. Can't you say good night?"

"G'night," mumbled Gramp obediently, his eyes continuing to study Rush. "I've been thinkin'—you ain't a bad boy."

"Why, thank you, sir," replied Rush a little surprised.

"I can tell, I can tell. I'm ninety years old an' I have my ways of tellin'. We ain't folks to pry. . . . But I was wonderin'—"

"Wonderin' what, Gramp?" asked Mrs. Tolman leaning forward, a bit perplexed.

"Well, this mornin' when I was alone on the boat sunnin', a raft drew alongside an' a man called out—"

"I thought I heard voices," interrupted Mrs. Tolman.

"The man wanted to know if we had a strange boy an' white dog aboard. I said no. Now I've been settin' here wonderin'," and the pale blue eyes almost stabbed Rush in their intensity, "why a good boy like you should be leavin' home. I jest can't figgur it out. Maybe you'd like to speak up."

3

THE GREAT RIVER

For a moment Rush was unable to speak. Twice his mouth opened but no words came. Mr. and Mrs. Tolman and Jake were regarding him in mute astonishment, Ezra sitting upright in his bunk oblivious of his injured arm. All the security and pleasant companionship were dispelled by a little old man in a black felt hat who had known from the first that people were searching for him.

"I'm sorry," the words came at last and Rush turned toward the door, "I'll be going along, I guess. There's nothing much to tell you—I only want to say that I really haven't done anything wrong—"

"Who says you have?" asked the old man testily. "Annie, give me some more tea."

By now Ezra Tolman had roused himself into action. Unobserved he had laboriously descended from the upper bunk and walked slowly to where Rush stood, his free hand tenderly supporting his arm. His dark eyes, bright with fever and pain, also held an angry light.

"You'd best leave, boy. You might bring trouble down on my family an' I'm not in any shape to take more'n I've got already. Is the law after you?"

"No—no, sir."

"You kilt somebody?" asked Jake, finding his wind at last and rather pleased with the excitement.

"No, no, Jake—it's just that—I want to work on the river and my uncle doesn't want me to."

"Well, he's right," agreed Ezra Tolman. "The river's no place for a boy your age."

"Easy," cautioned the old man. "Your nerves is sick, Ezra. You've worked too hard of late. An' I've got more to ask. . . . Did I hear you say your name was Jamieson?"

"Yes, sir."

"You a Wisconsin Jamieson?"

Rush nodded, his throat tight. These people, simple, kindly, might wish to believe his story but Sam Burton's influence and power would overshadow it. They would not dare take his side, and harbor him. However, the old man had not finished.

"I've known a lot of Wisconsin Jamiesons," the old man was saying. "Never knew one yet that was crooked. You got a father an' mother?"

"No—they're dead. My mother was a Jamieson," he de-

clared, and the thought sent a little flash of pride through
Rush. The Jamiesons were fine people and it had helped,
hearing it from a total stranger. "My uncle's no blood
kin," he added. "He's not like the Jamiesons."

Gramp was quiet for a moment, his eyes fixed on Rush,
as he waited to hear more.

"Everyone knows my stepuncle. Mr. Tolman's right, it
might make trouble for you if I stayed here. So I'll go.
. . . You've been very kind—"

Ezra Tolman stirred uncertainly and Mrs. Tolman came
a step closer as if to intercede.

"Jest a minit, sonny," said Gramp, then paused and took
a swallow of tea. "Tell me if I'm wrong. There was Silas
Jamieson, William Jamieson, 'nother Silas Jamieson, a
little girl Mary—least she was a little girl when I knew her
—was they some of your folks?"

"Oh, yes—yes, sir." The names had rung like sweet
familiar music in Rush's ears and he turned quickly toward the old man, his face lighted. "They're my folks! The
little girl Mary—she died when I was born—she was my
mother."

"Glory be!" Gramp set his cup down with a bang on the
table. "I knew t'was somethin' like that! So she was your
ma—Glory be! An' she's dead—"

"Gramp—Mr. Tolman, tell me about her. All you can
remember. Then I'll go—"

"I'll tell you all I can remember. But you ain't goin',
not til' you get good an' ready. Set down here, near the fire.
Annie—some more tea. You, Ezra, go back to bed. There's
somethin' wrong somewhere but it ain't with a Jamieson!
Why, I uster run logs down Black River for your Grandpa

an' once I held little Mary Jamieson on my knee an' told her stories. Such a purty mite with black eyes an' curls. . . . So you're Mary Jamieson's boy. Glory be!"

Two days later beneath an early afternoon sun, the Chippewa River had a gold cast to its clear waters. The same yellow sheen enveloped the flatboat, the marshes and meadows but stopped short of the dense forest with its line of black pine. Rush, watching from the bow of the Tolman's flatboat, shivered slightly and let his hand rest on Shal's head. Away from the cold and gloom of the forest, the sun had warmed his body as well as his courage and he had no desire to return. For two days he had enjoyed the comradeship and confidence of the Tolmans on their floating home and, now that he was approaching Foxtails Wharf, it was not easy to face the separation. The sway of the boat, the sing of the water, the genuine affection of those about him could never be forgotten. Would he see the Tolmans again —ever? Was it always to be this way, saying good-bye to people he loved? First Delos, then Len Slocum and now— the Tolmans.

There was Ezra Tolman now, standing by the sweep, ready to ease the boat into the trough should she swing to one side. Ezra's strong constitution had responded quickly to two days of rest although he still carried his arm in a sling. Ezra was grateful for Rush's assistance and now convinced of his honesty. Mrs. Tolman had mothered the boy and fed him generously. Young Jake had followed him about with worshipping eyes. But it had been Gramp, ripe with experiences of ninety years, to whom he had confided all, and who seemed the closest. The old man's tales of the early days of Grandfather Silas Jamieson's lumber triumphs in the forest and on the rivers, the vivid description of the little daughter Mary, had pieced out a picture never before quite clear in Rush's mind. Yes, it was hardest of all to leave Gramp. . . .

"There it is," called Ezra suddenly, nodding in the direction of the shore on the left. "Least, that's what they uster call Foxtails Wharf."

Young Jake, fishing for catfish over the side, rose quickly to his feet and Mrs. Tolman came to the doorway.

"You sartin, Ezra?" she called, her voice worried.

"Sartin. You won't change your mind an' go a piece further, boy?" asked Ezra, looking at Rush with concern in his eyes.

"No, this will do all right. There might be someone asking for me around the next bend. And I have directions how to reach a wood yard from here. There's a man named Pod who may let me have a cabin for the night."

"Ain't much of a place." Mrs. Tolman was now beside them, holding her light hair in place against the wind. "Jest one wharf an' a cabin. I hate to see you go, Rush. You kinder belong to us."

"I know—I feel that way—but you understand—"

"Of course, I know. I was thinkin', would it help you any to leave Shal with us? She's frien's with Milkweed an' Jake an' you could pick her up at Galena when you come by—"

"Oh, Ma, could we? Could we?" Jake, unobserved and just behind his mother, pushed himself between them, an excited figure in blue jeans.

"I couldn't, Jake—I couldn't leave her," and Rush felt

himself suffering with the boy in his disappointment. "Anyway, she wouldn't stay. She'd get loose and follow me. She's done it before. Maybe I'd better say good-bye to Gramp." Glad to be free of Jake's pleading eyes, Rush moved away. His feet made no sound as he walked a narrow path between boxes and kettles to a bench where Gramp sat, warming himself in the sun. Although the old man's eyes were closed beneath the brim of the black felt hat, he seemed to be aware of Rush's presence.

"You goin'?"

"We're almost across from Foxtails," said Rush as he sat down beside the stooped figure. "Gramp, I'll see you in Galena someday—soon." Rush paused, fearing the old man might surmise how unsteady he was. Somehow his voice sounded thick and strange.

"I reckon mebbe." Gramp had opened his eyes and he spoke slowly.

"You may like it there—a lot."

"We'll see, we'll see. Seems kinder queer movin' at my time of life. I never dreampt of bein' buried in the South. Everyone's movin' down the Mississippi, seems like."

"It will be warmer there—"

"That's true."

"Gramp, it's been wonderful to hear about my grandfather and my mother. Almost like knowing them. . . . I won't forget."

"No, remember best you can. It's history, kinder." And suddenly Gramp drew himself up straight and there was fire in his pale blue eyes. "An' blast his cheatin' hide! You keep a jump ahead of that stepuncle. Don't let him get a-holt of one tree. Remember that's Jamieson timber, fought an' bled for. The ol' weasel—I'd like to fix 'im proper! Now mind what I say—"

"I'll remember. . . . Good-bye." With a shy touch on the old man's shoulder, Rush stood and walked quickly to where the three Tolmans were waiting. Ezra had put a small canoe over the side. Within were a paddle, his pack, and a parcel wrapped in brown paper.

"I've got 'er hitched to a long rope," Ezra explained and nodded in the direction of the canoe. "Soon's you land, we'll haul 'er back. The dog'll swim?"

"Yes, she'd rather."

"Have you got some silver, Rush?" asked Mrs. Tolman anxiously. "You might not find work for a spell."

"Delos sewed some in my trousers. Someday I'll bring Delos to see you. . . . Thank you for the parcel."

"Just a few cookies an' some cold meat. T'aint nothin'. . . . Take care of yourself."

Rush nodded, stepped carefully into the canoe, and eased himself down on his knees.

"Hope you catch that catfish, Jake."

"I'm aimin' to ketch me a whopper!" Jake made a valiant attempt to appear cheerful but his eyes were fixed on Shal longingly.

"Good-bye. I'm much obliged for everything—everything. I'll see you soon—maybe very soon—there's no telling." Rush's fleeting smile included them all, even the motionless figure on the bench.

"No tellin'," echoed Mrs. Tolman.

"Follow, Shal!"

Shal was waiting for the command and she responded instantly. There was a jump, a splash, and in another mo-

ment the canoe was headed toward shore with Shal's white
head following in its wake.

The canoe was hauled back and restored to its place on
the flatboat long before the Tolmans disappeared from
sight. The faint sound of Milkweed's mooing still lingered
on the air when Rush waved his final good-bye and turned
to find the path described by Len Slocum. There was no
need to enter the old cabin which has once served as a trading post. One side had collapsed and all that remained
within was a rusty stove and empty shelves.

The path was almost obscured by brush but still visible
in places. The journey commenced, Shal ran ahead in pur-
suit of game, joyous with her new freedom. From the west,
like beckoning sirens, came the call of whistles of varying
tones and the occasional chime of a bell. Ahead lay a new
world and now Rush almost ran in his eagerness to see it.

Even before he saw the Great River, Rush heard the song
and swirl of its waters. And then from the top of a hill,
beneath a setting sun, he was able to look down and see for
the first time the Mississippi—a wide shining serpent, curling and twisting through the land. Green hills framed the
northern bend; there were flat meadows to the south. For a
moment he was unable to look at anything else. Although
he had heard many descriptions, its beauty and immensity
startled him. A moment later his eyes sought the shore below. It was all as Len Slocum had described—a wood yard
with wharves stacked with wood reaching out into the water
and nearby three houses of identical shape occupied by the
lumberjacks. Now and then he caught a glimpse of cabins
scattered among the trees. Somewhere close by was a man
named Pod. . . . But before Rush could descend the hill

to ask permission for the use of a cabin, he must carefully hide Shal. Once seen, she would not easily be forgotten.

Two deep blasts of a whistle sounded and instinctively Rush hid himself behind some vines. And then a gasp of surprise escaped him as he looked down at the river. Like a white-winged apparition came a large boat with upper and lower decks, hugging the shore, her gold trim seeming to take fire from the sunset. She advanced silently like a huge bird, until a wind from the northwest brought strains of music—the twang of banjos and men's voices singing. A moment later came the undertones of a throbbing engine and the churn of a paddle wheel. Leaning forward, he could see the dainty wooden lace along her upper works. Between two chimney stacks swung something bright—a gilded star! And atop the pilot house was a deer's head with antlers painted red. Beneath the flutter of flags, ladies strolled with gentlemen upon the upper deck, in gowns and shawls of every color of the rainbow. In all his life Rush had never seen so many gay and happy people.

For a long while Rush watched, crouched behind the vines with Shal beside him. Although a man ran the length of the wood yard's wharf below and waved, the boat did not stop but floated on—a regal lady with sweeping skirts of lace and foam, leaving behind her skies stained with smoke and snatches of music. The Mississippi! In the whole wide world there was no river to be compared. All rivermen said the same. Even Delos, who loved the forests, had said that "after a while if you lived beside or upon its waters the river possessed you—body and soul." And Rush, awed by what he had just seen, began to understand.

With Shal hidden in the brush and guarding his pack at

the top of the hill, Rush descended the path. Halfway down was a cabin, almost secluded in a grove of pines, not visible from the top of the hill. It appeared empty and more or less dilapidated but comfortable enough for one night's rest. The man who had run the length of the wharf waving, presumably Pod, was now lighting lanterns which he hung along the edge of the wood piles. A few lights had begun to shine in the three houses below. It was evident that the lumberjacks had not returned but were expected shortly. If only he could have Shal and himself stored away for the night before they came! And in case anyone had notified the wood yard of a missing boy and dog, he planned to keep a safe distance between himself and the man Pod. Within speaking distance, Rush paused a moment, cautious and uncertain of his welcome. The man had seen him but had given no sign.

"Are you Mr. Pod?" called Rush.

"Ay-up," grunted the man and he finally looked up. "Jest Pod—that's my name."

Pod was a short stocky man with red cheeks and a wheeze in his voice. His large bulging eyes gave him the appearance of being in a perpetual state of surprise.

"Did you see that blasted boat go by?" he asked suddenly with a burst of temper.

"Why, yes, I did—"

"Well, that floatin' mess of white an' gold junk shouldn't a-come so close to my wharves if she warn't goin' to stop for wood. Blew her whistle two times an' sprung me outer a sound sleep."

"That's too bad. What was her name? I couldn't see—"

Secretly pleased that Pod's attention was on the boat and not on himself, Rush went a step nearer.

"*Doctor Franklin Number Two*. She's a packet, dang her cats! If she'd stopped, I might have done a good stroke of business. Well, she didn't, and that's that. And jest what would you be wantin'?" Pod's bulging eyes were looking Rush over curiously. There seemed to be no suspicion in his glance.

"I'd like to stay in the cabin on the hill tonight—if it's all right with you. I'll be leaving in the morning."

"Stay there if you like. But don't build a fire. The boss— he's dead set agin fires. Light the lantern if you're keerful, but no stove. That all you want?"

"Yes, sir. I'm much obliged."

"Then I'll get goin'. It's time for the jacks to come in an' I've got to help the cook. Mebbe it's a good thing them whistles did jump me outer bed," he declared, and breathing noisily as he walked, Pod departed in the direction of the three houses.

4

CAPTAIN DAN WHIPPLE'S
CIRCUS BOAT

Pleased with his success in securing a shelter for the night and without questions asked, Rush lost no time in joining Shal at the top of the hill and leading her to the cabin half hidden in the pines. For some reason the dog seemed uneasy and growled continuously. With the creaking door closed behind them, she crouched to the ground and listened while Rush waited, somewhat dismayed by this quick turn of affairs. Once she looked up at him and wagged her tail as if asking him to be patient and then resumed her vigilance. This was not a new procedure between them and finally the silence was broken by the low murmur of voices, the heavy tramp of feet. As the sound gained in volume, Shal rose as though ready to spring should anyone attempt to open the door.

"Lumberjacks," Rush whispered softly. "They won't stop here. . . ."

The feet marched on, the men conversing in French with occasional bursts of laughter. Even when the last one had passed, Rush did not open the door for fear some belated straggler might come by. Through a crack between two logs, however, he was able to see them, some twenty burly figures in the distance, all wearing short jackets and caps. They were hungry and eager to reach their quarters, so there was little chance of their returning that night. When convinced there was no danger, Rush lighted a lantern which hung by the door and, turning the wick low, placed it on a table in a farther corner. Should Shal growl, he planned to extinguish it immediately. Meanwhile it was necessary to see if the bunk in the cabin was comfortable. If not, perhaps additional branches of pine could be added.

The bunk was amply supplied and there were indications that the cabin had been occupied that spring. A discarded woolen shirt hung on a side wall and on a lower shelf of the table lay several newspapers. Curious, Rush brought them nearer the light. Although they were torn and creased, he saw they were fairly recent newspapers named the *Journal*, printed in Hannibal, Missouri, and dated April 3, 1854—only two months old!

There were headlines of various subjects: Hannibal people and how they were faring in the State of California, having joined the gold rush in 1849; six hogsheads of molasses had been stolen from the town's largest grocery store; a fire had been set in the calaboose but extinguished before the prisoners were injured; the price of wood was now four dollars a cord. And then halfway down the smudged page the word "circus" caught Rush's eye. Captain Dan Whipple, owner of the Whipple Circus Boat, had stopped in his old home town, Hannibal, that very week on business. The show season was about to start, and "Captain Dan" and his troupers hoped to come that way very soon with a new line of powerful and exciting shows. His many friends were also eager to see his new boat which carried various animals being trained for a future "Big Top." Although there was considerable competition among the circus boats on the river, every citizen of Hannibal wished Captain Dan success, remembering him in his young manhood as upright and industrious and Madame Whipple, his mother, as a most gracious and charming lady.

Captain Dan Whipple's Circus Boat! Perhaps Jake, with his unbounded enthusiasm for circuses, would see this particular circus once he reached Galena. It was evident that Captain Whipple stood in high regard and had many friends. The printed article rang with genuine enthusiasm and Rush found himself curious to see a circus boat. There had been little or no talk in Eau Claire about such boats and visiting one would be an entirely fresh experience. As for joining a circus boat and letting Shal be trained under a stranger's whip—the idea was not to be considered. Surely there would be better opportunities elsewhere.

Suddenly remembering that he had not eaten supper, Rush untied the package so carefully wrapped by Mrs. Tolman. As she had said, there were slices of cold beef and cookies sprinkled with sugar. Having fed herself with a rabbit only a short time ago, Shal was contented with a small portion and the remainder of the food was saved for the following day. A few moments later, the door bolted and table propped against it, Rush blew out the lantern's light and, with Shal close beside him, fell asleep.

A loud whistle on the river half awakened Rush and, springing to his feet, he stood in the center of the room staring about him in bewilderment. The bunk filled with pine branches, the table propped against the door, the wool shirt upon the wall gradually brought him back to the cabin in the pines and yesterday's parting with the Tolmans. Shal, a bit excited by his actions, had run to the door. With the table removed, Rush opened it a crack and looked out. Daylight filtered through the pines but there was no smoke coming from the chimneys of the three houses and no sign of Pod. Perhaps, while the camp remained quiet, it would be wise for him to leave. So far he had not been seen by anyone but Pod, and the sooner he traveled south the better. A path skirted the hilltop above and by following it for a distance he could avoid passing the houses where the lumberjacks slept. Seizing his pack, he carefully closed the door behind him and quickly reached the path with Shal running ahead. Light was breaking brightly in the east, and the faint sound of voices could be heard in the camp below as he walked southward and descended to the next valley.

In the morning sunlight, the river was the color of a bluejay's wing and Rush's eyes sought it constantly, marveling at its great width and beauty. There were times when the path disappeared into dense growths of brush, but he always found it again by keeping close to the bank of the river. Meadow larks, orchard orioles, and song sparrows swooped low over the wild fields and filled the air with their songs. Unfortunately the berries on the blackberry bushes were still green, but a slice of the cold meat and two cookies sufficed for his breakfast while Shal hunted at the edge of a wood. Every mile away from Eau Claire brought him an increasing sense of freedom and he frequently stopped to gaze in wonderment at the passing boats.

Each boat was different—surprisingly different from the boats he had read about and heard described. There were side wheelers and stern wheelers, their great wheels noisily churning as they kicked out white spray. While some boats were trimmed about the texas and pilot house, others were plain. Blinds were painted red, green, or white and every whistle had a different pitch, every bell a different tone. Flatboats with their shanties and lines of clothes drying in the sun reminded him of the Tolmans, and he scanned each one eagerly in hope of seeing them. However, the main channel of the river had begun to swing toward the center and it was difficult to recognize people so far away.

It was close to the noon hour when Rush noticed that the narrow footpath was gradually merging into a cart road and that he was about to enter a town. Over the tops of trees ahead there were spirals of smoke and once he glimpsed a church steeple. There would be no way of knowing the name of the town until he passed a road sign or inquired. The place, however, was of little consequence as long as it possessed a wharf where boats docked. Here, he would begin to make his first efforts to obtain work—with a kindly captain who loved dogs. If no opportunity offered itself here, he would walk to the next town.

CAPTAIN DAN WHIPPLE'S CIRCUS BOAT

An old sawmill weathered and deserted, a row of sheds, a large barn and house appeared as the road smoothed out and grew wider. There seemed to be no people about, so he walked on, Shal beside him. After the next turn there were houses of all shapes and sizes on both sides, and to his surprise the street was filled with hurrying people. Girls and boys, housewives, farmers, and tradesmen in aprons were calling to one another as they hastened toward the wharf.

"Tell Nellie to hurry—she's just coming round the bend!" shouted one grown man to a neighbor.

"Nellie's down there already!" shouted back the neighbor.

It was a temptation to stop and ask the reason for all the excitement but, not wishing to draw attention to himself or Shal, Rush walked on. What was coming round the bend? The only way to find out was to hurry also to the wharf. On the edge of the crowd he and Shal would hardly be noticed and, as soon as the crowd dispersed, they could leave quickly. A poster nailed to the front of a large warehouse next caught his eye and he stopped to read, one hand holding fast to Shal's collar.

In the corner of the poster was a photograph of Captain Whipple, a pleasant-faced man with mustache and broad shoulders, and Rush stared at him curiously. This was the man whom all Hannibal loved and admired. Almost anyone might enjoy working for such a person and he felt a a little surge of excitement as he leaned closer. The eyes were kind and understanding. Captain Whipple owned his own boat and there would be no danger of any business connection with his stepuncle, Samuel Burton. He would feel safe with a man like Captain Whipple and if Shal

RIVER CIRCUS
TONIGHT!

AT THE RIVER

CAPTAIN DAN WHIPPLE'S CIRCUS BOAT

presents

From Rags to Riches
one of the world's greatest dramas

Starring

ELLIE SAMPSON
and
LESLIE WOOD

Adults 50¢   **Children 25¢**

Great care has been taken to provide ladies with comfortable and commodious seats. Every courtesy is extended to all!

could be placed in a happy role with only himself to train her, finding work on the Whipple Circus Boat might be a quick and easy solution. However, there was no date on the poster—only the word TONIGHT. He must begin to ask questions and he hailed a little girl in pigtails skipping by.

"What's happening down on the wharf?" he called.

"Why, don't you know?" she asked, her eyes round with surprise as she halted on the edge of the walk. "It's Captain Dan Whipple's Circus Boat! My brother says it's almost here now," and on she sped.

It was apparent that the Whipple Circus Boat had awakened interest in both young and old. The whole town seemed to have gathered at the wharf and all eyes were focused downriver. By walking around the fringe of the crowd, Rush was able to squeeze himself and Shal into a space between a board fence and a portly gentleman just as a loud shrill whistle announced that the Circus Boat was arriving. There she was—a strange box-like creation with upper and lower rows of windows, and a pilot house, pushed by a small red towboat.

"Well, that's the queerest thing I ever did see!" exclaimed the portly gentleman to his woman companion. "Looks like a box. Where does the audience sit and where do they keep the animals?"

"Anyone would know you were from the East, John," laughed the woman. "Why, we see these kinds of boats quite often. The amphitheater is on the top floor and the animals are probably kept in cages below. Generally the troupers live on the towboat. Ellie Sampson is Captain Whipple's leading lady and said to be a splendid actress. I don't believe the animals are ready to perform yet—"

"What kind of animals?" asked a small boy tugging at the woman's skirt. "Can I go and see them?"

"I don't know, dear. We'll have to wait a bit. . . . The Floating Circus Palace stopped at Alma a few weeks ago," continued the woman addressing the portly gentleman, "and they had Tom Thumb with them. My, and a lot of animals—" and the rest of the conversation grew indistinct.

As the Circus Boat drew near, Rush could see that she had been freshly painted white and at her bow were words printed in red—CAPTAIN DAN WHIPPLE'S CIRCUS BOAT. About her middle were paintings of animals, a small elephant, two cub bears, a lion, a galloping horse, and two monkeys. A small cannon on the flat roof was fired as the boat proceeded to dock, aided by long sweep-oars at the stern. And to the crowd's delight a very large lady in flowing skirts suddenly appeared and began to play "My Old Kentucky Home" on a string of bells fastened between two posts. She played easily and well, the bells resounding sweetly over the water.

"They're going to tie her up now—an' there's some people on the roof—circus people!" screamed the little boy excitedly, having almost pulled the skirt from his mother by this time.

The Circus Boat was now docked and Rush could see some of the faces of the people gathered on the roof— pleasant, smiling faces. Among them was a tiny old lady in a bonnet who waved to the crowd, a small bag hanging from her wrist. But his interest was quickly turned to a nearby door which had suddenly opened on the lower floor, and two attendants in blue coats and brass buttons were pushing out a stout wide plank which served as a bridge between the Circus Boat and the wharf. Almost immediately a prancing white horse bedecked in gold ribbons walked the length of the plank, lifting its hoofs daintily in almost a tightrope fashion. Its jaunty rider was dressed in red satin. Admiration swept the watching crowd and above all could be heard the voice of a small boy perched on the top of the board fence.

"You see that man on the hoss?" he called to a boy below. "Well, he's the trainer. My Uncle Moses down St. Louis knows 'im!"

The horse by this time had reached the wharf. When only

a few feet distant from Rush, the rider in red snapped his whip and suddenly stood on his feet, the horse continuing the same gait with no change whatsoever. Absorbed in watching the grace and ease of both man and horse, Rush was taken completely by surprise when someone grasped his collar and gave him a shove forward, ramming him into the back of the portly man.

"What are you—deef?" a harsh voice rasped in his ear.

The speaker, one of the attendants in a blue coat and brass buttons, was trying to push back the crowd to make room for a small ticket booth on the wharf. Startled, Rush turned to reply when he received a more violent shove. This was too much for Shal who was standing behind Rush, quiet and inconspicuous. With a roar of rage her white body leaped upward and landed on the attendant's back. In another moment the young man lay pinned to the rough boards of the wharf, face downward, while Shal proceeded to rip off his coat collar with her sharp white teeth.

"Help! Help! Get him off!" howled the young man flailing his arms, and then a woman's voice took up the cry, "Help! Help! There's a wild animal loose!"

"Up, Shal, up!" Rush immediately bent over Shal. "Let go—"

With reluctance Shal stood and relinquished her hold, but the fur along her neck and back stood upright as she watched the man rise to his feet.

"You'll pay for this—plenty!" the attendant shouted at Rush as soon as he had caught his breath. "That dog is ugly, he ought to be shot! Why, this town isn't safe with such an animal around—why, it's half wolf," he exclaimed in surprise as he looked at Shal more closely. "A wolf—"

"Stop your noise, Roscoe," called a woman's voice from above. "You aren't hurt a mite. I saw you push that boy—" It was the little old lady in the bonnet speaking from the roof and before Rush could thank her, another voice, deep and resonant, boomed in his ears.

"Well, young man, what have you to say for yourself? What do you mean by scattering my audience—" and then the voice paused as the newcomer stared at Shal. "What kind of dog is it? Some wolf blood?" Indignation had now given way to curiosity.

"She's part wolf, sir." So this was Captain Whipple! There was no mistaking him, the broad shoulders and mustache, the blue coat, brass buttons and gold braid. And there was a certain dignity about him which made the attendant step back in deference.

"Where'd you get your dog?"

"A Chippewa squaw gave her to me."

"She's not ugly?"

"Oh, no, sir. She was trying to protect me. I didn't mean to start a commotion." Rush gazed about him dismayed. It was as Captain Whipple said—most of the crowd had scattered. All of the women had disappered. The little boy had remained perched on the top of the fence and was now staring down with eyes like saucers while a few men were slowly returning, a bit timid but curious. From now on Shal would be the talk of the town and they would have to leave together—quickly.

"The beast's ugly, Captain Whipple," complained the young attendant, feeling of his torn coat collar. "I was only trying to set up the ticket booth—"

"Roscoe," interrupted Captain Whipple a bit wearily,

"you're always causing trouble. No matter what you do, you've got to show off. My mother says she saw you push this boy. Naturally his dog would jump. Between the two of you I've probably lost the sales to the evening show. . . . Go aboard and get your coat mended," he ordered Roscoe in no gentle tones, "and wash your face."

The attendant sulkily turned away and Captain Whipple then addressed Rush. "And you, young man—do you wish to sell your dog?"

The question came so suddenly that Rush could not reply but merely stared at the Captain.

"Well? Do you?"

"No—no, sir. I don't want to sell her," said Rush, putting one hand possessively on Shal's neck. "She's been my dog since a puppy."

"Do you live here in Alma?" The Captain's eyes were penetrating and keen as they studied first Shal and then himself.

"No, sir. I came here looking for work."

"I see." The eyes were now speculative as though the man were thinking ahead and about to make some decision. "Right now I've got to go up the street on business. Maybe you'd better come to the towboat in about an hour. You'll find me there somewhere—and bring the dog. Tell the man on guard that I'm expecting you." Captain Whipple pointed at the red towboat now docked beside the Circus Boat. "Perhaps we can talk things over a bit."

"Yes, sir, I'll come—but I'm not selling my dog—"

"In about an hour then," repeated Captain Whipple. Then he turned away and walked briskly up the deserted street of Alma.

5

TWO WEEKS' TRIAL

The next hour passed slowly. Seated with Shal and half hidden by some hogsheads piled on the levee left of the wharf, Rush quietly watched groups of people who approached the Circus Boat, studied the posters, sometimes bought tickets from the man in the booth, and then departed. In some way the rumor that an animal had escaped had been corrected, for there was no evidence of any timidity. There was now a row of curious small boys perched along the top of the fence, evidently waiting for the white horse and rider to return. But there was no sign of the outraged Roscoe. Smoke poured from one of the smaller chimneys on the red towboat which was named *Flora Belle,* and someone lowered a pail on a rope into the river from one of the windows on the Circus Boat and hauled it up again. In a little less than an hour's time Captain Whipple arrived. A man in blue jeans produced a loose plank for him to cross on and the Captain disappeared into the towboat. As the plank remained down and the man seemed to be waiting, Rush approached the towboat, leading Shal by the collar. It was his first experience aboard a large boat and he was curious as well as awed.

"Captain Whipple's expecting me, sir," Rush told the man in blue jeans.

"Sure enough. He said you were coming. Walk right over. That's some dog. . . . Going to put him in the Circus?"

"I don't know—where will I find the Captain?"

"In the texas I reckon. That's the Captain's quarters, on the upper deck," the man explained kindly. "If you don't find him there, look in the pilot house above. Is this the dog that jumped Roscoe this morning?"

"Yes—"

"The idiot needed it. Take the stairs to the left, son."

A narrow flight of steps brought Rush to the door of the texas and one glance inside told him the Captain was not there. The room was long, narrow but comfortably furnished with chairs and a sofa, and evidently the Captain spent much of his time there. Books and charts littered a desk in one corner and photographs covered the walls.

After climbing a second short flight of stairs Rush reached the pilot house, a small square room with glass windows on all sides and built above the texas. Captain

Whipple sat in a chair facing the wharf, reading his mail. Hearing Rush and Shal approach, he looked up and nodded pleasantly.

"Come in and take a chair. I'll be finished in a moment."

Rush seated himself, pulled Shal close, and stared about him. The pilot house appeared to be a most strange and fascinating place. As he waited his eyes took in every detail possible, and he tried to remember the various tales he had heard concerning pilots and their methods. The steering wheel was large, the wood worn by much handling; a high stool with soft cushions stood beneath. A series of brass and wooden rings swung in a row and were attached to ropes which passed through the floor—probably down to the engine room below. A pull on a certain ring rang a certain bell which meant "speed up" or "slow down."

A pilot was a very important person on the river and Rush wondered if Captain Whipple did his own piloting. Some captains managed it themselves.

In the room there were also speaking tubes connecting with the engine room, a chair or two, and in a corner was an old stuffed bear, faded brown with its front teeth missing, a strange ornament for a pilot room. Possibly the old bear had been a pet—

A slight sound made Rush turn his gaze back to Captain Whipple, who had finished his letters and was now placing them in their envelopes. And then the Captain silently directed his attention to them both, first noting Shal's thick neck ruff, the delicately pointed black nose, the slender forelegs, and finally meeting the gold-brown eyes of Shal herself, steadfastly watching him. Next, he inspected Rush, observing the boots, the sleeve of the jacket which had been torn by briars, and the pack which lay on the floor. It was a swift, keen, and calculating appraisal.

"So you are looking for work," the Captain broke the silence, "and you don't wish to sell your dog. What can you do—in the line of work?"

"I can learn anything," replied Rush eagerly. "Maybe I could help the cook, clean, saw wood—"

"At the moment I have two cooks, my chimneys are clean, and I can buy my wood sawed," returned the Captain instantly. It was plain now that the man was about to commence his bargaining. "What's your name?"

"Jamieson, sir."

"Humph, who taught you your 'sirs'?"

"My father. He's dead, sir."

"You have no home now?"

"I've been living with a friend in upper Wisconsin."

"Humph! So you think you'd like to be on a circus boat, where there's music, good food, and a lot of adventure and fun. I don't blame you. Most boys feel that way. However, you're the tenth boy who's asked for work this spring. Everyone I've hired says the work's too hard and leaves me at the next town. Matter of fact I don't need you—but I need your dog. You saw that white horse go ashore this morning?"

"Yes, sir."

"Well, I could put that horse and dog together in a tableau—both of them pure white against a black curtain. It would be a beautiful sight! And the dog would have a good home here and I'd pay you good money for her. How old is she?"

"Three years old. But I'm not selling my dog, Captain Whipple."

"There's wolf blood in her, you say," continued the Captain as though he had not heard.

"Yes, sir."

A long pause followed and again Captain Whipple studied the boy and dog before him. The eyes were kindly, but the man himself lost in some process of speculation. This was a business transaction, pure and simple, and the Captain was weighing every angle.

"Twenty-five dollars?"

"What did you say, sir?"

"I said twenty-five dollars. For the dog. Take it or leave it. It's a lot of money for an untrained dog—"

"She's trained, sir. She does quite a few tricks. . . . But I'm not selling her. I thought you understood. She's going where I go—and maybe I better leave now." Rush rose to his feet. Shal rose also as if in perfect accord, and upon seeing the two move together a flicker of a smile passed over Captain Whipple's face.

"Boy, you're a smart trader. Fifty dollars? You see I've doubled the money—"

"No—I'm not trading. I wouldn't trade Shal for any price. She's the best friend I have—right now—" and Rush left his sentence unfinished. Hoping the Captain could not read the bitter disappointment in his face, Rush crossed to the door.

"Just a minute, you've forgotten your pack. Now see here, don't be in such a hurry." There was a more friendly warmth in Captain Whipple's voice. "Of course I know you

love your dog, but wouldn't she be better off with me—
good food, shelter—"

"No, sir, she wouldn't. And you'd have to cage her to
keep her from following me," and Rush bent to pick up
his pack.

"Then as I understand it, your proposition is this: in
order to have the dog, I have to take you, too."

"That's what I had hoped—"

"Maybe I've sounded a bit hard, boy, but we do a lot of
bargaining along the river. You'll get used to it if you stay
around. So I have to have you—in order to keep the dog.
You won't sell. . . . Well, maybe we'd better try it for a
while—say, two weeks—"

The aroma of roasting meat suddenly assailed Rush as
he stood in the doorway. A good dinner was being cooked
somewhere below. The Captain had a well-fed look and
there was color in his cheeks. The man had not meant to be
severe—he was merely bargaining. Buying a dog was his
business. No doubt he had purchased the white horse the
same way. Only the owner could not have cared for the
horse as much as he cared for Shal. Or he would not have
let him go.

"I'll pay you for the use of the dog—and you can earn
your keep," continued Captain Whipple. "What I really
need is an advance agent to put up my posters in the towns
where we are playing. Not a boy to fill in. . . . The trainer
has been ill and we've had some severe setbacks. It will be
up to you to make yourself useful."

"We'd work hard to please you." Despite himself, Rush
could hear a little break in his voice and he swallowed hard

to stifle it. A home—with work for both himself and Shal! Here, he would be safe from Sam Burton. No more wandering, cold nights, and loneliness. No one would shoot at Shal, trap her— There was just one more hurdle to jump before he finally agreed, and Rush steeled himself and plunged.

"If we stay, I want to do her training, Captain Whipple."

"I'm afraid you won't have the training of her, boy. We have a regular trainer aboard—an excellent man."

Shal trained by a stranger! This was what he had most feared and although it was not unexpected, it came as a blow. As he watched him closely, the Captain's face sobered.

"You mean—you have a trainer—he uses a whip?"

"Why, yes, all trainers use whips. They have to. That doesn't mean they are necessarily cruel. The white horse didn't look abused, did he?"

"Shal has never been whipped. I'd never let her be whipped, sir. I'd have to do the training myself."

"Well, of all the blasted tomfoolery! Why, boy, you'd upset my whole system. You'd be in the way—we'd get our signals crossed. The trainer might leave and I've had enough trouble already—"

Captain Whipple was genuinely disturbed. Above the dark mustache, there was an angry flush of annoyance. But a swift glance at Shal, standing like a white statue beside Rush, appeared to calm him. The dog was worth fighting for, his glance seemed to say. A little more patience—

"What have you trained your dog to do?" he asked Rush, his manner more controlled. "Can you show me a trick right now?" and there was a challenge in his voice.

"Why, yes. Yes, sir."

Warmth began to seep back into Rush's body—there was still a chance. For a moment he had felt as though he had been plunged to the bottom of the river. All was not lost. Leading Shal, he placed her directly in front of Captain Whipple, then stepped aside. Shal's eyes remained upon him, her ears forward, alert. Never had he loved her more. . . .

"Attention, Shal."

Rush's voice was surprisingly crisp, commanding; and the dog steadied herself, waiting. It was as if she realized the importance of that moment.

"Shal—smile!"

Captain Whipple leaned forward at this unusual request in order to see better. And then a look of amazement lay on his face as he stared. The dog before him was actually smiling, both lips drawn back and curled upward. With her head tilted, one ear flat, the tip of her pink tongue showing, her face assumed a wholly feminine and simpering expression.

"Why, she is—she's smiling!"

"All right, Shal. Good girl." At Rush's words, Shal resumed her former pose. A wave of relief swept over Rush. He had not expected Shal to fail, but this was the first time anyone had seen her smile. It was their latest and newest trick.

"Tell me—" and there was frank admiration in Captain Whipple's voice, "how did you manage that, boy?" The Captain had lost his cool bargaining tone.

"I just talked to her," replied Rush. "Every time I said 'Smile,' I pushed her lips back with my fingers, tilted her head, and pressed down one ear. We did it over and over again. It took a lot of time. I didn't use a whip, sir."

"Well," and the Captain seemed to be searching for words, "I must say you've given me a surprise. She does other tricks?"

"Yes, sir. She already knows how to stand like a statue and won't move a hair until I snap my fingers. And then she makes a bow."

"Do you think the noise of a large audience would upset her?" There was suppressed excitement in the Captain's manner and voice. "If not, you win on the training of her."

"I'm sure I could manage it—"

Light quick steps sounded on the stairs outside and in another moment someone stood in the doorway. The newcomer was the little old lady he had seen on the roof of the Circus Boat that morning—the one who had rebuked Roscoe in his defense. She was no taller than he, and without her bonnet her white curls shone in the sunlight. Madame Whipple, the Captain's mother, described in the Hannibal *Journal* as gracious and charming! Indeed, she looked the part, with her bright black eyes and pink cheeks. One hand swung an empty bird cage against her black silk skirt and the other carried a small sewing bag.

"Daniel, have you seen Blackie?" asked the little lady in a demanding voice. "Someone opened the door of his cage and let him out. He's raised havoc with my sewing things. My thimble's gone—"

"Now, Mother," and Captain Whipple's voice was gentle, an amused smile on his lips as he rose to his feet, "don't blame Blackie for everything."

"He's a terrible thief and you know it, Daniel. You're always trying to shield him. It's my silver thimble, Daniel, the one your father gave me—I'm trying to mend Roscoe's collar. It's badly torn—why, it's the boy with the white dog!"

"Come in, come in, Madame Whipple. I have something to show you. A rather unusual young man and a beautiful dog. Here, sit by me," offered the Captain as he pulled forward a chair.

Madame Whipple entered with a little rustling sound of her silk skirts, bringing with her the sweet scent of peppermint. Without looking about she seated herself primly in the chair, placed the empty cage at her feet, and then lifted her gaze to Shal and Rush.

"Daniel, you're not scolding this boy for what his dog did this morning, are you? I told you that Roscoe was rough —I saw it all from the rake—"

"I'm not scolding him, Mother. We're just talking business."

"The dog's not ugly?" she asked Rush.

"Oh, no, Ma'am. She's gentle as a kitten. I'm sorry the coat was torn—" If the old lady took a dislike to Shal, it might be unpleasant for them both. It was evident that Captain Whipple was very fond of his mother. And her word might be law upon this boat.

"Roscoe's always in trouble of some sort. Most of the animals don't like him. What's your name, boy?"

"Rush Jamieson, Ma'am."

"That's a good name. You have an honest look about you—and manners, too, it seems," announced the old lady with unusual candor. "Is he coming to live with us, Daniel?"

"We've practically agreed on a two-weeks' trial. Right, boy?"

"Yes, sir."

"We can talk some more later. Let's go down now. Every time the wind blows from the north I smell lamb roasting."

"It will be a treat to all of us," and Madame Whipple rose nimbly to her feet. "I'll leave the cage here. But my thimble, Daniel. I must find it or I won't enjoy my dinner. Where has Blackie been perching lately? He generally guards what he hides—"

"Just a minute. Now you speak of it—" and Captain Whipple rose hastily and turned toward the stuffed bear in the corner. Stooping, he peered into the bear's mouth, ran an exploratory finger between the jaws, and then, with a little exclamation of triumph, held the finger up, capped with a silver thimble.

"I knew it! I knew it! The scamp!" With evident joy and relief, Madame Whipple deposited the cherished thimble in her silk bag.

"I'd forgotten," the Captain confessed. "Blackie perched on Salome's head quite a while yesterday. Blackie's a crow," Captain Whipple explained, meeting Rush's inquiring look. "We've had him since a storm blew him against one of our chimneys—with a broken wing. One of the things Shal will have to learn is not to chase any of the pets she may see about. That's one of your responsibilities, boy."

"Yes, sir. She'll learn."

"And now you'd better come with us. Leave the dog here for a while. Shall I close the door?"

"No need, sir. She'll stay with my pack. There's just one more question—" Rush hesitated a bit as though disliking to ask the favor. "Shal has always slept near me—always followed me. We've never been separated. She wouldn't bother anyone," and Rush's blue eyes were pleading.

"I suppose it's all right." The Captain gave a sigh of resignation as though he could argue no longer. "As I said, we'll test the arrangement for two weeks. Does your dog make friends easily?" he asked suddenly as an afterthought.

"There are some people she won't go near—"

"People unfriendly to you?"

"Yes, sir."

"She's a smart dog. I wouldn't think much of her if she did. Come, Daniel. Come, Rush," and leaning on her son's arm, the old lady led the way down the stairs.

6

DINNER ON THE
TOWBOAT

With Shal left to guard the pack in the pilot house and
gazing mournfully after him, Rush followed Captain and
Madame Whipple to the lower deck, happy and relieved
that all had gone so well. However, he was a little self-
conscious as it had been some time since he had mingled
with so many people, and he wished now that he had taken
time to improve his appearance. Pushing through brambles
and sleeping on the ground in the earlier part of his journey had not improved his clothing, and he had not washed
his face since he left the Tolmans' flatboat.

However, Madame Whipple seemed kindly disposed toward him despite any evidences of grime. The Captain was friendly but somewhat reserved, which was to be expected. But if his two weeks of probation aboard the boat proved satisfactory, Rush felt that the Captain would be more friendly. Possibly the Captain had lost confidence in boys, due to his recent experiences with them along the river. Shal was wanted—needed—but he himself would have to win his place and make a friend of every member of the company including Roscoe, if possible. And he had fourteen days and nights in which to accomplish it.

The white horse with the rider in red was just returning to the Circus Boat as Captain and Madame Whipple, followed by Rush, paused before a door which evidently led to the dining room. Having observed them, the rider wheeled his horse nearer and within speaking distance. To Rush's surprise, the man, though youthfully slender, was not young but middle-aged with hair graying at the temples. His eyes were dark and keenly alert, his face deeply tanned.

"Good prospects tonight, Cy?" called the Captain.

"Tolerable. No more rumors of a wild animal escaping. There are quite a few wood yards nearby and lumberjacks. I sent some posters upriver to them on a flatboat. They may come down but of course a lot depends upon the weather."

"It seems pleasant enough now," said Captain Whipple, scanning the sky. "Dinner's about ready."

"Yes, sir, I'll be right along," and the man Cy headed his horse toward the Circus Boat.

"Cy looks thin," remarked Madame Whipple to her son. "I'll be glad when he puts on some flesh."

"He says he's feeling better," replied Captain Whipple. "My, I'd hate to lose him. Just see how he goes ahead— notified those lumberjacks of the show. He's always wide awake and never asleep on his job."

Lumberjacks! Would they come from the wood yard he had left only that morning? And by now had Pod received word to watch out for a boy and white dog? Thanks to Len Slocum Rush had managed to keep Shal out of sight. And until he left that section of the river he knew he must continue to use every caution. The sooner the Circus Boat moved away the better, and for the next few evenings he and Shal must remain under cover. Again the old hunted sense returned to him and he felt himself tight and tense, wishing that he might put out one hand and feel Shal close beside him. As soon as dinner was over, he planned to go to her immediately.

A narrow passage, filled with appetizing odors of lamb and vegetables, led to a larger room. Other feet could be heard traversing all parts of the boat and voices called, each person reminding the other that lamb was to be served that noon. And in another moment he had reached the towboat's dining room.

Tall wooden partitions, open at the top, separated the dining room from the kitchen. From where he stood, Rush could feel the heat of the cooking stove as it penetrated the wooden wall. A long table with chairs in place almost filled the oblong-shaped dining room. The table was set with heavy white china, with a generous supply of bread and butter at each end. Madame Whipple, taking the lead, was seated by the Captain, near the window. By this time, not knowing what he should do, Rush paused halfway down the room, more conscious than ever of being an outsider.

"Over here, Rush," called the Captain. "Sit by my mother today until we find you a regular place," and he motioned to a chair on the other side of Madame Whipple.

"Thank you, sir."

In his eagerness to reach his place, Rush hurried, one of his boots smartly knocking the leg of a chair in passing. To his surprise he discovered it to be a high chair—such as young children and infants sat in. All ages seemed to be represented on the Circus Boat—from Madame Whipple to a baby!

By this time others were entering the dining room, groups of chattering people evidently happy over their mail received from the Alma post office. And there was Cy, appearing even more tan in the subdued light, his red suit replaced by blue jeans and a cotton shirt. There were several gentlemen with sideburns and of portly bearing, in company with a handsome young man carrying a large book under one arm. A young lady, pretty and blonde followed, with two elderly ladies wearing curlers in their hair. Not all the company had arrived when the Captain gave the signal to be seated. There was the noisy scraping of chairs drawn back and inched forward again, and then Rush, sitting beside Madame Whipple, stared in surprise at the high chair halfway down the room. The chair was being moved and he could not see who was moving it! A second later, someone was spryly mounting the steps to reach the seat. . . . No, it was not a child but a tiny man with a brown mustache, wearing long trousers and Prince Albert coat tails! As Rush watched, astounded, his mouth open in spite of his efforts to close it, he was conscious of someone else entering the room, turning sideways in order to pass through the door. She was the very large woman he had seen ringing the bells on the roof of the Circus Boat.

"Here comes Effie," called someone. "Last but not least."

Undisturbed by this reference to her weight, Effie smiled pleasantly, but before she seated herself she walked behind the high chair and pushed the small man closer to the table.

"Thanks, Eff," and the little man spoke in a high metallic voice. "But for you, I guess I'd starve."

Despite her weight, Effie was, Rush realized, a person of unusual beauty. Her eyes were amazingly blue with long dark lashes, her hair coal black, and her skin pink and white. Although her body resembled the round trunk of a tree, her feet and ankles were small and she moved with a rolling grace. With considerable effort, Cy pushed her to the table in a chair on rollers.

"If you get any heavier, Effie," he threatened, "you'll have to find someone else."

"My sister is a lot better," announced Effie, disregarding Cy's remarks and holding up a letter. "My nephew drove her to the levee and she watched the boats go by last week. She hopes to see the Circus Boat when it reaches Clarksville."

"Good!" came a chorus of voices and the entire company acted as one person. It was plain that Effie was a favorite.

"We ought to reach Clarksville in another month and we'll invite her aboard," promised Captain Whipple.

Effie nodded her thanks, her blue eyes lighting on Rush for a moment but expressing no surprise. There had been several other boys hired on the boat, Rush remembered.

Each one had left at the next town from the one where he had embarked. If possible he did not intend to be added to this mounting list. With all his senses alert, he watched and listened. . . . Was Cy the only trainer? Rush hoped so. . . . The man had handled the horse deftly and there was an intelligent kindness about him. At this point someone approached with a large platter, bearing the roast of lamb. It was Roscoe, wearing a very tight short jacket which gave him an overstuffed appearance. As he bent forward Roscoe deposited the roast before Captain Whipple and as he straightened he saw Rush for the first time. Surprise, anger, and then hatred flashed in quick succession across his face and, muttering to himself, he left the room hastily. If Captain Whipple or Madame Whipple saw or heard, they gave no sign. However, the little lady leaned closer to Rush a few moments later.

"Now that I've found my thimble," she half whispered, "I believe I could darn that tear on your coat so no one would notice. Shall I try?"

"Thank you, Ma'am," and to his own discomfiture, Rush felt tears welling to his eyes. And again, if Madame Whipple saw, she gave no sign and commenced to eat the dinner set before her.

The big roast, browned and crisp on the outside, was tender and juicy within. The turnips and potatoes were mashed and the onions creamed. There was plenty of brown gravy but somehow the edge was gone from Rush's appetite as he watched Roscoe come and go with the serving. Both Shal and he had made an enemy of the attendant, whose pride had been wounded before a gaping public that morning. No doubt Roscoe had been twitted more than once about the ludicrous spectacle he had made, flat on his face with Shal standing over him. From now on, Rush warned himself, both he and the dog must be watchful, careful to keep on guard. Even now Shal was waiting alone in the pilot house and he wished that he might run up the stairs just to see if she were safe. Busy with his own thoughts, he lost the trend of conversation until he heard one of the older men with sideburns mention *Doctor Franklin Number Two*.

"So Cap'n Harris has got her now," exclaimed the man. "I was surprised not to see Cap'n Blakely."

"Yes, Dan Harris is her captain now and Steven Hanks her pilot. It's a great team and hard to beat." Captain Whipple spoke with ardent enthusiasm.

"You used to work with Captain Harris, didn't you?" asked one of the prim elderly ladies.

"Yes, Miss Dorset. We were together on the *Smelter*. Dan Harris is a fine man."

With his mind returning to Shal, Rush was about to slip a chop bone into his pocket when Madame Whipple forestalled him, leaning close to whisper.

"No need of it," she told him briefly. "All of the animals are fed at two o'clock in the Circus Boat. Take the dog over there."

"Yes, Ma'am," and Rush felt his face redden.

"It's just a habit, isn't it?"

"I suppose so, Ma'am." He felt better when he saw that she smiled. Taking advantage of the moment, he decided to venture a question.

"Would you mind telling me, Ma'am, is Cy, the man who rode the white horse, the only trainer?"

"Yes, Rush, Cy's a good man. He's not well, so help him all you can."

"Roscoe!" suddenly called the little man Bertie, whose voice soared high above the others, "you look awfully queer somehow. Got your little brother's coat on or is it one of mine?"

Apparently Bertie was unaware that Roscoe had had his coat torn that morning, and was innocent in his banter. He was somewhat amazed when Roscoe, without answering, slammed the platter of meat down on a side table and hurriedly disappeared into the kitchen. However, a welcome burst of laughter covered the unpleasant break and Effie could be heard appealing to Captain Whipple.

"But Captain, Bertie's not eating his dinner. Can't you do something?"

"I'm not expected to eat as much as you," the little man defended himself promptly, apparently dismissing Roscoe from his mind. Who was Effie to judge an appetite anyway, he wanted to know. Already she had passed her plate back four times to be refilled.

"You'll have to anchor yourself down somehow, Bertie," advised the Captain. "Remember we nearly lost you in that last blow."

"Are the storms pretty dreadful on the Mississippi?" asked the blonde girl breathlessly. She was evidently a stranger on the river and undoubtedly the leading lady. "My uncle said he saw a horse lifted off a road in Iowa and blown to a field in Illinois. I never quite believed him—" and she appealed to the handsome young man who Rush decided was the leading man in the cast.

"Why, that's nothing on the Mississippi, Ellie," Cy told her quickly. "Horses, cows, sheep, chickens, and even roofs fly over—just as though they had wings," and he grinned teasingly at the girl. "But we've never lost anyone yet because when a storm comes, we tie onto Effie here. There isn't a blow strong enough to budge her."

"Thank you, Cy," came Effie's voice good-naturedly. "Folks, I'm your bulwark in any storm. But right now I want something done about Bertie's appetite. Maybe a dose of herbs, Captain Whipple, or some dandelion greens?"

Dinner was climaxed by two large custard pies served by a young boy, since Roscoe did not come in again. After a short announcement by Captain Whipple that there would be no rehearsal that afternoon and anyone who might wish to shop in the village was free to go ashore, the company disbanded. Most of the people drifted off toward the bow of the boat. With no desire to linger, Rush hurried up the stairs to the pilot house, still uneasy over Shal. Roscoe's black look of hatred still hung like a shadow over him, and as he finished his pie all sorts of questions turned in his mind. Who fed the animals in the Circus Boat? Roscoe? Would he find some way of poisoning Shal—or when alone with her, claim she attacked him again? Possibly shoot her in self-defense? As he reached the last step, a short, sharp bark greeted him. Shal was glad to see him—but she was also excited by something else, although she still stood guard by the pack left in her care.

"What is it, Shal? There—there—I'm just as glad to see you. . . . Something in the corner?"

The pilot house appeared to be empty. Curiously, Rush followed the dog's gaze and then gave a sigh of relief. A large black crow, clinging fast to the bear Salome's nose and almost standing on its head, was peering into the bear's mouth. Blackie! Searching for the thimble. Evidently the bird had just arrived.

"It's all right, Shal," he told the mystified dog. "That's Blackie—not a wild crow. You must be friends and there'll be others, too. Quiet, Shal."

Perplexed but obedient, Shal stood still. Blackie, now convinced the thimble was gone, regained his normal position, his bright black eyes taking stock of Rush and Shal. There was almost an accusing look in his face.

"Here, Blackie—"

There was a small bone button in Rush's pocket and he offered it to the bird. Blackie gazed at it but did not move.

Walking forward a few steps, Rush placed the button on the Captain's chair. Blackie showed more interest now, shifted his wings a little, and as Rush retreated, floated down to the chair. There were hoarse little sounds of approval as he pecked at the button, and then carrying it in his beak, Blackie was gone, flying in a direct line to the top of the flagpole outside.

"There goes my button," observed Rush as he watched, and then feeling Shal's tongue against his hand, he leaned over her, the top of her white head soft against his cheek.

"We've got to work hard these next two weeks," he told her. "And then maybe they'll let us stay. It's a nice place. . . ."

7

RUSH VISITS THE
ZOO

For fear Shal might become excited at her first glimpse of
the zoo animals, Rush led her by a leash as they crossed the
narrow bridge which connected the Circus Boat with the
towboat. A gently sloping ramp led to the animals' quarters,
but before he descended he paused, his ears catching the
sound of soft music. A light hand moved over the piano
keys and a voice hummed softly. Following the sound, a
moment later he stood in an open doorway and saw for the
first time the theater auditorium. It was a large room occupying the very heart of the boat, with an elevated stage

at the farther end, now dim with partially drawn curtains. At the foot of the stage the blonde girl Ellie sat practicing at the piano, intent upon her work. Behind her stretched rows of benches, the first ten rows offering backs for support, the seats softened with blue and white striped cushions. Kerosene lamps with bright tin reflectors hung along the walls.

Not wishing to disturb Ellie, Rush silently tiptoed away and walked toward the ramp, impressed by what he had seen. The boat was truly a floating theater and he found himself wondering who took the different parts. Just where did Effie fit in—and what of Bertie?

To prevent one's feet from slipping down the ramp, horizontal boards had been nailed across the entire length. What kind of animals had passed along this strange structure? In a few moments he would know. . . . Already the warm air from the hold blew against his face and indicated the presence of animal life. Even though it mounted to a stench, it was not wholly unpleasant. Shal, however, was distressed and came to a halt, her eyes anxious and a growl in her throat.

"Easy, Shal. You'll get used to it. Easy, girl," and Rush pulled the leash even tighter. "These animals are different —they're not wild. . . . They can't hurt us."

At the end of the ramp, both Rush and Shal stopped short before a tall arched doorway, startled by a shrill trumpeting cry within. And for a moment Rush caught his breath with a slight gasp.

A small grayish-black elephant stood directly opposite, his short stumpy legs braced apart in defiance. Outside the cage, scattered about the floor, lay hay which the animal had evidently found distasteful and tossed back to the keeper. Over the iron gateway of the large cage was a name-board and on it was printed TINY TOM. An elephant! The first he had ever seen in real life and Rush stared, eagerly absorbed in the strange creature. Oddly enough, Tiny Tom had no tusks and he stood only six feet high, with large pinkish freckles on his forehead. Although there was unmistakable wrath in Tiny Tom's eyes, his ferocity seemed somewhat lessened by the accidental bouquet of hay which had landed on the top of his head and still clung there.

"It's an elephant, Shal—named Tiny Tom. There's a picture of an elephant in my geography book just like him. The ones with little ears come from India. Look, there are more animals!" exclaimed Rush, and, gripping Shal's leash firmly, he walked toward a second cage. In the center of the cage floor was a squirming mass of black-brown fur from which came squeals and grunts. Upon closer inspection Rush could distinguish short tails, clutching forepaws, and open mouths with white teeth. Over and over rolled the mass of fur and finally became disentangled as one of the heads struck the bars of the cage with a sickening thud. Two cub bears—and their names above were TWIST and TURN. A moment's pause and they were in another embrace, the larger of the two now at the bottom. The scent of a bear was nothing new to Shal, whose control was severely taxed. Rush pulled her away, and they next faced a big lion who sat dozing in the third cage, undisturbed by the turmoil close by. His closed eyes, his two crossed forepaws, and the gray streaking his reddish mane made Rush wonder for a moment if he were real. DIGNITY, printed over the door, seemed a very appropriate name.

Farther down the line there were smaller cages but Rush did not stop to look within. To the right, in a box stall, was the white horse he had seen that morning and the name overhead was DAZZLE. Black harness, shining with silver trim, hung from a nearby peg and Rush wished he might go nearer for the horse had a friendly face. But Cy was more important now. Undoubtedly the room ahead was the feed room, as from within came the steady sound of chopping. If Cy were preparing the daily food, possibly he needed help. Once there was a steady job to do—no matter how menial—Rush knew he would then feel part of this big family aboard the Circus Boat.

Dressed in blue overalls, his back to the door, Cy was hacking at some meat with a big knife on a wooden table. Beyond were a cook stove, a refrigerator, and a sink, with another door leading beyond. Upon hearing Rush's footstep, Cy wheeled quickly, his dark face expressionless. For the first time Rush noticed a scar on the man's right cheek. It had healed evenly and was hardly discernible.

"Someone send you down here?" Cy asked after a pause.

"Yes, sir. Madame Whipple said this was the place to feed my dog."

There was no further question and Cy resumed his cutting of the meat. But for a peculiar hoarse rumbling which seemed to come from Tiny Tom's throat, there was no sound and the silence was not encouraging. Cy was unfriendly. Undoubtedly Captain Whipple had spoken to him about Shal's training and Cy did not wish a stranger, particularly a boy, foisted upon him as an assistant trainer. The man was reacting just as Captain Whipple feared. Meanwhile the elephant's cries had excited Shal, whose every desire and instinct was to crouch low, her ears flattened back, and to crawl toward the cages beyond the doorway. She was almost in position and had inched away several feet when Rush discovered her.

"Stay, Shal."

With a deep sigh the dog lowered her body to the floor and remained motionless, her eyes on Tiny Tom. If the man Cy saw her, he made no sign.

"Is the elephant sick, sir?" Rush knew that his voice did not sound natural but the lack of conversation had become oppressive. "Is there anything I can do to help?"

For a moment the cutting ceased. Cy's voice was impersonal, uninterested. "Thanks. Nothing you can do. Tom's mad. Doesn't like the weeds in his hay. Roscoe's gone for some more," and the cutting resumed.

Roscoe! Was Roscoe helping Cy? So this was the reason Madame Whipple had remarked to her son that some of the animals did not like Roscoe. The thought of Shal left to the devices of Roscoe for training sent a cold shudder down Rush's back. More than ever he was now determined to hold his ground. He alone was to train Shal—no one else. If only he and Cy might talk a bit—

"How long are you here for?" asked Cy, suddenly breaking the silence.

"Two weeks. If I'm able to fit in all right, Captain Whipple says I can stay."

"Well, I reckon you can be of help right now, if you've a mind to." Cy looked up at the clock, mopping his forehead with a handkerchief. "You might fill the sink with water and scrub some of those carrots in the basket. There's more water in the pails on the floor. I'm late today."

"Yes, sir."

It was clear that Cy was not feeling well. His hands shook and he perspired freely. Welcoming the chance to be useful, Rush took hold with alacrity, scrubbing the carrots with a brush. There were also cabbages and apples in the basket and he found himself wondering which animal ate the meat. The lion most likely. . . . And would there be some left for Shal? The dog was now interested, dividing her time in watching the elephant and the preparation of the red beef. Hungry, of course. For several hours that morning, she too had sniffed the savory lamb dinner cooking on the Circus Boat and it was time she had her share.

"Could my dog have a little meat, too?" asked Rush bravely. "She hasn't eaten today."

"I suppose so," and there was a weary note in Cy's voice. "I'll save out some. See that cart over there?" He pointed to a large boxlike affair with trays. "Pull it over here and we'll fill the pans. Cut the cabbage in quarters and the apples in halves. . . . Will your dog stay here while we feed the animals? I don't want a fracas—"

"She'll stay right where she is," promised Rush quietly. "You can count on it. But if you don't mind, I'd like to feed her first. She hasn't been eating very regularly, sir."

The roll of cart wheels across the floor brought every animal to attention except Tiny Tom, who now appeared to sulk in a corner, turning his back on the entire room, his wisp of a tail hanging dejectedly.

"Cheer up, Tom," encouraged Cy. "There's more hay coming." But Tom only crowded his fat little body tighter into the corner, refusing to look around.

"We'll stop here first," directed Cy. "The meat goes to

the lion. Sometimes I add a little oil to keep him in condition. You open the door and I'll push the pan in."

Rush obeyed the directions, conscious that Cy watched to see if he were timid. The lion stirred, opened his eyes, but the door was closed again before he could get to his feet.

"Dignity's pretty old, isn't he?" asked Rush.

"Too old," replied Cy. "He's just an ornament now, poor old fellow." Cy was beginning to be more friendly. "The carrots, apples, and cabbage go to the cubs."

The cubs had stopped wrestling for the moment and stood looking out.

"We won't open the door. . . . Just push the stuff through the bars. Look out for their claws."

Twist and Turn lost no time in greedily grabbing their food and choked in their haste as their sharp teeth crunched into the cabbage.

"Maybe I should show you something else while we're here," and Cy reached up and lightly touched an iron ring which was attached to a short length of chain at the top. "Whenever the cubs get fighting too much, pull this ring. It lowers a partition of iron bars from the ceiling and makes two compartments out of one. Put a cub in solitary confinement and he'll quiet in no time. But be sure the cubs are at one side before the partition comes down. The wall is heavy and they might be hurt. Did you see the leather gloves in the feed room?"

"No, sir, I didn't."

"Well, they're hanging on the wall. Wear them when you separate the cubs. We use the right-hand door when they are together in one room. The left door is locked. And always bolt all doors when you leave the cages. This is the law of the zoo. You will notice that every door has a lock and key as well as a bolt. We are forced to lock the cages sometimes when we have inquisitive visitors aboard. Now over here—"

At this point, in passing an apparently empty cage, Rush was surprised to feel something clutch at his sleeve—a small black hand—and then he gazed down into the questioning wrinkled face of a monkey!

"Well, well, Lily," and there was considerable astonishment in Cy's voice just behind him. "Wait a minute, boy. She wants you to stop."

Rush waited, putting his own hand lightly over the small leathery black one and feeling a keen sense of joy. Madame Whipple, and now Lily, a strange little brown-faced monkey, were his two new friends. But Lily had such a worried expression, looking up into his face as though trying to ask him something. If it were not for her anxiety, he would have thoroughly enjoyed himself. Such a comical little flat nose and human ears, and her brown hair growing up straight in a pompadour!

"It's all right, Lily," he comforted her.

The monkey slowly withdrew her hand and settled back watching Cy as he placed a slice of apple in her pan. A moment later her eyes returned to Rush.

"She happens to like you," observed Cy. "Know much about monkeys?"

"No, sir."

"They are strong in their likes and dislikes." Cy was silent the rest of the time the food was being distributed. As they approached the box-stall he suddenly turned and spoke again.

"I can manage the rest. I wish you'd go back to Lily and see if you can get her to eat." Cy's voice was more natural now, as though some barrier had been broken down. Was it Lily's gesture of friendliness and Shal's good behavior? The dog had not moved from her post but sat tense, her eyes never leaving Rush as he walked about with Cy. In this strange place of sound and smell, she had shown magnificent control, and surely it had not been lost on the trainer. And now—if he could persuade the monkey to eat—

It was dark in Lily's cage, which was half covered with a burlap bag, placed as if purposely to shut out the light. The apple lay where Cy had placed it, untouched.

"Lily," Rush called softly.

There was a slight stir beneath the tan blanket which covered her, and Lily appeared almost immediately, squinting up at him. If only she put out her hand again, he would be sure that she knew him.

"What's the trouble, Lily?" and gathering his courage he thrust his own hand between the bars. A second later he felt her clutch his forefinger and heard her give a faint whimper.

"It's so dark here, Lily. . . . I wish you were in the sunshine. . . . See, here's some nice apple." He picked up the fruit with his free hand. "Couldn't you eat just a little?"

The monkey sniffed at the apple and then drooped wearily, trembling a little as if chilled, still questioning Rush with her eyes as she leaned closer, supported by the bars.

"Can you get her interested?" asked Cy's voice just behind him. "She seems weak. I've tried milk—"

"I wish I could have her where it's warm and quiet. I think she's cold."

"We've tried everything. No one's touched her before. She's new—came from Mexico two weeks ago. It might be the noise in here. . . . She's sort of a favorite with Madame Whipple."

"Let me try, sir. I'll just keep talking to her."

"There's a room with two windows off the feed room," Cy said slowly as though thinking aloud. "Might push the barrels in there to one end. I planned to do it before but was laid up sick."

"Is there some milk?" Rush's eyes followed Lily as she moved into the shadows of her cage once more.

"Fresh this morning." Cy was now looking at Rush, his black eyes keen as though it were the first time he had really seen him. "You like animals—all kinds?" he asked abruptly.

"Why, yes, sir."

"That lion over there—could you get to like him?"

"I don't know why not, sir. He's old—sort of helpless. I'd like to make friends with all of them." There was a little pause and Rush drew a deep breath. "I was hoping we could get on together, sir. And that you'd let me talk with you. . . . I've spent a lot of time with my dog. It doesn't seem as if I could let a stranger touch her. Captain Whipple said I could stay and try it out—"

"He told me." Some of the old crispness was back in Cy's manner.

"I can make her go through the acts—I know I can. I just don't use a whip—"

"Well," and Cy interrupted with a little flare of indignation, "anyone would think I abused these animals! All trainers use a whip. The animals simply know there's one ready in case they're disobedient. What I don't like is to have my discipline upset. Training one animal isn't like training a dozen. How do you suppose I could train a tiger —with words? See this scar here?" Cy pointed to his cheek.

Rush nodded.

"A tiger caught me off guard—in my younger days. I'm wiser now. . . . But I'll admit," and the trainer's voice softened, "that you've done a good job with your dog. I'm not blind. But there's a lot of complications here in this department—you wouldn't understand—"

"Of course Roscoe won't want me around. My dog jumped him. You saw how he felt about it this noon—"

"Yes, I saw it. That's just one of the complications. Roscoe's not an ordinary hand around here. His father is one of the Captain's friends. He's—er—a little used to having his own way. Truth is, I haven't the patience or the energy to tackle a whole new program. I've only a little time left for training. We've had a lot of bad luck. You see how I feel—maybe the Captain better find a new man, a younger man—"

"Oh, no, sir," and Rush must have looked the distress he felt, for Cy stopped and shrugged his shoulders.

"Well, do the best you can for Lily. She's wasting away. Of course, homesickness may be part of it. Can you manage the monkey and dog together in the same room?"

"Yes, sir."

"Clean the room before you move Lily. And try some milk. Might be she'd take some from you. It looks like I've got to go to town for that hay myself," and Cy was gone, striding up the ramp in his blue overalls and a torn straw hat on the back of his head.

8

LILY

Except for the ticking of the clock on the wall overhead, the big room was quiet when Rush approached the monkey's cage, carrying a cup of milk and a narrow-lipped spoon which he had found among the supplies of the feed room. It was evidently the hour when all the animals were accustomed to nap, their appetites appeased and their stomachs full. Even Twist and Turn lay motionless, locked in a strangling embrace. All slept but Shal, quiet and guarded in the doorway, and Tiny Tom, who, still unfed, turned hopefully at the sound of a strange footfall and peeked with one eye over his fat shoulder.

"The hay'll be here soon," called Rush encouragingly, hoping the small elephant understood some of the words. Tom's only response was a soft whistling sigh.

Lily now lay very still beneath her blanket and did not move when Rush called. After a moment of waiting, Rush opened the door and laid a light hand on the slight figure. She breathed regularly but did not attempt to rise. His first inclination was to pick her up—and then he hesitated. Had she the strength to fight? Cy had said no one had been able to touch her until today. . . . Would she behave like the baby wildcat which he and his father had nursed back to health only their last summer together? However, it was impossible to feed her lying down—her head in the farthermost corner. If he were to succeed, he knew he must risk her displeasure and resistance.

"Don't worry, Shal," he called to the dog who had risen to her feet, sensing his dilemma. "She's sick—she can't hurt me."

Wrapping the blanket about Lily, pinning her arms to her sides, Rush gently drew her toward him and finally through the door. The monkey made no attempt to escape. She lay limp against him, and the blanket falling away revealed one hand clutching a tiny brass bell, evidently her most cherished plaything. It was the tight grasp of the black hand upon the bell that gave Rush the strong conviction that Lily was not physically sick. She still had strength and her sickness was mental—homesickness. Perhaps, in some mysterious way, she had divined his own loneliness when she reached out her hand to clutch his sleeve. And the questioning eyes. Yes, Lily was homesick, wasting away with longing for the old and familiar, nothing else.

"Lily," he half whispered, cradling her in his arms as he seated himself on a nearby box, "you aren't going to be alone any more. You, Shal, and I will have a nice room together. And you'll forget. . . . But you must eat, Lily. Now open your mouth—and take this milk. Open your mouth." Dipping the narrow spoon into the milk, he pressed the tip against her lips.

The mouth did not yield but Lily's eyes opened instead and looked directly into his. She was tired, the eyes seemed to say, and did not wish to be disturbed. What was the use —and the little bell dropped from her hand to the floor with a slight tinkling sound. Rush leaned over, picked up the bell, and pressed it into her hand once more.

"Shal and I feel strange here, too, Lily. But we're going to like this new home. Just a little bit, Lily, please."

Lily's eyes were still open, fixed upon him as he tried to pry her lips apart with the tip of the spoon. But her jaws remained set and a little stubborn expression crept into her face. The milk spilled, ran down her neck and over the blanket. There, her eyes seemed to say, why waste the milk—

"There's plenty more," Rush answered her, "and I shall keep trying until you change your mind. I'll clean the room now—"

There was a small round drop of milk on Lily's upper lip, balanced precariously on a few tiny hairs. And with the spoon removed, the ordeal over, the monkey's pink tongue unexpectedly appeared and licked her mouth clean. A single drop of milk. . . . From now on, if she refused to open her mouth, Rush determined to wet her lips. Slowly but surely she would absorb food even though it was so little at a time. So very little—but how much better than none at all! Happy with his slight success, he suddenly hugged her closer. What a mite she was. . . . If only he could give her the strength to live, the will to live.

Early afternoon sunshine now flooded the big room from the upper windows and the boat swayed gently, rocked by the passing of another boat. He had spoken truthfully to Lily—she would soon like this new home. And as he looked about him, he was suddenly aware that every animal watched him intently. Shal from the doorway, Tiny Tom peeking over his shoulder, Dazzle from the box-stall, Twist and Turn upright on their hind feet, and even Dignity, looking out from beneath heavy bangs. All eyes were upon him in silent appraisal. Motionless, he waited. There was a quietness and peace within, a friendliness which warmed him even more than the sun. Somehow, deep down, he felt that these animals liked him. And without words they were telling him so, as he nursed a small homesick monkey back to life.

Shal took exceptional interest in the cleaning of the new quarters. She followed Rush at every step as he rolled and piled the barrels at the farther end of the room. Now and then she surveyed the animals outside, to make sure they were in their cages.

"We're staying here, Shal—for a while. The monkey's coming with us. Here, get out of my way before I hit you with the broom—"

With the floor swept, the new quarters took on more promise. And Rush discovered two bunks built in a side wall, hidden by the barrels. A blanket from his own pack

made up the bed, and the hay discarded by Tiny Tom made
a comfortable pillow when rolled in an old shirt. Finally,
using a barrel for a table, he was able to carry Lily's cage
inside, placing it directly in the sunlight. Shal smelled of
the cage and Rush did nothing to stop her, talking gently
and smoothing her head.

"She's different, isn't she, Shal? Remember the little
wildcat who was so sick? Well, this monkey is sick—and
we've got to take care of her. Now, go over in the doorway
where you were. I'm going to feed her again and she might
be frightened to see you so close. That's a good girl, Shal."

Time passed quickly. Tiny Tom butted his head against
the wall, and with his trunk squirted drinking water over
his back and finally added a layer of dust, sticks, and
debris. Twice, Lily cleaned away drops of milk from her
mouth with her tongue and then swallowed with a look of
surprise in her eyes. She had been outwitted but did not
seem to resent it. Once she looked at her bell, examined it
carefully, and then softly rang it. But Rush knew that it was
the attention she had received, and not the milk, that had
revived her spirits.

The afternoon was half gone when hurried footsteps
came down the ramp. Shal growled softly and Rush rose
from his seat on the edge of the bunk. Through the two
doorways he was able to look beyond into the large room,
and it was possible to see Tiny Tom's cage without being
observed himself. The owner of the hurrying feet soon appeared, and none other than Roscoe bowed down with a
load of hay, his face red, perspiring and angry. Silently
Rush watched as he cut away the binding cords of the hay
with a jackknife, muttering the while. The young elephant,

half facing him, stood guarded, his ears slightly lifted, his trunk curled protectively. It was evident that there was bad feeling between the two. With a jerk, Roscoe opened the cage door, pitched the hay inside with a pitchfork, and banged the door shut again. And then for a moment he stood looking at Tiny Tom, who had not moved—a strange little figure with the skin bagging at his knees like old stockings.

"You don't get any water—see? You fat lummox! Just cause you don't like the hay, you go and spoil my afternoon! This is the second time—no water—see?"

Alone, a few moments later, Rush approached Tiny Tom's cage and looked inside. An empty metal tank stood in a corner, hardly noticeable from the front. Attached to the tank was a round pipe which ran along the wall, passing through the bars of the cage to a window outside. Walking closer, he discovered a pail with a length of rope tied to the handle, just beneath the window—the same pail he had seen from the wharf only that morning. Used as a well-bucket, of course! With the elephant watching, Rush lowered the pail through the window into the river four times and poured the river-water into the open mouth of the pipe. The tank filled, he turned away, conscious that Tiny Tom, still motionless, followed him with his eyes.

For the next hour Rush persisted in his feedings, and finally Lily, won by his attentions, half-heartedly opened her mouth. Twenty minutes later she obligingly consented again and now seemed to be enjoying herself as the sun warmed her cage; there was a look of contentment on her face as she clung to her bell. Shal watched the proceedings tolerantly. . . . This was not the first time she had watched

Rush bring some ailing animal back to health. Moreover, her attention was mostly taken up by Dignity, who appeared possibly to be another dog, but with unusually long hair and who never barked. Not for a moment had she slept; she had remained alert, catching every sound, watching every movement, even to a tiny mouse which dashed across the floor of the feed room into a box of grain.

But for Cy's news that the posters of the Circus Boat had been sent up the river to tempt the lumberjacks near the wood yards, Rush would have felt at ease and even napped in the quiet about him. However, the possibility of being pursued by strange messengers whom he could not recognize kept him tense and anxious. If only Shal and he might remain with Lily in the new quarters that evening, all might go well. Should he be stationed outside on some wharf duty, he would be the target of all eyes. Pod himself might even decide to help search, provided there was a substantial reward offered. . . . Mr. Bissett, the lawyer, was a thorough man and would leave no stone unturned. As soon as the Circus Boat quit that particular vicinity, how happy he would be!

The sudden sound of laughter brought Rush to the window. A small group of people stood on the wharf looking up at someone on the second deck of the towboat. The troupers had returned and Cy was with them, carrying a basket of apples on his arm. Miss Dorset was holding up a strip of orange-colored cloth against Bertie, whose woebegone face peered over the top.

"Is it the right color, Madame Whipple?" called Miss Dorset. "It was a real bargain and I found it at the bottom of a pile in the store here."

"Just right for the jacket," came Madame Whipple's voice.

"Don't look so mournful, Bertie," comforted Effie's voice. "I hope there's enough for a hat for Tiny Tom, too."

"Yes, and an elastic to hold it on," replied Miss Dorset gleefully.

Bertie and Tiny Tom were about to have new costumes, it seemed. And Bertie appeared most unhappy about it all. Rush had left the window when steps came pounding down the ramp. Shal did not growl. Her heavily plumed tail began to wave slightly and Rush knew it must be Cy even before he saw the blue-overalled legs descending. The dog liked the trainer and started to walk forward to meet him. Rush watched, feeling a great sense of relief. Give her time and the dog would make her own friends.

"Hello, Shal," came Cy's voice in recognition, and in another moment he saw Rush, also coming to meet him.

"How's Lily?" asked Cy, his eyes sweeping the room in search of the cage.

"She's in there," said Rush, pointing toward his new quarters. "And she's taken a little milk." Rush's happiness was unmistakable. "At first," he explained eagerly, "she just licked the milk off her mouth—but now, she swallows. She had two teaspoonfuls and slept in my lap—"

"In your lap? You mean you picked her up?" There was considerable surprise in Cy's voice. "I meant to tell you—" and then the trainer paused as if uncertain how he should go on.

"Wasn't it all right? I couldn't reach her in the cage." Rush's face was anxious.

"Sure it was all right. But you took a chance, boy. She's

a strange animal here and how'd you know she wouldn't bite? Let me see her," asked Cy as he led the way through the feed room. "Looks nice here," he commented at the door of the cleaned room. "Hello, Lily, been a good girl?"

Lily, sitting in the last rays of the sun, propped against the bars of her cage, stretched lazily and yawned, showing small white teeth and a pink mouth. A veritable lady of leisure. . . .

"Well, some difference," exclaimed Cy, a pleased expression on his face. "Your dog seem to mind?"

"Not too much. The lion seems to bother her. I suppose she thinks it's some kind of a dog."

"She'll get over it. Dignity just sleeps and eats." Evidently Cy's jaunt to town and Lily's recovery had heightened his spirits. Perhaps now was the time to ask a favor—

"If you don't mind, sir, I'd like to stay right here tonight and keep on with her feedings," and even as Rush spoke, he realized that his voice sounded over-eager and unnatural. "She's pretty thin," he added lamely.

Cy turned and let his dark eyes rest on Rush a full moment. "Most boys would be asking to see the show tonight," he commented quietly. "I don't doubt but what you have the monkey's interest at heart—but—there's something, an expression in your face. I've been thinking about it, quite a bit. You wouldn't be running away from someone, would you?"

Suddenly all the strength Rush seemed to possess flowed out of his body and he felt his face drain white. Instinctively he reached out one hand toward Shal, feeling for her collar. When he spoke finally, his voice had a choked sound, almost as if he were talking to himself.

"I promised. . . . I won't lie. . . . Ye-es, Mr. Cy—"

"So you are running away from someone. I thought so. . . . We've had other boys like you before and they caused Captain Whipple no end of trouble. He had to ship them back home and I'm surprised that he did not ask you more questions."

"He wasn't interested in me—it was my dog."

"Even so—I can't help feeling surprised. Would you have told him the truth if he had asked if you were running away?"

"Yes, sir. . . . I promised—"

"Promised who—promised what?" Cy's voice had a note of impatience.

"My father, sir—not to lie."

"Where's he now?"

"He's dead, sir."

"Oh." The silence which followed, with Cy still staring at him, was broken by the sound of a bell.

"Well, I guess we'll have to finish our talk later. Time for supper," and Cy turned to go. "It's only right that you tell the Captain. Maybe tomorrow. He's had a trying day."

To Rush, through blurred eyes, the ramp appeared like a long steep hill. Stumbling, he followed Cy, guided by the rail.

Supper began as a quiet affair, each person occupied with his own thoughts, quite different from the earlier meal. Rush was seated beside a Mr. Baker, who had a pompous manner and sideburns, and opposite Cy, who rarely looked his way. Madame Whipple, cheery as a cricket and dressed in lavender taffeta and lace kerchief, had nodded and smiled; but Captain Whipple, who looked weary and spent, merely sank into his chair with a long sigh. Roscoe waited upon table as usual but in a bored fashion, forgetting several times to replenish the little butter plates. The girl Ellie appeared nervous and actually giggled hysterically when Mr. Baker pulled a script from his pocket and began to memorize his lines in a loud whisper.

"Why are you having such a struggle over a few lines, Mr. Baker?" asked one of the ladies with curlers, in a plaintive voice. "You didn't have any trouble last year."

"Annie Dorset, mind your business," reprimanded the other lady with curlers, and Rush now decided they were two old-maid sisters. "Do you expect a big audience here tonight, Captain? It's been quiet all afternoon."

"Most of the folks will come from little nearby towns as soon as their work is done," replied Captain Whipple. "Yes, I expect a big audience," and conversation livened as the Captain talked. All ate heartily of the cold ham, potato salad, hot biscuits and applesauce, except Rush, whose every mouthful seemed to choke him. Perhaps after tomorrow he would be leaving these kind people. Tomorrow, such a short time away. . . . Cy was keen, observing. What had his face expressed—the hunted sense he had been feeling? Had he done wrong not to tell Captain Whipple his whole story? But the Captain had not appeared interested. His eyes had been upon Shal, studying and admiring the dog, and had he asked leading questions, Rush would have answered truthfully. Did Cy believe him? There would be more talk later. However, this was Cy's rare opportunity to be rid of him. Cy had not wanted him interfering with the training discipline in the first place.

"There'll be less money and more vegetables tonight,"

the Captain was saying. "We're now in the farm country. Randolph," and he looked appealingly at Mr. Baker, "you know your part all right—and you know sound vegetables. I wish you'd take over the box office tonight. There'll be time as you don't come on until the last of the second act."

"Of course, Captain. Just so long as I don't have to nibble and sample each thing. I'm no good on the animals, though."

"I'll be around," encouraged Cy.

"Now that the roast of lamb is gone, I hope someone walks up with a young steer. A few juicy steaks wouldn't go amiss."

"Pink in the middle for me," almost shouted Bertie.

"We'll keep our eyes open," replied Captain Whipple. "I must say I'm tired of eggs. In a week or so we'll be in the land of the fish pole."

"And remember, always be watching out for bananas," instructed Cy. "Some boat or other may be carrying them."

"I understand that Lily has been moved," and Madame Whipple directed her conversation to Rush. "Has she eaten anything yet?"

"Yes, Ma'am . . . a little milk," said Rush in a voice so low it was hardly audible.

"Good!" Madame Whipple's white curls bobbed with her enthusiasm.

"How'd you do it, young man? With a tube or something?" asked Mr. Baker, turning to survey him.

"With a spoon, sir," replied Rush, not too happy at being the center of attention. How generous was Cy? Would the trainer resent his success?

Cy had not looked at him since they sat down. How he

would miss these jovial, warm-hearted people. . . . And Lily, would she take her milk from anyone else?

"By the way, Captain," called somebody from the foot of the table, "didn't someone promise you another monkey as a gift? Some man from Kentucky?"

"That's right," and Captain Whipple sighed heavily. "We had two monkeys painted on the Circus Boat for that reason. I guess it was all talk as usual—people don't keep their promises these days. One man promised me a lion cub to take Dignity's place. I held the boat back two days waiting. No lion. Another man said he'd send me some peacocks. No peacocks. No, people don't keep their promises these days." And the Captain gave another deep sigh.

"Don't be despondent, son," murmured Madame Whipple.

"I still know one or two persons who keep their promises, Captain," said Cy after a pause. And for the first time during the supper hour, the trainer's dark eyes rested on Rush and he smiled a little.

9

FIRST EVENING

Supper finished, Rush returned to the Circus Boat, descending the ramp much happier than he had ascended, a brief hour ago. Cy's first show of friendliness, the warm smile of appreciation from his dark eyes, was heartening. If the trainer found him useful enough, he might persuade the Captain to let him remain on the Circus Boat, despite the fact that he was a runaway. Rush felt that in time he might be able to tell his story to them both and win their protection.

Conversation at the supper table had also revealed the news that the next stop would be downriver at Trempealeau and then on to La Crosse. He was glad to be traveling south-ward, into the larger cities and as far from Eau Claire as possible. Perhaps by tomorrow night, if he were still aboard, he might even feel free enough to leave Shal and Lily together and join the audience in seeing the drama played in the auditorium, *From Rags to Riches*. What a stirring and encouraging title the show had! Unconsciously Rush's hand felt of the rent in his sleeve. The drama could easily be applied to himself. Yes, Cy's show of friendliness had lightened his whole horizon and he found himself call-ing out to each animal as he passed their cages.

"Hello, Tiny Tom, that hay's all right, isn't it? Say, Twist and Turn," and he knocked gently on the bar to at-tract attention, "don't you ever get tired of wrestling? I hope I never have to pull that partition down and separate you! You're a nice old fellow, Dignity. I never knew lions could be so tame. . . . Hello, Dazzle, someday I'd like to ride you," and on to Shal, still posted in the doorway, her ears pricked forward, her tail waving vigorously, a little gleam of envy in her gold eyes because he did not speak to her first. "You come first—always—don't you know that, Shal?" Rush smiled as he saw the dog ease beneath his touch.

Lily lay asleep, her head thrown back and mouth half open. The bell was still clutched in one hand and there was a bright gleam of red about her neck and more of the same color draped over her shoulder. It was ribbon. Yes, Lily was wholly feminine. She had fallen asleep while attempt-ing to decorate herself with a bit of cheer and there she lay, content, with almost a smirk upon her small brown face. Apparently there were other treasures hoarded somewhere in her cage, and as her prospects had taken a favorable turn she was bringing them out, one by one. For the moment it seemed a pity to disturb her although it was time for her milk. Cy had spoken of bananas. Were they for Lily? A picture in an old copybook which he had once owned flashed across his mind as Cy spoke. A myriad of small monkeys seated upon the limb of a tree, eating bright yellow fruit. . . . He himself had never tasted a banana. If possible he meant to procure one for Lily. . . .

Someone with a heavy tread closed and locked the gate at the head of the ramp. There was a jingle of keys and the feet moved away. With little to do at the moment, Rush perched himself on the sill of the nearest window and looked out. From where he sat, he could see some of the lights of the Circus Boat. With all her lamps aglow, she was like a blazing jewel against the blue night, sending out yellow shafts of light over the moving water. By leaning out still farther, he could see the bows of other boats, which had arrived during the supper hour. He now vaguely remembered having heard their landing bells and whistles during the supper conversation, although they scarcely reached him through the fog of his deep discouragement. How would the lumberjacks come? Would they walk or arrive by boat?

A fierce bright blaze of light made him jump and draw back into the shadows of the room. A torch basket! It was suspended from a long pole leaning out over the water from a nearby boat, illuminating the levee and enabling the dock hands to see as they unloaded crates at night. The chips of wood in the basket, probably saturated with powdered rosin, sent up clouds of black smoke. Back at the window and now seated on a box inside, he continued to watch, warning himself to be careful. Tonight, of all nights, he must remain under cover. A foolhardy move and he might play directly into the hands of those searching for him. He was not very far from Eau Claire, he kept telling himself. The torch basket was an exceptionally large one—like an angry sun suddenly come up out of the water—and it was a few moments before he felt calm again.

There were more bells, more whistles, and people shouting. The whole night outside seemed to be breathing with excitement, making him wish that he could be in the center of it. How different from the quiet of the wilderness! To add to the feverish confusion, the bells on the roof above burst into a lively tune, "Turkey in the Straw," which made everyone pause and look up. A lone figure undoubtedly stood there though he could not see her. Effie, of course. Meanwhile Shal, roused by the loud blasts of music, had come close and rested her head on his knee, her ears flattened back in disapproval.

"It's just a song, Shal. Kind of loud. . . . We'll get used to it."

Shal was not alone in her disapproval. Tiny Tom could be heard between beats, roaring wheezily as he stumped up and down; and once Dazzle neighed. Lily slept on, however, and the bears continued their wrestling. However, the bells had whipped the world outside into action. Captain Whipple, wearing a high silk hat, crossed the stage plank and proceeded to nail a poster on the front of the ticket office. Shortly after, Mr. Baker hove into view, also wearing a high hat and carrying a cotton bag. With a deliberate pompousness, he disappeared into the ticket booth and seated himself behind a wire-mesh window. Engrossed in watching the scene as he leaned on the window sill, Rush heard a boy's voice suddenly ring out, almost in his ear.

"Look! There's a fellar in there with some of the animals! I can see something white—an' a cage—"

The faces of four boys, younger than himself, were now staring at him, having approached from the darker end of the wharf. A roar from Shal scattered them in all directions and they were about to return when someone from the towboat called.

"Keep away from there, boys! No one is allowed near those windows!"

It was the voice of the man in blue jeans who had admitted him to the towboat only that morning and was still on guard. No one seemed to have noticed the incident and, evidently impressed, the boys dissolved into the crowd. Rush, scolding himself, had retreated to the back of the room. Unwittingly, he had gone close to the window in order to look out. He had done exactly what he had warned himself not to do. . . . For a few moments he remained listening. No more feet approached, but from where he sat the glint of brass buttons caught his eyes. Yes, it was Roscoe. The coat had been mended and Roscoe strutted about in the crowd with his usual air of assurance. With his hair wet and combed in a side part, he made a smart appearance. It was now even more easy to understand how his false pride had suffered when he was pinned to the wharf in all his finery by Shal only that morning.

The bells stopped with a loud crash and the silence which followed was almost painful. Some live coals fell from the torch basket, and even at that distance Rush could hear the hot coals sizzle as they struck the water. Then voices began calling from across the square where already people were arriving in farm teams.

"There she is! . . . My, see the lights! . . . Captain Dan Whipple's Circus Boat!"

On they came, men, women, and children, their faces shining with anticipation as they passed the torchlight. And how Rush longed to join them! Not a lumberjack among them as far as he could determine. Even in that light they would be distinguishable by their heavy boots and short jackets. And meanwhile, above all other noise, the dogs left behind to guard the horses and wagons howled mournfully.

It was not long before a line formed, a jolly laughing crowd. Little boys chased each other, ladies called back and forth, and white-bearded old gentlemen brandished canes like swords. Finally at a given signal—three blasts of a whistle—the gate at the farther end of the stage plank was opened and the line passed across, Roscoe taking the tickets of admission. At last Dan Whipple's Circus Boat was ready to receive its first nightly audience from the little town of Alma. And as yet there was no sign of a single lumberjack. With a sigh of relief, Rush drew the box closer to the window, seated himself, and leaned against the wall. There was less cause to worry now. After a little while, when the torch basket had burned low he planned to sit on the window sill.

Lily stirred and Rush fed her. After admiring her ribbon and tying it in a bow, he returned her to her cage, sleepy, and relaxed. By now the line of waiting people had shortened and for the first time Rush saw farm produce exchanged for tickets of admission. A tall lean man with two live hens, their legs tied together and slung over his shoulder, had approached the window and was timidly dickering with Mr. Baker while his wife and two children hovered anxiously at one side. Mr. Baker, red of face and perspiring, his tall hat pushed to the back of his head, had lost his pompous manner and appeared somewhat wilted. With a final glance at the hens held up for inspection, he jerked his head in assent and the family joyously crossed the stage plank, transferring the hens to Roscoe who placed them in a nearby coop.

"Hooray! We're goin' in!" shouted one of the children, a fat boy in a white blouse.

Nor was this all, and Rush leaned forward a little to stare with increased interest. For a moment later a young man arrived with a gray and white goat, with the intention, no doubt, of adding it to the Circus Boat's zoo. However, the goat, alarmed by the blow of a whistle from a nearby boat, ran its length of rope dragging the youth with him into the midst of some young ladies who had just arrived. There were screams, a flutter of skirts, and flying heels. The day was saved by the owner, who with presence of mind reached out and clung to the side of the ticket office, which rocked precariously while Mr. Baker, an agonized expression on his red face, strove to keep balance within. Bystanders intervened and the young man and goat departed and were not seen again.

The last of the customers served, Mr. Baker closed the window and, hugging the cloth money bag, made his way into the Circus Boat, his lips moving noiselessly as he rehearsed the part he was to play that evening. Roscoe also left immediately, a bundle under his arm, glancing furtively about him as he became lost in the shadows of the village square. For a few moments there was no one guarding the entrance of the Circus Boat. Then came the sound of feet and Cy appeared, looking right and left as if in search of someone.

"Roscoe! Roscoe!"

There was no response and, plainly disturbed, Cy walked back and forth in the light where Rush had full view of his face.

"Roscoe! Roscoe!"

It was in the next moment of listening that Cy and Rush must have heard the same sound—the tramp of boots, faint at first, then louder, louder. Lumberjacks. Even Cy remained to watch. Across the square came groups of men, marching in twos and threes. Their gait, the lurch of their bodies confirmed Rush's suspicions. With hands gripping the edge of the window sill, his face hidden in the shadow, he waited. The men were within speaking distance when a spokesman emerged ahead of the others, wearing the usual red mackinaw and cap of the lumberjack, and approached Cy.

"Show commence?" asked a voice with a French accent.

"Ten minutes ago," replied Cy pleasantly.

"How much zee ticket?"

"Two bits—fifty cents. The office is closed but I have some tickets here."

There was a muffled jingle of coins as each man produced his money and received his ticket in return. The last man in line loitered behind the others, looking about him curiously.

"You see boy an' white dog at Circus tonight?" he asked Cy.

"A boy and white dog?" repeated Cy, gazing intently at

the man. "No—no boy and white dog in this crowd to-night."

For a moment Rush could hardly believe what he had heard. . . . But Cy's voice had been distinct, decisive, and the man crossed the stage plank along with the others without further comment. Cy had not even questioned the stranger—not even shown curiosity but had cleverly protected him. "No boy and white dog in this crowd tonight." Now it was clear that since their talk before supper, Cy had decided to become his friend. But would the lumberjack inquire of others inside—or become engrossed in the show and feel he had finished his mission?

There was nothing to do now but remain quietly hidden until the evening performance was done. Curled in the darkest corner of the bunk with Shal beside him, Rush waited. Just above, with only the wooden floor between, was the messenger sent in search of him. Rush could picture him now, seated between two other lumberjacks, his black eyes staring about. . . .

Cheers, laughter, long pauses from above. Would the show never end? The little room seemed stifling and it was evident that in the next room the animals were still restless. Tiny Tom thumped the end of his trunk upon the floor with a strange metallic sound and Dignity let out a muffled roar. At each sound Shal's ears stood upright, alert, and Rush soothed her with his hand. He must leave—soon—as soon as the show was over. It was not wise to go now, as a second messenger might be lurking in the darkness outside. He would feel safe—so much safer back in the deep forests than on the river. Why had he not realized it before?

Madame and Captain Whipple would classify him with

the other ne'er-do-well boys, who disappeared without saying good-bye or thank you. However, it would be impossible for him to tell them his story. No one would believe him. Samuel Burton was too well known up and down the river, a supposedly respectable and influential person. Cy, who was beginning to be kind and understanding, could do little for him. And Cy was ill. However, there was Roscoe to help the trainer as he had before, and Cy was slowly gaining. No one would miss him—only Lily. Who would continue with Lily's feeding—Roscoe? He hoped not. . . .

With a final burst of applause, feet pounded on the floor above and down the stairs, and Rush knew the amphitheater was being emptied. Like liquid from a bottle, people poured over the stage plank, their laughter and chatter suddenly drowned by the loud chimes of bells playing "Oh Dem Golden Slippers." Yes, there was the messenger in the midst of some lumberjacks, and with a sigh of relief he watched them go out of sight. In a few moments he would slip away the best he could. Only the roustabouts would be around then. He wished he might say a few words to Cy— and then he became conscious of two voices nearby, Captain Whipple's and Cy's. Both men were standing on the wharf at one side of the stage plank.

"He's disappeared," Cy was saying. "I walked the whole length of the levee looking for him and then I went to his room. All of his things are gone. There's only his uniform hanging in the closet—"

"Roscoe gone? Why, Cy—" There was no mistaking the shocked surprise in Captain Whipple's voice. "Are you sure? Have you inquired at the different boats? He might be visiting—"

"I've done everything. He's gone, Cap'n. And I think he's gone downriver to join some theatrical troupe. He made a lot of talk this week about acting. Stage-struck—like the most of them and thinks he can become a great actor. He never cared for the animals. That's where he's gone, Cap'n," and Cy's voice expressed strong feelings of disgust.

"Well, he was of little help around here." Captain Whipple gave a long sigh. "I think I imposed on the troupers, keeping him here. But his father, as you know, is an old friend and I was trying to help knock some sense into his boy's head. I haven't time now, nor the inclination to chase him. I'll see his father in Cairo."

"You did your best, sir," comforted Cy. "I've another piece of news for you—"

"I hope it's good—"

"Not too good. The *Elsie* is across the river. I heard some rivermen talking."

"So that blackguard Sam Burton is around again!" exclaimed Captain Whipple.

"He's never far away."

"Thinks he's going to run me off the river with his dirty tricks," mused Captain Whipple. "Well, we'll see. Keep a sharp lookout, Cy. It's all we can do now. . . . How are you feeling? Roscoe's leaving means more work for you. How's the new boy doing?"

"To tell the truth I don't know what I'd do without him. He's a worker and the animals like him. That's half the battle. Of course he's on trial for two weeks, but if he keeps up the pace he'll be the best help I've ever had. As to how I'm feeling—there are good days and bad. But I'm gaining. The doctor says I will be well within the year."

"Good. Well, we'll hang on and show Sam Burton a thing

or two. He'll run himself off the river before he's through.
. . . Strange, my mother predicted Roscoe would run
away . . . the overgrown lummox . . . no brains. . . ."
And the Captain walked slowly in the direction of the
towboat.

To Rush, listening, the news that Roscoe had run away,
lured by the footlights, was overshadowed by the name
spoken by Captain Whipple—Sam Burton! Hardly conscious of moving, he found his way to the bunk and sat
upon its edge. Sam Burton! Was he never to hear the last
of that name? What was the connection between Captain
Whipple and Sam Burton? The Captain's voice had been
bitter and he had called his stepuncle a blackguard and
said, "Thinks he's going to run me off the river with his
dirty tricks." Cy had called his stepuncle's boat *Elsie* . . .
and "never far away."

A fresh burst of light from the torch basket flooded the
room and Rush moved deeper into the bunk. Roscoe's disappearance affected his own plans now. The sharp fear of
his own danger lessened as he thought of Cy's position,
carrying on alone and still weak with illness. Cy was his
friend now—depending upon him. Not only had he protected him from the messenger but also he had not reported
the incident to Captain Whipple. Cy's praise had been sin-
cere. In the short time he had been on the Circus Boat, he
was beginning to make a place for Shal and himself. Should
he sacrifice it all now? Question after question poured
through Rush's mind. It was like a searchlight turned glar-
ingly upon himself, his own hopes and fears, and Cy's
predicament. And for a moment the wind from the river
blew against him. Though warm—it chilled him.

The wharf and street were deserted. There was still time

for him to go. Rush rose to his feet and then sat down again. No, he could not leave Cy, and there was also a certain sense of security in the fact that Captain Whipple and he had an enemy in common. In a way, the Circus Boat was a haven. . . . Possibly the news of his disappearance from Eau Claire had not reached his stepuncle. Moreover, it had been a long time since Sam Burton had seen him. He would not recognize him, should they come face to face. Why should he leave the Circus Boat? And if he remained, should he acknowledge his relationship to Sam Burton, tell his whole story to Captain Whipple? What would it accomplish? Nothing. . . . Despite the acknowledgment, Captain Whipple might think the uncle had planted him there in their midst. Any relation, close or distant, of Sam Burton's might prove abhorrent to the Captain. He must remain silent . . . if he stayed . . . if he cast his lot with the Whipple Circus Boat.

A heavy voice from the towboat was shouting orders. Voices answered and then came the throb of an engine—like a great heartbeat. Was the Circus Boat leaving or shifting her position?

In an instant Rush was at the window looking out. The stage plank had been removed. . . . The lights in the village still shone. There were no lumberjacks—only men in the distance unloading crates. The dark water between the Circus Boat and levee was widening. A torchlight on the wharf grew smaller. Yes, they were moving southward, leaving Alma. He could not leave the boat now, even if he wished, and this erased all torturing uncertainty for the moment. Shal nuzzled his hand, and he bent down to rest his cheek against her head.

"It's all right, Shal. We're safe for tonight, anyway. We can sleep now. What's the matter, Lily?"

Lily was standing upright, whimpering for attention. As Rush went closer, she reached out one hand.

"Why, you're cold, Lily."

A few moments later Rush lay in the bunk, Lily nestled against his shoulder, Shal stretched at his feet. The little room no longer seemed stifling and the wash of the current on the side of the boat held an even song. As though eager to leave Alma and reach Trempealeau, the towboat, pulsing strong and steadily, pushed the Circus Boat down the wide waters of the Mississippi.

10

THE TRAINING OF
TINY TOM

The two things seemed to happen together. Cy called his name just as the throb of the engine stopped. Yes, it was morning and there was Cy, fully dressed, standing by the side of the bunk with Shal vigorously wagging her tail. However, Cy was not looking at him but at Lily who lay across his chest, sleeping placidly.

"For Heaven's sake!" and Cy bent down to look closer. "Did she sleep there all night?"

"Yes, sir. I guess so. . . . She was cold."

By now Lily was awake. She yawned, looked up at Cy and, after feeling of her throat with one hand, began to search about diligently, finally pulling forth a red ribbon and small bell which had been tucked beneath the corner of Rush's collar.

"For Heaven's sake!" came from Cy again and a smile lighted his dark face. "Made herself right at home, didn't she? Looks to me as if Lily hadn't been sick at all—just lonesome."

"I think you're right, sir." With Lily balanced on his shoulder, Rush rose to his feet. "Am I late? Is this Trempealeau?"

"No, Fountain City. We've stopped for a time to take on two men here. A new cook and an engineer. By the way Roscoe's left us," and Cy's black eyes watched Rush carefully as if to see the effect of his words.

"I know, sir. I heard you and the Captain talking last night."

"That so?" Cy looked a little surprised. "We were right near your window, weren't we? . . . Had you any idea Roscoe was leaving?"

"No, sir. He wasn't down here much—"

"I guess not," said Cy with a wry smile. "Well, it leaves just us two on the job now. It's rough on you because I'm not able to do a full day's work." Cy's eyes continued to study him.

"I'll do my best—as long as I stay. I—I heard that man asking for me last night. You didn't tell about me—"

"I didn't like his face," replied Cy quickly. "Now let's drop the whole thing, for the time being anyway. I'm asking no questions because, well, I have confidence in you. You're needed here—you've done a fine job with Lily. The animals like you. Do you enjoy your work?"

"Oh, yes, sir."

"That settles it. And I think the Captain will be willing to pay you something each week, too. Shal appears to be fitting in. I notice she watches you every time you go near the cages."

"She's still worried but I think she's beginning to understand."

"Good. Now this morning, I want to try out Tom. He's only a calf, you know. His mother was killed in an accident and he was raised on a bottle. We bought him of a Burmese who had started training him. Trainers in India are called oozies."

"Oozies?"

"Yes. Tom's oozie went back to Burma. Captain Whipple paid a big price for Tom—bought him in New Orleans. I saw the oozie put Tom through a few tricks and I wrote them down. I'll bring my notes and we'll see how much Tom remembers. They say an elephant never forgets—but I don't know. He's still pretty young—"

"How old is he, sir?"

" 'Bout four years. Calves are nursed by their mothers until they are five. So you see, Tom has had a different background than most. He's a scamp and can make a lot of trouble," and Cy smiled indulgently. "For some reason," said Cy, his smile fading, "he doesn't like Bertie. Maybe it's Bertie's voice."

"Is Bertie to help train him?"

"Not exactly. He's supposed to ride him, though, at the

head of the parade which we're training for. I think the whole trouble is that Bertie's afraid of Tom and Tom knows it. We'll have to work it out somehow."

"That's why Bertie isn't happy over that orange cloth? I heard them talking yesterday."

"Yes, he's pretty miserable. Doesn't want to wear an orange jacket. But it's the Captain's pet plan for Bertie to ride Tom. I guess Tom has played a few tricks on Bertie. You see," and Cy's eyes shone with enthusiasm, "once we get the parade going—it will make a great hit and draw crowds. We've only started. . . . There will be more horses added and a band as soon as we find the right players. By the way, there are brushes in the feed room. Be sure and give Shal a good brushing every day. She and Dazzle will start work together soon. There goes the first breakfast bell." Cy turned away as a shrill gong sounded from the towboat. "Don't forget to put Lily back in her cage. She might wander off—up a smoke stack! We'll start with Tom as soon as I exercise Dazzle," and Cy was gone, his last words drifting back through the doorway.

With Lily on his shoulder and Shal by his side, Rush remained standing in the middle of the room. Never had Cy been so talkative, so friendly; and the acknowledgment that Rush was needed to assist in the training work sent his spirits soaring. How strange that Bertie should fear Tom! Perhaps the elephant seemed very large to the midget who stood only three feet high. But to ride Tom at the head of a parade! In all his life nothing had appealed to Rush so much, and he gave such a long deep sigh that Shal looked at him curiously.

"It's just something I want to do," he told the dog gently.

And then again, as his mind turned to Bertie and Tom and his own desire to ride at the head of the parade, the seriousness of his own position brought his dreaming to a halt. The *Elsie,* owned by his stepuncle Samuel Burton, was not far away; there was danger. . . . By now, perhaps his stepuncle had heard of his disappearance from Eau Claire and would be watching for a boy accompanied by a white dog. No, riding Tom might be his ruin. He could not hope to head a parade, the target of all eyes. From now on he must content himself with training Tom. Already the little freckle-faced fellow had shown evidence of friendliness, advancing a step or two to meet him when he opened the cage door and making a little purring sound of welcome. Perhaps, someday, when the Circus Boat had traveled farther south, he might be allowed to substitute for Bertie and ride Tom down some village street—just once.

Meanwhile Cy needed him. He was even needed by the frail little monkey who now perched on his shoulder. As though sensing his dilemma and longing, Lily clung to his arm as he placed her back in her cage. And then the second breakfast bell rang.

While the people of Fountain City slumbered quietly, surrounded by high brown bluffs, the troupers of the Circus Boat ate their breakfast. Little clouds of fog swirled past the windows, and as the sun climbed higher cowbells tinkled in the distance. Early as it was, everyone seemed to be in good humor and all had a pleasant nod for Rush as he took his seat at the table. Evidently Lily's recovery and his work had been appreciated.

There was, however, no mention of Roscoe's sudden departure and Rush had the feeling that the matter had been discussed before his arrival. To his surprise, mid the homelike aromas of bacon and coffee, Blackie the crow sat upon Captain Whipple's broad shoulder, leaning forward to peer curiously at every mouthful that passed to the Captain's mouth. And for the first time Rush was able to catch a close look at the leading man, Leslie Wood, who was a tall handsome youth with dreamy eyes, always memorizing parts from his big volume of Shakespeare. Ellie, the leading lady, seemed quiet and shy in his presence, asking questions of the table in general but seeking the young man's final approval with her eyes. Conversation did not lag but took quick and devious turns.

"When we reach Trempealeau, we'll probably receive a corn beef brisket," Madame Whipple announced during a discussion on food supplies. "Last year a man from there brought one and we let his whole family on the boat. They took up eight seats but the meat was worth it."

"We got two nice pullets last night," added Mr. Baker. "But I certainly didn't want that smelly goat!"

"No," and Effie shook her head over her ruffles and coffee cup, "no goats! But I'd love a boiled dinner. Bertie," she said, leaning forward as far as possible to gaze into Bertie's plate, "you haven't eaten your egg."

"These morning mists take all the curl out of my hair," complained Miss Annie Dorset. "I know I'm a sight in curlers but what can I do—"

"I must get Dazzle's saddle mended in Trempealeau," Cy told Captain Whipple.

"Bertie! You must eat your egg!" exclaimed Effie again.

"If you get any smaller Sam Burton will be running off with you—"

"Not me," replied Bertie firmly. "Anyway," stated Bertie, before cramming the entire yoke into his mouth, "I shan't get off the boat here to give him a chance."

"We'll wait a few hours and if by that time the men don't appear, we'll go along," announced Captain Whipple. "Yes, Cy, get the saddle mended in Trempealeau. There's a fine saddler there."

For the next two hours, while Cy exercised Dazzle along the shore, Rush cleaned and tidied the cages, swept the floor, and brushed Shal. He had barely finished when Cy returned a little breathless and a trifle pale beneath his dark tan.

"I'll rest a bit," he told Rush, seating himself on a stool, "and then we'll see what we can do with Tom. I didn't try any stunts today. Madame Whipple was watching with the Captain's glasses." He smiled knowingly. "She's given orders for me not to do any stunts until I'm better."

"Madame Whipple seems to take care of everybody," observed Rush. "Just like a grandmother."

"Everybody," repeated Cy. "She knows what goes on— and don't think she doesn't. Well, let's get down to work," and Cy pulled a notebook from his pocket. "First, you go in and talk to Tom a bit. Get him in good humor. Does Shal mind your being in Tom's cage?"

"Not too much. She watches, though. Will she make Tom nervous?"

"She might. As a rule elephants don't like dogs. Shut Shal in your room for this time."

With Shal removed, Rush placed two apples in his pockets at Cy's request and then approached the gate of Tom's cage. Upon hearing his gate opened, Tom gave a low squeaking sound of pleasure.

"By the way, Rush," warned Cy outside, "always let Tom see you approach. Elephants are easily startled. If they hear a noise and can't see the cause, they get panicky."

"Yes, sir—seems natural, doesn't it? Ready for a lesson, Tom?" asked Rush as he entered. "Here, boy, look in my pockets."

Tom's trunk lost no time in worming its way into both pockets for apples. The two apples disappeared quickly into his mouth.

"Now, pat him a bit on his trunk. Don't be afraid."

A brisk patting followed while Tom stood motionless as though enjoying it.

"There, you're getting acquainted. Remember, he's an awful thief at times. Loose in a crowd, he can make quite a haul. I've seen him. Bring him out, Rush."

Tom was delighted to come through the gate into the larger room. There were many things he wished to investigate but at Cy's sharp command to halt he paused and coiled his trunk protectively. Cy now held a long-handled spear in his hand.

"This is the spear the oozie used," explained Cy. "I hope just the sight of it will be all he needs. You notice how he has coiled his trunk? He's on guard. All right, Tom—we'll see how much you've remembered. Stand away and give him room. Here's the word . . . *hlà-cha* . . . I hope I pronounce it right. He's supposed to lie down when I say *hlà-cha*. Hlà-cha, Tom, hlà-cha!"

Tiny Tom was not too anxious to remember the few words he had been taught before leaving India. Upon hearing Cy's first command of "Hlà-cha!" he slowly turned his body sideways and stared at the trainer with one searching eye as if trying to make sure he heard aright.

"Hlà-cha!" called Cy a little louder. The elephant continued to stare, one ear pricked higher than the other.

"He remembers," muttered Cy beneath his breath. "But he's hoping we'll think he's forgotten. The little beggar's lazy—lazy as they come! "Hlà-cha! Hlà-cha!" and Cy walked closer holding the spear before him. "Might as well obey and get it over—"

Tom eyed the spear and made a little complaining sound in his throat.

"You're lazy—getting soft, Tom. Hlà-cha! No, you don't," objected Cy as the elephant wheeled about and ambled toward the open window. "Thinks it might be fun to douse us with river water." Cy gave Tom's plump hindquarters a slight prick. Tom squealed, switched his skinny little tail, and hurried for an opposite corner. By now he realized that Cy meant business. Momentary indignation faded as Cy held out a handful of salt toward him.

"It's yours, Tom, if you'll lie down."

Slowly, reluctantly, Tom came closer and swung his body to one side, his eye on the spear, then the salt. After a long moment of indecision, he partially crooked his hind legs in a feeble courtesy and then straightened. . . .

"Not enough, Tom. He does remember!" Cy told Rush softly as he tried to restrain a chuckle. "No, you don't get the salt yet. Hlà-cha!"

A wisp of hay on the floor now drew Tom's attention.

In an attempt to delay matters, the small fleshy fingers of his trunk picked it up and thrust it in his mouth. Then suddenly, as though realizing it was useless to procrastinate any longer, his hind legs slumped and he sat down like an overstuffed toy, wrinkles of gray skin sagging from his waistline. He remained in this position tentatively, regarding the salt in Cy's hand, evidently hoping he would not have to complete the trick.

"All the way down—no salt til' you finish," and Cy walked a step closer.

With a sigh of resignation which was almost a blast, Tom lolled to one side, his front feet slipping toward the trainer until his right side and head lay flat upon the floor. Cy mopped his forehead with his handkerchief and smiled at Rush. It was evident that the trainer was greatly relieved to find that Tom had remembered.

"Hadn't forgotten after all. The rest will be easier. . . . All right, Tom, you're a good fellow. Now, Hta! Hta!"

Tom rose with a willingness, pushing with his forelegs until he sat on his hindquarters, the loose skin pulling taut as he labored. His trunk was now uncoiled, reaching for the salt even before he gained his balance. With a wheezy inhale, it disappeared into the end of the trunk and was then blown into his open and waiting mouth. Ah, yes, Tom had remembered.

Meanwhile the two expected men, an engineer and a cook, arrived and were hired. Almost immediately the Circus Boat got under way and headed towards Trempealeau. The time passed pleasantly, Rush taking charge of the zoo as Cy rested. There was no further talk about riding Tom—only a few references to "foot aids" and the general care of an elephant's feet. At the dinner table that noon, Cy had announced that Tom performed successfully and everyone looked pleased and exclaimed. All but Bertie, who was twitting Effie about something. At the mention of Tom's success, his face sobered and Rush looked up to find Madame Whipple's black eyes watching. Cy was right —nothing escaped the old lady. As they left the dining room she had turned to Cy: "You'll be resting this afternoon?" and "I see you kept your promise this morning— no stunts." Yes, Madame Whipple mothered each and every one, knew their hopes, fears and little weaknesses, from her son, the Captain, to the assistant stoker in the engine room. So it was not surprising that she visited the zoo that afternoon, her sewing bag swinging from one arm and a small box in one hand.

"I've come to darn that hole in your sleeve, Rush, and to see Lily. Why, how clean and snug you are down here," she exclaimed as she seated herself in his small room. "And Lily, you're a new girl. Yes, I've brought you a present," and to Rush's surprise, Madame Whipple opened the box and produced a doll-sized hat of red velvet trimmed with iridescent green and blue feathers. Lily, completely hypnotized, sat staring, and made no move.

"See, we'll put it on and make sure the elastic is not too tight." Madame Whipple placed the hat gently upon the monkey's head. "The elastic goes under the chin—so! And the feathers always hang down the back. Can you remember, Rush?"

"I guess so," replied Rush a little helplessly. "When is she supposed to wear it?"

"Whenever she wishes. The idea is to let her become accustomed to a hat. You like it, Lily?"

By now Lily had come out of her trance and had removed the hat, staring at it with fascinated eyes. Madame Whipple smiled with satisfaction. "Let her play with it. The feather came from a duster but she won't mind." And then she addressed Shal, who had come forward and laid her head upon her knee.

"You beautiful creature—your coat has been brushed, hasn't it? Everything looks better, cleaner down here. You like the work, Rush?"

"Yes, Ma'am," and Rush spoke so earnestly that Madame Whipple smiled.

"I believe you do," she replied gently, "and you've come to us just at the right time. Now take this jacket off and I'll start work. I can't bear to see anyone go ragged. Someday I'll come down and we'll have a real visit. Today, I have only ten minutes before the rehearsal begins upstairs. Did you see the show last night?"

"No, Ma'am."

"I didn't see you around. Maybe you'd like to see the rehearsal this afternoon. Would you?"

"Why, yes, Ma'am. But Cy's asleep—"

"That doesn't matter. You can come down between acts. It would do you good. You're alone too much."

Child of the Storm, written by a brother of Mr. Baker's, was one of the first dramas that Rush had seen. Eau Claire had not as yet boasted of an opera house, and only occasionally had Rush been taken by his parents to see Shakespearean plays in nearby cities. Melodrama was quick to affect him, since he had passed through stirring experiences of his own. Even the actors seemed scarcely familiar. Leslie Wood, pacing the stage, appeared taller and more handsome than ever and Ellie, mouselike and painfully shy, wearing a long dark cape, almost whispered her lines. Mr. Baker seemed to have the play in charge, directing with unusual vim, and even taking parts himself in order to help.

"Now, Leslie, lower your voice and don't move so fast. You two ought to be getting used to each other by now. See, stand like this—when you speak. Ellie isn't deaf. Now, Ellie, remember you are a little lady sitting on a bench," and Mr. Baker pretended to spread his skirts daintily as he seated himself on a box. "You like Leslie. Push your bonnet back so the audience can see your face—" And so it went, Ellie never losing her self-consciousness or losing sight of Leslie as Leslie Wood.

"I know you can act, Ellie, because I've seen you," stormed Mr. Baker. "Now, now, don't cry about it—" and his voice softened. "You aren't afraid of Leslie, are you?"

To his surprise Rush found himself deeply engrossed in the two young people's problem. Mr. Baker, later taking the part of a cruel landlord and hounding the orphan Ellie into the stormy night, appeared astonishingly real. Between the shifting of scenes, Rush hurried to the zoo to make certain all was well with Shal, left in charge, and returned breathless and expectant to a dim corner behind the stage. Madame Whipple smiled at him each time, glad to see his enjoyment. Present at the finish of the first act, he was as embarrassed as Ellie herself, flushed peony-pink, who was pushed into Leslie's stiff embrace by the zealous Mr. Baker.

"Fine! Fine!" Mr. Baker congratulated the young couple. "It will be easier the second time. Remember, it's only a play and the audience doesn't know you from a hole in the ground. To them, Ellie is Pansy Perkins and Leslie— Archibald Crane. It's spring . . . and you're in love. Come, try it again and don't wait so long, Ellie— You're the child of the storm and there's refuge in Archibald's arms!"

On went the rehearsal into the third act, with Bertie, bonneted and bibbed for want of an infant, being rocked in a cradle. Despite the fact that Rush knew he was seeing a mere drama, the struggles of Pansy Perkins, the cruelty of her landlord, the courage of Archibald, and the thin wails of the infant were so vivid and true that after the green muslin curtain had descended, he found himself clinging fast with both hands to the edge of some stage setting—a cardboard tree. Indignation, sorrow, joy, rolled over him like the waves of the sea. Unwittingly he had laughed and cried with an imaginary audience.

"Pretty good for the first try, isn't it?" asked a harsh voice at his elbow, and Rush looked down through the dim light at Bertie. The infant's cap and dress were now gone and Bertie was himself in long trousers and coat tails. His hair, however, was mussed and stood upright.

"Yes. . . . I guess I forgot it was a show," admitted Rush, loosening his hold on the cardboard tree. "Seemed awfully real. Mr. Baker's not as cruel as that—it's hard to believe—" Embarrassed, Rush left his sentence unfinished.

Bertie gave his queer little metallic laugh. "You've given Mr. Baker a fine compliment. Ellie and Leslie will do better as they go along. 'Tween you an' me," and Bertie lowered his voice, "they like each other and that's what's the matter. Would you like to substitute some time?" Bertie gazed at him directly, as if curious to see if Rush had secret ambitions for the stage—like Roscoe.

"Oh, no," replied Rush as he drew back a bit. "I'd rather work with the animals. I wouldn't be good on the stage at all. Cy says you're going to ride Tiny Tom as soon as we have him trained. It will be wonderful—"

"I suppose so—" Bertie's voice lost its usual happy note and became listless. "That's what Captain Whipple has planned. They want me to get acquainted with him and I've tried. Now I'm telling you," he added in a burst of confidence, "that Tom's a devil! You watch out for yourself! Why, last week when I went in with some grass, he stood me on my head and pulled off my buttons. There's nothing tiny about him—he looks pretty big to me." Bertie managed to give another short laugh. In the dimness backstage the midget looked pathetically small. The entire cast of troupers had hurried off to the kitchen for a cup of tea and only Mr. Baker remained at the farthur end of the stage, sorting out costumes from a big trunk.

"Perhaps if you work with Cy and me—" encouraged Rush.

"But I don't like it, I tell you. It's more fun taking over different parts up here. I'm not always a baby—why, last week I was an old man sitting in a chair with make-believe legs. Say—" and Bertie's face lighted with a new idea, "why don't you take over that job? That is—if," and his face sobered a bit, "if Captain Whipple will let you. The Cap'n's awful set—once he has a plan fixed in his mind. Awful set. But you'd do a better job, I know you would. All you've got to do is stain your face a walnut brown, wear a turban on your head and a jacket. Madame Whipple and Effie are going to make the costume any day now. You're not much bigger than I am and there'd be enough cloth. Would you like it?"

In his enthusiasm, Bertie had drawn closer and stood looking up at Rush beseechingly, one hand tugging at Rush's sleeve.

"If Captain Whipple—"

"I'll go find him—talk with him. Don't say a word, let me manage it. He's set—set as the hills, but we can try. Don't count on it too much because he might have the hand-bills ordered with my name on 'em. TINY TOM AND THE TINY DWARF—that's what he's planned!" There was disgust in Bertie's voice. "Who wants to be a dwarf—I'm no General Tom Thumb—not when I can play parts of regular human beings. I'll see you again—good-bye." And Bertie was gone, his coat tails the last to disappear around the corner.

Shal was guarding the doorway of the zoo and the big room was quiet and peaceful. Each animal was in his cage contentedly munching or dozing. Tom turned his head expectantly. Already he had learned to know Rush's footsteps. Slowly he ambled toward the gate, his little tail swinging, and Rush met him halfway. Never had the little elephant seemed so appealing. If Bertie failed—

"Tom," and Rush leaned against him, "I want to ride you—so much—"

There was no doubt that Tom understood. He gave a soft purring sound. However, always with an eye to business, his trunk began to search Rush's pockets like a small suction pump and, finding an apple there, he clapped it into his mouth. The purring sound continued.

"Maybe the handbills are all printed. . . . The Captain's set on Bertie's riding you and maybe he won't change. . . . It would be wonderful, Tom, if he decided—"

What a relief it was to talk and it seemed to strengthen the bond between them.

"Maybe Bertie won't fail. And no one would know me all dressed up—no one. My face would be painted and I'd wear a queer hat. . . ." The warmth of Tom's body was comforting, reassuring, and he pressed closer, an intense longing within him.

"I'd be safe on your back—and we'd head the parade together, Tom." A moment later, without warning, Tom wound his trunk about Rush's waist and lifted him gently, so very gently, and set him down again.

11

A STRANGE VOICE
GIVES WARNING

A large juicy corn beef brisket was brought aboard the Circus Boat at Trempealeau by a family of eight and exchanged for tickets of admission—just as Madame Whipple had hoped. Besides the purchase of supplies and having the saddle mended, some new-style hair curlers were discovered in a dry-goods store by the Dorset sisters and immediately applied. Still fearful of being followed, Rush did not leave the Circus Boat but remained in the zoo and Cy, making no comment whatsoever, gave him plenty to do as an excuse for remaining there. When Rush was solicited to help outside on the wharf for the evening's performance, Cy insisted that Rush remain in the feed room to overhaul boxes and rid the place of mice which were eating the grain. Rush looked his gratitude and Cy merely nodded.

"As long as you do your work well," Cy told him later, "it doesn't matter where you've come from. It's no one's business. You haven't stolen, murdered—"

"Oh, no, sir—"

"And the Captain needs you on this boat."

"Thank you, sir."

A light mist slowed the Circus Boat the first night out of Trempealeau but Captain Whipple sat doggedly at the wheel in the pilot house on the towboat, determined to keep his engagement at La Crosse. Bells down in the engine room jangled constantly as he steered his way past shoal, snag, reef, and slough. However, before dawn the mist turned to milk-white fog and Captain Whipple found it necessary to tie up at a small town, finding it impossible to keep the engagement at La Crosse.

"It's the law of the river to tie up in a fog as bad as this," explained Cy, chopping meat in the feed room after breakfast. "The Captain's a fine pilot. I would trust his steering through a fog because he knows every stump and sawyer on the river. But the danger comes from colliding with a less skilled pilot."

"What's a sawyer?"

Cy looked up a little surprised and then smiled. "Somehow I forget you haven't always lived on the river. A sawyer is a tree which has become loose and leans over the water, moving back and forth. It plays the dickens with passing boats. The Mississippi is a conundrum—always changing. An island can disappear in a few weeks' time, washed away by a changing current."

"Where would you say we were now?"

"By my map on the back of the door I would say we were some distance above La Crosse. I'm glad the Captain decided to stop. There's a bad place below La Crosse called Crooked Slough and that's hard to take even in clear weather. Hello, someone's calling!"

"Whipple! Dan Whipple!" called a hoarse insistent voice.

Because of the fog there was nothing to be seen outside. However, a window in the pilot house on the towboat was noisily raised and then came the Captain's voice, strained and tight.

"Here—right here. What do you want?"

"Fellar on a boat says to tell yer he ain't goin' to take yer backwater no more. He's goin' ahead an' fer you to watch out."

"That all?" and there was biting scorn in Captain Whipple's voice.

"Fur's I know—"

The slam of the window in the pilot house finished the conversation and then came the dip of an oar. Cy gave a low whistle.

"Trouble's brewing again."

"Was that message from Sam Burton?" asked Rush after a pause.

"Yes. . . . How'd you hear of Sam Burton?"

"I heard you and Captain Whipple speak of him the night Roscoe left."

"So you did. . . . Yes, that message came from Sam.

He hires people to remind us that he's always around. Tries to wear down our nerves. Some day the law will catch up with that coyote!"

"What started the trouble?"

"Captain Whipple's boat rammed Sam's boat two years ago. That often happens on the river. Well, Captain Whipple paid the damages—but it wasn't enough money to suit Sam. He's always hounding and threatening to collect more. We know now that Sam arranged the collision—it's one of his tricks. Last year he hired some thugs to break up our show. Captain Whipple called the sheriff and made arrests but there was no proof that Sam was back of it."

"What do you think he'll do now?"

Shal, feeling the tension, had come close and Rush put his arm around her. Cy smiled and offered her a piece of red meat.

"That dog senses a lot. . . . She knows there's trouble. Well, it's anyone's guess what Sam will try next. Maybe cut our lines some night. Dan Whipple is an honorable man and I think this whole affair is getting under his skin. Sam has cost him money, scared his troupers and crew. That's one reason we got two new men at Fountain City."

The voice in the fog with its ominous message lingered for some time in Rush's ears as he went about his work. There were more questions he would have liked to ask but Cy seemed unusually preoccupied. The warning shouted through the cover of fog brought disquietude and fear.

"Don't let it get you down," encouraged Cy, and a little smile warmed his sober face. "You'll get used to it. Wonder what Roscoe's doing now? My best guess is that he's memorizing his lines on an empty stomach somewhere north of here. How many poses can Shal do now?" asked Cy, with an obvious attempt to change the conversation.

"Two," replied Rush, glad to speak of Shal. "We're starting another soon. I have trouble though, keeping her steady when the boat rocks. She and Dazzle touched noses yesterday and I let her eat her dinner in Dazzle's stall. I think they'll work together soon."

"That's progress. How's Lily?"

"She's a lot better. I'm afraid she's going to wear all the hair off her head putting that hat on, though. She puts it on and I take it off because the feather aims the wrong way."

"That doesn't do any harm, does it?"

"Yes, sir. Makes her cross-eyed."

Fresh, spontaneous laughter escaped Cy, and Rush joined in, both forgetting for a little while the threatening voice which had hailed Captain Whipple.

"The ways of a woman," chuckled Cy. "Here, cut this meat for me—finer, so Dignity won't lose his loose teeth. By the way, we'll be taking Tom ashore one of these days and teach him to march. This afternoon, I'll oil his skin. I use that floor mop in the corner. The oil softens up his dry scaly skin—and then I shall cut his toenails and cuticle. Did you notice that the flesh around his toenails is ragged? An elephant's feet have to be watched. It's surprising the care it takes to keep an elephant in good condition."

"I wish he'd stop throwing all that dirt and stuff on his back. I keep brushing it off—"

"Well, don't bother. All elephants do that—it's an old habit started in India. The sun is hot there and elephants don't like the heat on their backs. So they cover themselves.

They get easily chilled however. . . . You should have seen Tom three weeks ago. He stole some sugar, stuffed himself, and I had to rub hot linament on his stomach."

"Linament?"

"Then I tied a sheet about his middle. He was a handsome sight, I'll tell you."

"Is Tom too young to have tusks?"

"Oh, no—he broke one of them and I took the two out. Better for him and for us if he developed a bad temper. Ever hear of a squeeze?

"No, sir—"

"It's a log pen, made so small that the elephant cannot move about inside. The driver or oozie is lowered from above and sits on the elephant's neck. In that way the animal gets accustomed to a person's weight. Now and then I'll put a rope ladder over Tom's back and you might try crawling up there. He likes you and I doubt if he pulls you off. We haven't a squeeze here and I don't think we'll need one. You don't object to trying?"

"I'd like it."

"Then we'll try the foot aids. What will you do this winter, Rush?" asked the trainer suddenly. "Go to school?"

"I plan to, sir."

"Father and mother both dead?"

"Yes, sir. This boat is more like home than any place I know now."

"Not a bad place," agreed Cy. "Some nice folks aboard here."

Late on the afternoon of the following day Captain Whipple docked his boat safely at the wharves in Lansing,

Iowa, a good-sized town located beneath a towering hill. Released from his wheel, the Captain appeared red-eyed and weary, with lines about his mouth, and swaying a little as he walked.

"Mr. Baker, put out the posters. It's still raining but the show goes on." With this final instruction the Captain hied himself to bed for sleep richly deserved. The show went on —with only a few wet, bedraggled people for an audience.

There was only one reminder of Sam Burton at Lansing. A shifty-eyed roustabout on the pretext of assisting one of the engineers coil rope managed to deliver another message.

"Friends of yourn jest left. . . . Says to tell yer Cap'n that the river may seem high but there still ain't 'nuff water to float the two of ye."

"So Sam's passed us—gone ahead," added the engineer after relating the message to Cy and Mr. Baker who were unwilling to disturb the sleeping Captain. "Slimy as an eel an' works in the mud. Keep your eyes open—we can expect anything from now on."

Skies were blue and hillsides an emerald green the following morning. To the north stretched a meadow of a mile's length and Cy declared it to be a perfect spot in which to try out the foot aids on Tiny Tom. By now, after several spills, Rush was able to maintain his seat on the back of Tom's neck and it was an achievement which delighted him not a little. The feel of firm flesh beneath him, the lurch of the body in movement, were exhilarating— exciting. Moreover, Tom seemed pleased to have him there and made soft grunting sounds of conversation when Rush leaned forward and talked to him. So it was in the early morning hours when Cy, armed with the spear, led Tom forth with Rush mounted and Shal following, eager for a run on land.

"It's good to get away from that boat," exclaimed Cy, breathing deep of the morning air. "We've had too much of Sam Burton. Looks like no one's up yet."

Not a household stirred as the four moved down the principal street. The small elephant, wearing a breast strap of red leather, kept an even pace but fell into a little trot upon seeing the green meadow ahead.

"Let him have all he wants," advised Cy. "He's hungry for something of his own choosing. Watch close though and see that he doesn't head for the river all of a sudden. The rascal is crazy for a swim and June is too early for deep water."

"Tom can swim?" asked Rush.

"Very well indeed," replied Cy. "All elephants love water. They spend most of their time along the rivers and brooks in Burma. They don't like hot weather. If you notice carefully, you'll see little bits of wool on Tom. You may not have noticed it in the zoo. Elephants came from the north originally. There—I think he's had enough for now," and Cy approached Tom, who had been steadily stuffing his mouth with grass.

"Time to stop, Tom." The pointed spear was persuasive and Tom obediently refrained, giving Rush a moment to look at the elephant carefully. There were little patches of gray fuzz on the broad gray back and some behind the ears. At some time in the north, Tom's ancestors had worn fur coats.

"Ready, Rush? Now when I say 'Left,' you push with

your left foot back of Tom's left ear. Hold it there and I will lead to the left. We'll have to do this until he gets the idea. We'll make a big circle. It's the only way I can figure out and it ought to work in time. I wish I'd asked more questions of Tom's oozie. Left! Left, Tom!"

Pulled by the rope attached to his breast strap and prompted by a spear point, Tom had little choice. He marched despondently, his fat legs mechanical, slyly tweaking with his trunk at several clumps of grass as he passed.

"He's doing fine," called Rush enthusiastically. The fresh morning air and the wide sky above were doubly pleasant after a sojourn in the zoo of the Circus Boat. Shal was enjoying herself, too, running ahead at full speed. From his post on high, Rush could now see they were making a complete circle of trampled grass. Tom's obedience was almost too good to believe.

"Right, Tom! Right!"

Holding his right foot behind Tom's ear, Rush waited. Pulled by the rope, Tom moved slowly to retrace his route but not quite so anxious to obey as before. His eyes had caught the distant gleam of water.

"Come on, Tom. Right! Come on, boy. Push hard with your right foot, Rush."

Tom plodded slowly, as though conceding to a new form of drudgery, finishing the circle with great effort. However, he had managed on the way to pick a few wild geraniums which he tossed over his back.

"Good! We made it. Now it's just repeating this performance until he learns those words and associates them with your foot pressure. Look at that dog streaking it!

She's been housed too long—we must see that she gets her runs. Must be a brook at the farther end—she hurdled that spot going and coming."

Through the green meadow Shal appeared a swift white flash. Twice she had leaped across an open space, exuberant with joy.

"It's a brook. I've seen her do that before," and Rush felt a surge of pride as he watched her. "Couldn't we give Tom a drink?" he asked eagerly.

"If he'd just drink—nothing more," replied Cy slowly. "I've always wanted to see an elephant by a stream. The sun's out—it's getting warmer. . . . I've got the spear. . . . We might try it."

With Cy leading Tom and Rush still mounted, they crossed the field passing Shal on the way. It was a wide shallow brook, and once Tom caught the sound of the flowing water he lost no time. It was evident that he had a keen sense of hearing. With his front feet in the stream and his body tilted forward, he filled his trunk noisily.

"You'd better get off," advised Cy worriedly. "He's not that thirsty. Why, he's almost sucked the place dry. Now if it comes our way—"

Cy had not finished before a stream of water hit him, face-on, and with some violence. Like a huge hose the shower then swerved to Rush, who had just dismounted and was forced to shield his face with both hands. The water was cold, seeping down his collar.

"Tom! Tom!" came as a chorus from both victims.

However, Tom was now on his own, engaged in merry debauchery. With his two forefeet he pounded and splashed in the deepest pools. Soft black mud issued from his trunk.

"Come over here," called Cy, hurrying for a safer spot. "We might as well let him have his fun for a while. Look at you—you're all mud—"

"So are you." Rush gave a shout of laughter at Cy's appearance. "How will we ever get him out of there?"

"I'll go behind him with the spear—if he doesn't see me first. Might as well let him play awhile. I doubt if he's seen a brook since he left Burma. It's my mistake—I should have known he'd do this. Wonder what Bertie would say now," chuckled Cy, mopping the mud from his face. "Better call your dog back," he warned Rush, peering out from the folds of his handkerchief. "You'll have a black dog in five minutes if you don't—"

From a distance, Cy and Rush spent the next half hour observing Tom's antics. Like a child the elephant reveled in his freedom as he trampled in the mud, squirted water on his back, rolled stones, and uprooted any bush which hindered his activities. At last, satisfied, he sat down in the stream at its widest point.

"I can almost hear him purr from here," announced Cy, making ready to leave. "We'll have to be sure there are no brooks in the next training field or he'll think that's what we've come for. Stay where you are until I get him out."

Tom, prodded by the spear, rose and hastened for shore, crossing the meadow in an amiable frame of mind. To Rush's surprise, instead of following, Shal led the way, head up and plumed tail waving, like an advance guard. And watching her, Rush wondered if he imagined that she lifted her forepaws a little higher than usual. By now the village was awake and a school bell rang as they passed down the central street. As though moved by some uncontrollable impulse, a group of boys and girls carrying dinner pails and books turned about and escorted the party to the Circus Boat. Rush, mounted on Tom, could not help but enjoy his position on high, noting their upward and admiring glances. Meanwhile Cy was bombarded with questions. What a wonderful white dog! What kind was he? Where had they been and what had they done to get so muddy? How much did the elephant weigh and how old was he? Would they be in the show that night and was Rush, beneath the mud, a white boy, or did he come from Burma, too?

As though aware of his importance, Tom marched along with unusual dignity. Only as he crossed the ramp which bridged the wharf and boat did he give way to a final fling at freedom by stealing an apple from a boy's dinner pail and tossing a little girl's red hood into the river.

A storm with even greater force tore down the Mississippi Valley at dawn the next day. It came suddenly, vicious and without warning, the wind singing on a high wailing note. Awakened by a loud crash and the sound of splintering wood, Rush struggled to his feet, Lily clinging to his neck and Shal by his side. The next moment all three were hurled to the floor. Dazed, Rush lay there, conscious of Shal lapping his cheek and Lily whimpering in his ear. What has happened? Had Sam Burton made good his threat? Were the animals safe? Where was Cy?

Gaining his feet and holding fast to Lily, Rush made his way to the door of the zoo, moving unsteadily, as the boat spun round and round and then lunged forward as though

seized by a mighty current. Above the rush of water he
could hear the cries of the animals, and then his own
voice—

"Cy! Cy!"

There was no answer. In all probability Cy was assisting
Captain Whipple in the pilot room. The job at hand was to
care for the animals—left in his charge. The cubs were
squealing with fright. Tom lay on his side, his back against
the bars, apparently uninjured. Dazzle and Dignity had
kept their feet. With Lily held close against him, he had
reached the cubs' cage when the boat began to spin about
crazily once more. It was then, for the first time, that Rush
realized with growing horror that the Circus Boat had been
separated from the towboat—and that he and the animals
were drifting down the Mississippi—alone.

12

STORM

For a few frantic moments, his legs weak and trembling, Rush clung for support to the cubs' cage. Then dropping to his knees, he crawled to a center post, encircling it with one arm as he lay on the floor, Shal beside him. What had happened to the boat and where were they headed for? Above the cries of the frightened animals and Lily's wailing in his ear, he tried to remember the map of the Mississippi River as he last saw it hung on the back of the feedroom door. The river flowed to the east beyond Lansing. Then came Lynxville and Prairie du Chien on the east shore and McGregor on the west. The Wisconsin River flowed in from the east and this was as much as he could remember. There was no telling how far the Circus Boat had traveled that night. Meanwhile there would be snags, towheads, reefs, and islands ahead. Wrecked midstream in the storm, they might not be discovered for hours—if ever.

To break the darkness about him and lift his own spirits as well, Rush decided to light the lantern in the feed room. Groping his way, he found it hanging on its usual nail, also the matches in their tin box close by. Once lighted, the lantern sent out a steady glow and brought back the familiar things about him. It seemed to comfort the animals, too. Their cries lessened as he approached the different cages, struggling to maintain his balance over the swaying floor. In an effort to make his voice heard above the rushing water outside, he had almost to shout. And Lily's tugging at his shirt collar gave him a choked sensation.

"Easy, Lily," he soothed, trying to loosen her small hands. "You'll rip my shirt. It's all right, Twist—all right, Turn," and he patted the two heads through the bars. "See, I'm right here—and Shal, too. Stay where you are, Tom," he advised the elephant, who still lay on the floor and had raised his head inquiringly. If only he could make Dazzle lie down! Should the horse fall and break a leg, he would be powerless to help him. Dignity alone remained calm, his eyes glowing through the shadows with a yellowish-green light. On second thought it seemed safer to keep Lily in her cage even though she cried. His weight might injure her if he fell. Accordingly, he half crawled, half walked to his own room and returned dragging the cage after him with the monkey inside. If possible he meant to keep all of the animals together within reach. And if the boat crashed, he intended to unlock the cages and let each animal go free. It was the best he could do under the circumstances.

Time moved slowly. Despite its rough voyage the clock in the feed room ticked steadily. It was necessary now and then to quiet Shal, who, excited by the cries of the other animals, joined them with short sharp yelps of distress. Occasionally the boat ceased its mad dipping and swirling and kept an even balance as though following the main course of the current. There was nothing to see from the windows. The glass was opaque—as though someone stood just outside and constantly swashed it with buckets of water. Also it seemed difficult to breathe. As he stood trying to look out, lightning, sharp and blinding, lashed at him, accompanied by deafening thunder. Stumbling in his hurry and vaguely conscious of a sick uneasiness in his stomach, he made his way back to the animals. They were watching for him, and their dependence upon him gave him a feeling of awe. He was their sole caretaker, and how well they knew it, helplessly locked behind iron bars!

"I'll do my best," he promised them. "I'll do everything I can."

By now Tom was on his feet, reaching out with his trunk, asking for attention. When the boat dipped, he took little running steps to keep his balance, complaining the while. Lily rattled her door. The cubs climbed to the top of their bars as though to escape the tumult below. Dazzle stamped and whinnied. Dignity shifted his position only once and stared before him, his eyes two disks, strangely alight. Although the cages were on rollers, they were securely fastened in the wall behind with large iron hooks and despite the roll and toss of the boat remained stationary. A storm on the Big River. . . . All his life Rush had heard tales of the Mississippi's furies and eccentricities. Little had he dreamed that he would experience his first storm alone, in the strange company of caged circus animals.

And where was Cy? Safe with the troupers on the towboat, battling with wind and rain—or tied securely to some wharf? At least they had each other for company. Captain Whipple would mourn the loss of his Circus Boat. He would be shocked and disheartened. However, the little white-haired mother would console him, perhaps expressing faith in Rush, a strange boy from out of nowhere who had shown a singular love for animals in the one week he had worked in the zoo, and saving them if possible. But the most skilled of rivermen would be helpless in a storm such as this, the Captain would most likely argue. And closing his eyes, Rush could almost hear them speaking.

Lightning flared through the windows. Added to the noise of thunder came the slam of the benches above as they shifted back and forth across the amphitheater floor. They were now, no doubt, a tangled heap of wreckage. More grief for Captain Whipple . . . and how pleased Sam Burton would be to hear of the Whipples' misfortunes. And again the question—ever ready to haunt him—were Sam Burton and his underlings responsible for the separating of the Circus Boat from the towboat? There had been the two warnings, one in the fog and the other at the dock in Lansing . . . and hadn't Cy mentioned the possibility of Sam's cutting the Circus Boat's lines? Would he ever know the answer?

Another glare of lightning illumined the zoo so brightly that Rush was forced to shield his face. But not before his eyes caught sight of a narrow trickle of dark water flowing across the floor toward him from the direction of the cubs' cage. A leak? Tense, his hands clenched, he waited, his gaze riveted ahead. Another flash of light and yes—it was water. Water coming in from outside. Had some seam given way? According to Cy the Circus Boat had been built in Pittsburgh by the best of shipbuilders. Every seam had been carefully calked.

The pangs of nausea at the pit of his stomach were more definite as he rose and, holding the lantern high, walked unsteadily toward the cubs' cage. Seeping water—there it was—a darkened spot in the wall where the cubs had reached through the bars and clawed at the wood. It was a small spot but could prove dangerous should it increase. So far he had kept the river out, and now like a sinister enemy the river had crept in. The very sight of it was frightening—he had not thought of leaks before. He would need oakum and a board nailed tightly across to mend it. Possibly a piece of tin to cover the boards—anything to keep the water out. Cy's tools were in the feed room.

Conscious of Shal's cold nose against his hand, the dog almost blocking his way in an effort to keep close, Rush crossed to the feed room, carrying the lantern. If only the boat would stop its motion, the dizziness and nausea would lift—

"Don't worry, Shal," he told the anxious dog. "It's just that I—can't walk straight."

The box of tools. . . . Yes, everything was there, nails,

hammer, and a few boards in a corner with a sheet of tin. All but the oakum, the most important thing of all. A short length of rope with frayed ends hanging on a nail caught his glance, and swaying near, he pulled it toward him. The rope, shredded apart, would be the same as oakum. How fortunate he was to have seen it! Returned to the larger room, he seated himself by the post and in the lantern's light began to pluck open the twisted strands. Every preventative measure must be taken, he told himself, no matter how weak or sick he felt. Perhaps his life and the lives of the animals depended on the very thing he was doing. But for his own physical discomfort, he would have laughed to see so many eyes following the movements of his hands—especially Shal, who kept sniffing of the rope as if questioning his purpose.

"It's to mend the leak," he told her. With the cubs' cage pulled away, the rollers blocked by a piece of wood, Rush padded the hollow in the wall, nailed two boards across, and sealed the entire surface with tin. He worked with feverish haste as if against all time and a world of water outside, and had about finished his task when an onslaught of wind, more violent than the others, struck the boat and sent it whirling. At the same time from above came the wrenching sound of wood, the crash of glass, and then a wild discord as though something had fallen across the piano keys. Had the roof gone? Or was it the pilot house with its many windows and the big oar sweeps as well? Perhaps some of the debris had fallen down and hit the piano beneath.

There was another sound—a dull thud close by. This time, one of the cub bears, Twist, had lost his hold on the upper bars of his cage and had fallen to the floor below. A wild duet of squealing followed from both cubs, the other animals soon joining in. However, Twist was not seriously hurt, but mostly dazed, and rubbed his head with one paw as he blinked up at Rush.

"Why, that's nothing," he told them all bravely, his voice scarcely disguising his own fear, "you've got to expect things like that. It's a bad storm. It won't happen again."

Kerosene—did he imagine that he smelled its pungent fumes? Possibly it was leaking through the ceiling, spilled on the floor upstairs. It would never do now to keep the lantern lighted, much as he enjoyed the feeble glow. Many a boat had been burned to a cinder because of spilt kerosene—so drawing a deep breath he blew out the lantern's flame. From now on he would have to be content with the pale gray light coming from the windows. Once more he seated himself with his back against the post—waiting. All he asked now was that the Circus Boat keep to the main stream, trusting it to carry them past reef and island. When it sailed a smoother course, he would ascend the stairs and see what happened above. Meanwhile his eyes frequently sought the square of bright tin, shining through the subdued light. Had he packed the hollow with enough hemp—had he used too many nails?

The clock in the feed room struck eight jangled notes. Eight o'clock in the morning. Already he felt as though he had lived a lifetime and a long day still lay ahead. . . . No matter what happened, Shal would never leave him. In the dim gloom he knew he could always put out his hand and feel her near.

By noon, the wind made less noise and the boat traveled

a more even course. With the exception of strange scraping sounds beneath—old tree snags probably embedded in the river bottom—there were no new disturbances. The tin patch over the leak emitted little moisture and gradually Rush ceased to watch it so closely. His stomach bothered him only at intervals and at the calls of birds perching on the roof, he felt greatly encouraged. Surely the storm was waning or they would not be able to remain there. Perhaps now it would be safe to climb the stairs to the amphitheater and see what damage had been done. Also he might get a better view of the river from the upper windows. Even now, it would be utter folly to go to the roof.

Grasping the banisters of the stairs, he mounted, Shal running ahead. At the top he paused, after giving a gasp of dismay. All that he had feared had happened—even worse. There was a hole in the ceiling where the small pilot house had once stood above. The entire house was gone, taking some of the amphitheater's ceiling with it. Windows were broken and lamps had crashed. Several trunks had dropped from the stage to the floor level and lay open, their contents strewn about. Wigs, beards, bustles, shawls, parasols, and clothing of all kinds. Even as Rush stood there, a black silk top hat, usually worn by Mr. Baker, came rolling toward him. However, as he stooped to catch it, Shal barked loudly and a voice called from outside.

Had the towboat caught up with them? Was it Cy? Leaping over the hat and every obstacle in his way, Rush quickly reached the other side of the room and leaned out from a broken window, Shal crowding in closely beside him. To his amazement, he looked into the face of a stranger, directly opposite, who was lying full length upon the flat roof of a house. The man was heavily bearded and hoarse from shouting. Behind him were two bedraggled children sitting on a mattress, wrapped in blankets.

"Throw us a rope! Throw us a rope!" and the man held out his hands beseechingly.

Swiftly Rush looked back into the disordered room behind him. There was no rope in sight but in a closet nearby—

"No rope here," Rush shouted, "but I can get some—"

"Hurry—" but already it was too late. The house moved by, dipping, swaying, while the man gazed back with hopeless eyes. From the roof came the shrill cries of the two children, mingled with the plaintive mooing of a cow whose head showed from a back window below. And then, like a screen, rain blotted out the picture.

"Oh, Shal! It was a house—a whole house—and people—"

Loneliness, his failure to throw a rope, the cries of the children were almost more than Rush could bear, and he stumbled across the floor of the amphitheater and down the stairs. In the zoo he knelt and unwound from a buckle on his boot a scrap of gold lace which had fallen from an overturned trunk.

"Here, Lily, something to play with."

At the look of glad surprise on the small monkey's face as her hand reached out to grasp it, some of the disappointment lifted from Rush. How fortunate, how very fortunate, they were with a roof overhead and a dry floor beneath!

Pangs of hunger reminded Rush that neither he nor the animals had partaken of food that morning. Cy had re-

plenished the supplies from the big warehouse at Lansing
—meat, apples, crackers, oats, hay, and even a bit of molasses for the cubs. There was plenty to eat but each animal
ate moderately. Tom, down on the floor again, did not even
rise but fed himself languidly as though he always expected
to recline thereafter while taking his meals.

"Cy said you were lazy, Tom," Rush told the elephant
as he watched him, "and this proves it. That's a good girl,
Lily," he praised the monkey, who, with the red velvet hat
on the back of her head, finished her apple with one hand,
clutching the piece of gold lace in the other. For himself,
Rush ate crackers sweetened with molasses and drank water. The meat was doled out sparingly for Dignity and
Shal. If they succeeded in landing safely, Shal could hunt
her own food but until then she and Dignity must share
alike.

The murky light from the windows offered little induce-
ment to keep awake. Although Rush sat upright and focused
his eyes on the bright square of tin covering the leak, it
seemed impossible not to doze. Sleep weighted his eyelids,
exhaustion pulled at every muscle of his body. Gradually
he slipped to the floor and lay with his head pillowed
against Shal. Meanwhile the Circus Boat sped on. . . .

The clock in the feed room was striking nine when Rush
awakened with a jump. The boat had come to a stop and
appeared to be listing on one side. Again from above
came the cries of birds resting on the roof, and in the distance—a hoot of an owl. Land could not be far away!

Hastily lighting the lantern, Rush hurried to the rear
door. There were stars overhead, unusually large and

bright. Quiet water lay to his left and to the right stretched a white line of beach, rocks, and the blur of woods beyond. Land! Relief like a torrent of the storm itself swept over him. The Circus Boat floated, every animal was alive and well, and they had come, through the night, to this calm haven.

"We're safe." Rush put down the lantern with a shaking hand and knelt beside Shal. "We're safe. The towboat'll find us now. . . . I never was so glad—in all my life. We're safe, Shal," and he hoped that the big dog and the listening animals did not notice the tremor in his voice.

13

MAROONED ON AN
ISLAND

Morning brought the sun. Rush awakened with a little start
of surprise to discover long ribbons of yellow light stream-
ing across the floor, almost reaching him where he lay near
the center post. Sunshine after three black days of storm!
Still a bit dazed with sleep, he rose with an effort, forced
to swing his body about before he could stand, as his feet
seemed to be higher than his head. The Circus Boat had
listed; the floor of the zoo stood on a decided slant. The
end occupied by the cages sank at least three feet lower
than the opposite side. Dazzle, looking out from his box-

stall, whinnied for attention as soon as he saw Rush stir.

"I know, Dazzle. You can't stand up straight. I'll go out-side and see what's happened. Come, Shal."

Eager for a run on land, Shal leaped gracefully from the doorway to the shore. It was a drop of several feet and Rush, in following, was obliged to jump wide, barely clear-ing thick black mud below. Once he was on dry land, how-ever, a quick glance around told him the cause of the un-even floor. The Circus Boat was half on land and half afloat in water, due to the sudden receding of the river. Another deluge of rain would be necessary to dislodge the craft from its bed of muck, shallow water, and rocks.

"We're stuck—until it rains again. I'll have to find someone to pull us off," Rush told the dog and shook his head slowly.

Faced with this new dilemma, Rush mounted a bank for a higher view of the Circus Boat. The roof, with its hole in the center where the pilot house had stood, was a com-pletely flat surface, shorn of its white painted rails, flag-poles, and trim. Moreover, the big sweep-oars, lashed to the sides when not in use, were gone as well as the little cannon and bells. It was a desolate scene of destruction and Ellie's story of the horse blown from Iowa to Illinois was now more convincing. However, the main body of the Circus Boat was intact and could still float. Perhaps there was a towboat near at hand and some kindly engineer who would advise him what to do.

Following the bank farther to the north, Rush was able to see more of his surroundings and the sight which met his eyes made him stand still in utter dismay. Floating logs and debris, backwash from the storm, had accompanied the Circus Boat in the night and now lay in a huge mesh surrounding her. Even though the boat was able to float, it would be impossible for her to plough her way through such an entanglement. Blocked, cut off, she could not receive aid from others until the debris moved away. An old stump of a once enormous cottonwood tree appeared to be holding back the main body of the refuse. Beyond, to the west, lay islands, shutting off his view of the river.

Still hopeful of discovering some other human being sharing the same plight, Rush descended the bank to the shore, his eyes searching the debris for some sign of life. It was a sad picture of waste . . . young green trees uprooted as well as old black snags with crooked arms. The beams of a wharf with a few planks still attached, a roof of a house, and a shanty boat tipped on its side were all imprisoned by logs, broken loose from some lumber raft. The only living creatures in sight were birds perched along the edge of the shanty boat, filling the air with raucous cries. Where were the house, the father, and two children who floated by only yesterday in the storm? The Great River had spent its fury and taken a heavy toll.

There was no more to be seen from the shore, and turning about Rush faced a dense wall of willows with a large cottonwood tree beyond. Surely there must be a higher place from which to look around. A hill rose to the south, a little distance beyond the Circus Boat. From its top he might be able to locate a farm, some sign of civilization on the mainland. At that moment he longed to hear a voice other than his own, someone to answer his questions and lend him a bit of courage.

"We're going back," he told Shal, "and climb that hill. I've got to know where we are. Maybe there's a house, a road somewhere—on the other side."

Glad to leave the depressing wreckage behind, Rush retraced his steps and began to ascend the hill. As it was thick with cottonwood and sassafras trees, trumpet vine and sumac, he was obliged to make his own path upward, often slipping in the black earth, moist with leaf-rot. Breathing hard, his shirt soaked from wet leaves, he at last came to an opening—a flat rock level with his chin. A single tree without branches grew in the center—no, looking closer, he saw that it was a ship's flagpole wedged in a crevice, weathered by time and broken at the top. It had evidently been placed there a year or more ago, and it was the first indication that anyone had lived in that vicinity.

"Look, Shal," exclaimed Rush, pointing eagerly, "someone else has been here! Maybe they were wrecked just like us and put up a signal for help."

But Shal was not interested. There were many trails of small game to follow and she wandered off, her white tail disappearing through the brush. Finding some toe holds, Rush climbed the rock, walked to the pole, and stood gazing before him. So much land—so much sky! Spring had wrapped the whole countryside in green. Below swept the Mississippi, dull gold and wide, sparkling in the morning sunshine. At the foot of the hill lay the half-beached Circus Boat with torn roof, hemmed in with litter. Small green islands lay beyond the litter, the channels between clogged with the same debris. Quickly, hopefully, Rush turned away to search the land behind him. Surely there would be a clearing nearby, a house, a patch of garden—but no, miles of timberland, a vast solitude stretched as far as he could see. Looking down at the foot of the hill, he caught the gleam of water. Slowly, he wheeled in a complete circle, still looking down. Water—was there water all around him? And then he drew in his breath with a sharp gasp. He was on an island, wild and uninhabited—in a world apart.

With this discovery came a feeling of helplessness, panic,

"Shal," he called, "Shal!"

The dog came running and stood upright, her forefeet against the rock as she looked up at him.

"Just wondered where you'd gone," he told her a little shakily. "We're on an island, Shal. I can't see a single house. We're hidden away from everyone. It gives you a queer feeling to be—to be so alone."

The dog seemed to sense his need of her and remained standing as Rush looked about him once more. Unconsciously, perhaps, he had taken for granted that he would be within the reach of people, at least a remote farm or even a road leading to some township. However, there was none of these. He was marooned on an island, long and narrow, and quite some distance from the mainland. There was not a path, a single patch of clearing on the island— only dense green timber and rocky shore. And now he realized why some castaway, like himself, had raised a distress signal. Had the call been answered? Was it possible that someone still lived here? Perhaps the light wind blowing from the north might carry his voice—

"Hello!" he shouted as loudly as he could. "Hello! I'm up here on the hill. Can you hear me? Hello!"

Leaves rustled in the wind. . . . Birds cried from the edge of the shanty boat. And that was all.

A little way down the hill, Rush paused and listened again. Sounds seemed to be coming from the Circus Boat —wails of grief and anger. There were the high-pitched squeals from the cubs and Lily, the loud neighs from Dazzle, and last but not least, staccato roars and barks from Tom. What was happening? When he arrived at the boat, one swift glance from the doorway told the story. The leak which he had mended behind the cubs' cage had given way due to the pressure of weight, and a foot of water lay on the floor at the lower end. With his back to the door, Tom stood ankle-deep, hilariously spraying the cubs who had climbed to the very top of their cage to escape the onslaught of water. There they clung, their cries of distress unheeded, their fur flat against their bodies reminding Rush of some wet kittens he had once seen. Water dripped from the ceiling, walls, and windows. Dignity, next in line for a ducking, was crouched in the one dry corner of his cage as if ready to spring.

"Tom! Tom!"

Engrossed in purging the cubs, Tom gave a little start of surprise upon hearing his name and suddenly shut off the stream of water. Very slowly he turned and surveyed Rush with one eye. Wet himself, the pink freckles on his forehead stood out with a rosier glow than usual.

"Tom—this is the worst thing I've ever seen you do! You know better! Those poor cubs—I'm going right now to get the spear!"

Still scolding, Rush turned to leave when a stream of water, adroitly aimed at the back of his neck, shut off all further conversation. A moment later, armed with the spear and carrying the breast strap, he walked toward Tom's cage, realizing that now or never he must teach the young elephant obedience. But how would he go about it? Cy had aimed the spear point at Tom's fat hindquarters and the single prick had achieved wonders. Would he do the same?

However, in the short time he was gone Rush saw that Tom had changed his position. He now stood facing the door, his hindquarters safely backed against the wall.

"If Cy were here, you wouldn't get away with this," Rush warned.

For reply, Tom made a little plaintive sound in his throat and managed to look quite dejected, his ears flat and drooping, his head lowered. What a rascal he was!

"I don't want to punish you, Tom. But you've got to mind. I'll give you another chance—I'm going to put your collar on. Hold still or I'll—"

The breast strap went on without trouble and Rush fastened a rope to the loop on the top. Then he opened the cage door.

"Out, Tom! I'll tie you to a post until I decide what to do. Maybe the boat will balance better if you move in the middle."

Always eager to leave the cage and relieved to have escaped punishment so easily, Tom moved willingly. As Rush had hoped, the floor of the boat leveled. Possibly, with Tom entirely off the boat, the leak might rise above the water line. He could try . . . but where could the elephant go? Tie him to the big cottonwood tree beyond the willows? The day was warm and pleasant and no harm could come if the elephant were fastened securely. Meanwhile the cubs and zoo could be dried and the leak mended once more.

"There's a big tree down the shore a piece. A nice place —I think I'll take you down there, Tom."

Before Tom could walk through the door, however, something would have to be done about a ramp. Between the doorsill and ground there was a drop of four feet and Tom was not built for jumping. What would he use for a ramp? Ordinary planks might not bear the elephant's weight. . . . Why not fill the gap with stones and spread earth over the top? If it were built solidly and on an even slope, Tom could march back and forth in comfort.

Tied to the post, Tom watched the proceedings with interest as Rush sorted rocks, packed them in tightly, selecting smooth surfaces for the outer grading. It all took more time than he had planned and he was forced to stop at noontime to feed the animals and himself. By early afternoon the stone structure of the bridge was complete. An hour later, after carting pailfuls of earth from a banking and spreading it over the stones, he considered the job finished. Perspiring and covered with mud, Rush stood back and surveyed his work with satisfaction.

"It's really a fine bridge," he told Lily, who was sunning in her cage by the doorway. "Now I'll move you back while I lead Tom out."

Meanwhile the view of the green world outside, so close and almost within reach, had whetted Tom's appetite for a stroll. Several times he had pulled surreptitiously at his rope and at the moment of release he started for the door, making low squeaking sounds of pleasure. Free at last! At the doorsill he halted, turned his body sideways in order to look down at the newly made incline.

"Don't be afraid, Tom. It will hold you—just one step at a time," encouraged Rush.

MAROONED ON AN ISLAND

But Tom had other plans. To Rush's amazement the small elephant deliberately seated himself in the doorway. With a backward push of his forelegs, a lurch of his plump body, Tom slid the length of the new bridge on his bent hind limbs, his tail trailing after him. Arrived at the bottom, he sat a moment while he looked about him and then rose slowly to his feet. In the furor of Shal's barking, Rush's shouts of laughter, and general noise in the zoo, Tom appeared unconcerned and moved calmly to one side where he began to pluck at a tuft of grass. It was now apparent that he had no intention of moving on.

Tom was young, poorly trained and unpredictable. How could he be made to walk toward the old cottonwood tree? Without Cy close by with the spear, Rush did not feel confident to mount the elephant nor would it be possible to pull Tom forward by means of the rope. Once the elephant became stubborn, he would not budge. Perhaps a little persuasion would turn the trick . . . an apple or something sweet, like molasses. There was an old wool sock in the feed room, used for polishing Dazzle's harness. Perhaps—

A few moments later, Rush appeared with the sock washed clean and sweetened with molasses. The scent was quick to reach Tom.

"Come on, boy—follow me and I'll let you have it—"

Tom followed, slowly at first, then increased his pace with Rush hurrying ahead. Beneath the cottonwood tree at last, Tom was allowed to suck and chew on the sock while Rush held fast to one end. Later as Tom turned his attention to the grass beneath the tree, Rush climbed and fastened the end of Tom's rope to an overhanging branch, allowing the elephant enough length to enable him to walk

a bit or lie down. The knot securely tied, he was about to
descend again when he caught a glimpse of a structure
of some sort beyond the next group of willows. It was more
of a shed than a house, hardly noticeable, with the corner
of the roof extending beyond the sweep of willow branches.
Just above he could see the top of a stone chimney. In his
haste he almost tumbled from the tree, barking his shin
and tearing his shirt. However, even before he reached the
doorstep he knew there could be no one there. No path
led to the door and Shal, who had been foraging in that
direction, would have barked and warned him. Regard-
less, he had the desire to call.

"Hello!"

Parting the branches of the willows which had grown
across the doorway, he stepped in. An old pilot house—
salvaged from the river! With the exception of one, all
the windows had been boarded up. Yes, this must be the
person who had raised the flagpole. His eyes growing accustomed to the darkness, he was finally able to distinguish
the objects about him. A stove with an old kettle on the
top, a bed built against the wall, and a box which served
for a seat. Over the stove hung a ship's name plate in black
with gold lettering, NELLIE K.

"The *Nellie K*—that was his boat," he told Shal, who
suddenly joined him by coming through the unboarded
window. "I wonder how long he stayed. Look! He forgot
his pipe," and Rush held up a corncob pipe, blackened
with smoke. "And what's this?"

Beside the pipe lay an object covered with dust—about
the size of a harmonica—it *was* a harmonica. Wiping it
against his shirt, Rush examined it eagerly. Would it play?
He had missed his own, left behind in Eau Claire. Placing

it to his mouth he blew, then inhaled, the length of the small keyboard. Every tone sounded, singularly sweet. A real loss to its owner to have left it behind, he told himself— but what a joy to the finder!

There was nothing more to see. Cobwebs hung thick in the corners and mice had built a nest under the floor. With the harmonica safe in his trousers pocket, Rush walked back to the boat, passing Tom on the way. The elephant appeared contented, reaching out for weeds and grass and sampling them. He did not even turn to see Rush go by but stood quietly, looking up at a little yellow and green bird which sang and swayed at the very top of the tree.

Before the day was over, Rush decided to hang a signal on the flagpole at the top of the hill. It had apparently brought release to the dweller in the pilot house and it might do the same for him. No doubt by now Captain Whipple and the troupers on the towboat had begun their search for the Circus Boat. They would be watching the shores on both sides of the river, and he selected the brightest cloth he could find—an old cape lined with scarlet satin, hanging in a closet at the back of the stage, and used frequently in the different acts. It was possible that with the aid of glasses the Captain might even recognize the cape! This accomplished, Rush spent the remainder of the day making the animals comfortable. The floor since Tom's departure was level and Dazzle was able to walk up and down its length for exercise.

Before settling down for the night, Rush took one last look at Tom from behind the willows. The elephant had made a soft bed for himself in the deeper grass, as far from the tree as the rope would allow, and lay contentedly looking up at the stars. Tiptoeing back to the boat, Rush made up his own bed of blankets in the doorway beside Lily's cage, where he could hear every sound. Shal joined them after prowling about—happy in her freedom to come and go.

Although Rush was weary, his mind teemed with plans for the morrow. If possible he wished to pull the cubs' cage and Dignity's cage to the doorway for sun. Lily could have a little outing in the sun, perhaps. Dazzle could be walked along the shore. If it rained, possibly Tom could be squeezed into the old pilot house for shelter. In a spare moment he hoped to catch some catfish. However, one of his biggest jobs was to check the supplies and distribute portions as evenly as possible. Food was important. . . . Meanwhile the distant blow of whistles told him that the river traffic had commenced again. It might be only a question of hours before he would be seeing Cy again—and Madame Whipple, who was probably worrying about him that very moment!

Suddenly remembering the harmonica in his pocket, Rush brought it out and looked at it in the moonlight. Was his own still in Delos' cabin in Eau Claire? It had seemed a long time since he had played. Softly he blew a few notes and then slipped into his favorite tune, "Oh Dem Golden Slippers," and ended with "Home, Sweet Home."

As the last note faded away and he was returning the harmonica to his pocket, he thought he heard a little sigh. It was Lily, standing upright, her face pressed against the bars, listening.

"You like music, Lily?" Rush asked and smoothed the top of her head. "Maybe you can learn to sing—" and that was the last he remembered. A long day was done.

14

A GREAT LOSS

Before dawn Rush was up and had lighted the lantern. Shal was uneasy and when she finally returned from one of her pilgrimages, lapped his cheek, and tugged at the blanket, he knew something was wrong. With little throat-cries, she led him down the shore and turned through the gap in the willows toward the large cottonwood tree. All of which pointed to one thing—Tom was in trouble. What had he done now—

There was no Tom. Holding the lantern high, Rush looked in every direction. One end of rope which appeared as though it had been chewed by Tom's square teeth and finally snapped apart, dangled from the half-broken limb of the tree. . . . The grass was still flattened where he had lain the earlier part of the evening. Something seemed to be amiss with the old pilot house. Ah, yes, most of the chimney stones had been removed and piled neatly at one side of the unboarded window. Finding it impossible to enter, the elephant had reached through with his trunk and seized the rusty kettle from the stove. It now lay upside down on the doorstep. And Tom was gone on an adventure of his own.

"We'll have to find him, Shal. He can't be far away."

Shal started off with a will, her nose close to the ground, her tail waving vigorously. Tom's trail proved disastrous for the young trees and green growth which had stood in his way. He had advanced in a sweeping triumph, laying low anything which hindered his progress. Even a large rock had been rolled aside, and down one bank was the telltale print of a joyous slide. Close examination showed that the slide had been repeated several times. Instinctively the elephant had headed toward water. Later, still holding the lantern high for guidance, Rush came to a broad shallow stream. Here, Tom had sprayed the rocks with mud and sand, then followed the water eastward, leaving Shal no scent to follow.

"Tom! Tom!" called Rush, wondering if his voice would cause the elephant to travel faster in the wrong direction rather than return to him. At first he had felt no great alarm. The island was small and Tom would not go far. At every turn of the stream he expected to see him, standing in the water, a silent gray shadow awaiting his coming. However, as the water grew deeper and the current swifter,

Rush felt his first qualms of fear. If Tom had followed the stream to the Mississippi and was now floundering in the Big River's depths, affairs would take a serious turn. Meanwhile, scouting ahead, Shal had given no sign of having caught up with the runaway. How much farther did the stream flow? Rush began to run now, splashing through the water, laboring to keep his balance on the slippery stones. Twice he fell full length, the second time crashing the glass lantern chimney into bits. Scolding himself for his carelessness, he left the tin frame at the foot of a tree, planning to pick it up again on the return journey. Fortunately there was a second chimney in the feed room, and on he hurried, grateful that day was breaking in the east.

Wet, breathless, and thoroughly alarmed, he reached the shore where the stream flowed into the river and searched carefully for evidences of Tom. Shal was waiting, her coat bedraggled and snarled with briars, her tail wagging apologetically.

"Isn't there some sign, Shal?"

However, there were no large round footprints, no branches stripped of leaves, no overturned rocks. It was as if Tom never existed.

"He must have been in a hurry and gone right into the river. . . . Can you hear anything, Shal?"

For a long moment they listened, hoping in vain to hear a noisy splash above the flow of river and stream. It was still impossible to see the opposite shore of the mainland.

"We'll wait here until it's light. Oh, Shal, if I'd only left him in the cage last night. Then he'd be safe this morning—"

Seated upon a rock, Rush waited for the mists and

shadows to clear, scarcely conscious of the beauty of the morning's changing lights, his mind striving to follow Tom. Undoubtedly the elephant had walked in the middle of the stream, not a foot touching the land. Had he been swept southward? According to the most skilled pilots, the Mississippi was an enigma, the waters always in the process of change. That which appeared calm on the surface might harbor maelstroms below. Poor Tom—so eager for a swim. Cy had said that Tom could swim "very well, indeed," but where was Tom now? Battling with the currents, hidden by the morning mists? Tortured and grieving, unable to sit still, Rush now walked back and forth pausing to listen and call.

"Tom! Tom! Come back! Come back!"

Added to his sorrow was the humiliation of his own failure to care for Tom. Through his carelessness, his lack of wit and common sense, one of the most valuable animals in the zoo had been lost. Unknown to Captain Whipple, there was another great misfortune in store for him—there was no small elephant to head his Circus Parade, for Tom had disappeared into the air like a bubble. Cy would be bitterly disappointed—and Madame Whipple. How would he ever explain his heedlessness—how could he ever atone? Undoubtedly he would be dismissed as inefficient and he and Shal would be forced to seek work on another boat. If only Shal would give one joyous bark, telling him to come—that he had found Tom. But Shal was silent, out of sight. Never had Rush felt more alone.

The mists were lifting. At the water's edge he waited until the dark line of opposite land loomed clear. In another moment all of the gray swirled upward as if by magic, pierced by the sun, and he could see the distant green shore, black rocks, and lighter patches of beach sand. Nothing seemed to stir. No plump gray figure played among the reeds in the shallow water, nor walked the fields of wild grass farther on. Nor did birds flying overhead show timidity or alarm. He wished now that he knew more about elephants, their habits and reactions.

For a little while Rush wandered along the shore, his eyes searching for a gray head above the current, condemning himself, his throat heavy and choked with tears. Tom drowned—at the bottom of the river. This was the picture which haunted him most. Tom—with his little tricks of naughtiness. Would he ever again feel the affectionate squeeze of Tom's trunk about him—lifting him gently from the floor? There had been so many ways in which the small elephant expressed himself. The little grunt of appreciation at the gift of an apple, the two ears pricked up at the sound of his footsteps, the playful tweak at his hair whenever he bent forward— Perhaps, right now, Tom was eating poisonous berries. . . . And who was there, in the wilderness which stretched about them, to apply hot linament to an aching stomach? Once more he tried to call. But no sound came—only tears, hot and blinding.

Wearily Rush made his way back to the Circus Boat, almost forgetting the lantern left on the bank of the stream. Shal followed at his heels, her head low, feeling his dejection.

"You've done your best," said Rush as he stopped to comfort her. "I'm the one to blame. In a little while we'll go back—maybe walk around the island. There might be a cave or something he's hiding in."

There was no change in the Circus Boat. All was as he

had left it. Tom's cage, empty and unusually neat, and the huge mound of hay in the corner brought a fresh lump to his throat but Rush doggedly measured out food for the remaining animals, checking the different supplies at the same time. Dignity's meat was fast dwindling, the ice in the big chest fairly gone. Shal would have to hunt for game if Dignity were to survive. . . . Fortunately for Lily, the apples continued to remain sound. Perhaps later in the day the bears could be staked outside to forage for bugs and tips of green leaves, and if so he could cut down on their daily quota of apples. The supply of molasses in the hogshead was lower than he realized. From now on he determined to go without himself, and save the molasses for the bears. Dazzle could be tethered on some grassy spot. As for his own meals, catfish and coarse grain steamed into mush would be ample. Cy had said that one could use the stove for cooking. Every mouthful must be accounted for from now on, every animal kept well and happy as possible. Captain Whipple and Cy must find order and cleanliness. All would be well but for the tragic absence of Tom. . . .

With the cages cleaned, the drinking water replenished and the animals fed, Rush climbed the hill, munching the last of the crackers. From now on he would be eating catfish and grain-mush, he told himself. Possibly there would be wild fruits and berries later, if he stayed on the island that long. However, food became unimportant when he reached the flat rock on the top of the hill. All his attention was focused on the land below, as he strove to catch some glimpse of Tom. Had he crossed from the island to the mainland? The red flag still waved in the breeze and for a long time he stood beside it, noting the slightest stir in the trees. Tom might be hiding. However, in time he would be forced to walk to the shore to drink. His one remaining hope was that a cave harbored him, somewhere at the end of the island. And he did not intend to give up his hope until he had thoroughly explored every foot of the shore line.

"I'll get my heavy boots, and then we'll go," he told the dog.

In the Circus Boat, Lily climbed up and down the sides of her cage continuously, little sobbing sounds in her throat. A sensitive creature, she had begun to reflect some of Rush's dejection and was restless and unhappy. Wishing to quiet her, Rush unbolted her cage and took her out. She clung to him tightly, her hat on the back of her head, both hands clenched to the collar of his shirt.

"I've got to go out again, Lily, but I won't be gone long—"

Later he found it impossible to release her hands without hurting her.

"I can't take you—it's a long walk."

Lily had been outside her cage only for a sunning and the idea of taking her on a journey was almost unthinkable. Yet Rush knew that for the next three hours she would continue to grieve and climb up and down the walls of her cage and he hesitated. The monkey had gained in health but not enough to offset a state of exhaustion. In a way, she might prove good company and the tight hold of her hands and arms might be comforting. She needed him. . . . Eventually she would perch on his shoulder and balance herself as he walked. He called Shal, and the three started off over the same ground they had covered before, Rush hoping to discover fresh clues in the daylight. The monkey, with her hat in reverse, was now happy, peering at every-thing about her through the feathers which hung over her eyes.

"If you must wear the hat the wrong way, Lily, push it back. Yes, that's a tree," Rush answered her incessant chat-ter. "Someday I'll let you climb one."

By the time Rush reached the bank of the Mississippi there had been only one new clue, hardly important. Tom had stopped by the side of the stream, placed a ponderous foot on the end of trailing rope, snapped off a portion and left it there. Only a few feet remained to dangle from his breast strap. Shal sniffed of the remaining rope and whined a little.

"He's smart, Shal. Probably the rope tripped him. Of course he's better off without it."

Nothing stirred on the mainland. After waiting a few moments, Rush began his journey around the island, which proved difficult from the very beginning. Sharp rocks cut his boots and the sun sent down blistering rays. Now and then he stopped to call Tom's name but there was no an-swer. Lily appeared contented even though they were forced to cross a swamp and cut their way through dense briars. Her chatter finally gave out but her eyes saw every-thing. Interest in her reactions served to lift Rush's disap-pointment in not finding rock caves which might have con-cealed Tom. For the country about him consisted of pebbly shores and dense timber which Shal was already foraging —nothing more.

Rush had covered one half of the distance when he paused to rest a moment beneath a group of young birches. Conscious that Lily was reaching for something, he turned and was amused to see her feeling a birch leaf with one hand. Impulsively he placed her among the branches.

"Go ahead, Lily, and climb. See what it's like."

Lily hesitated, her mouth open a little, and then to Rush's surprise she ascended rapidly to the very top of the tree, the red hat perched on the back of her head. The tree, slender and pliable, dipped with her weight, and the downward swing through the air caused her to squeal with mingled joy and fright. Encouraged by Rush, she mounted again. This time she showed less fright. And then Rush watched, his own gloom lifted by the little monkey's happiness. Four, five, six times she swung through the air from above with soft cries of ecstacy. Noting her rapid breathing, he finally caught her as she tried to ascend for the seventh time.

"No, Lily, you're all out of breath—and you might get away from me. Why, you're trembling. . . . We'll try to find a birch near the boat so you can swing when we get back. It's the first tree you ever climbed, isn't it, Lily?"

From then on every time she passed a birch tree, Lily held up her arms, asking for another taste of freedom. But time was slipping by and there was still some distance to go. It was not long before Shal suddenly appeared with a rabbit in her mouth. The animal was dead though still warm and Rush petted and praised her in genuine enthusiasm.

"Go get another, Shal. That's what we need—meat! This will keep Dignity going. Good work, Shal!"

Shal, spurred on by Rush's praise, produced a second rabbit on the last mile homeward. With the two brown bodies tied to the back of his belt, Rush now felt the need to hurry. The sun was already riding toward the west and Lily had begun to nod, struggling with sleep. For fear she might fall from his shoulder, he carried her on one arm. The Circus Boat was almost in sight and he could see the red cape blowing on the flagpole on the hill when Shal, a little distance ahead, suddenly stopped and gave a warning growl. Something was wrong and she turned to tell him, her fur standing upright on the ridge of her back, an angry glow in her eyes.

"What is it, Shal? Quiet—don't bark—quiet. I'm coming. . . . It isn't Tom, is it? No, you wouldn't act this way—"

It was only a short walk to some willows by the river's edge. From behind the green screen Rush could see the square outline of the Circus Boat. Soothing Lily with one hand to keep her quiet, he waited, Shal crouched beside him. Yes, now he could hear voices. But for Shal's strange attitude, he would have run forward, glad for the help in answer to his red signal. However, he had long ago learned to heed her judgment and she now indicated trouble—that something unpleasant lurked near. Only the word "quiet" and the touch of his hand on the back of her neck prevented the dog from springing forward in an angry attack.

Two voices—and neither of them had he heard before. A thin nasal voice seemed to do most of the talking. Now and then a second voice, slow and measured, of a softer tone, answered. It was difficult to catch some of the words at first but gradually Rush's ears became accustomed to the sounds and his mind fitted them together.

"As likely a bit of horseflesh as I've ever seen," the moderate voice was now saying. "This is the horse the

trainer rides through the towns. Whoa, there, you white
devil, or I'll give you a lacing."

There was a gleam of white through the willows and
Rush could now see Dazzle, standing outside the Circus
Boat. The horse was uneasy, frightened, and pulling away
from the stranger who held his bridle. A hot anger whipped
through him at the sight and he had an almost overpowering
urge to run to Dazzle's aid. But caution held him back—
the horse as yet was not hurt and he needed to hear more.
The man was evidently someone who had seen Cy ride by
on Dazzle. . . . Who was he? . . . What right had he to
lead the horse out of the Circus Boat? Were these two
newcomers here in answer to the red signal, and how had
they managed to reach the island? Ah, yes, a white towboat was anchored farther out. He had not noticed it before.
The strangers might have rowed around the floating debris
in a rowboat.

"Guess the kid's out airin' the el'phant," offered the nasal
voice after a pause. "Say, this is powerful good 'lasses.
There's a half hogshead of the stuff. Wanter taste?" A lean
tall figure in a red shirt and wide-brimmed black hat came
into view, one hand holding out a dipper which was used
for measuring grain in the feed room. Molasses! The molasses he was trying so hard to save for the cubs—and what
had the man said about a "kid airin' an el'phant"?

"Don't be a fool—this is no time to eat molasses," and
there was a sharp knife-like rebuke from the man holding
Dazzle. "Here, take the horse back to his stall. He might
break a leg out here. Then go up the hill and pull down that
red flag like I told you. There'll be half a dozen other boats
trying to get in here if you don't hurry. Get going!"

"Yes, sir. Yes, sir."

The sound of Dazzle's hoofs sounded on the wooden floor a moment later and Rush knew the horse was back in his stall. The tall man appeared again, licking his fingers which were apparently sticky with molasses.

"That man sez there was a big dog in the winder, remember?" he asked, his twangy voice full of apprehension. "Looked like a wolf, he sez. I ain't aimin' to mix up with wolves, Mr. Burton—"

Mr. Burton! Then the man holding Dazzle was Sam Burton! A cold chill ran up Rush's back and there was such a pounding in his ears that he scarcely heard Sam Burton's reply.

"I'll take care of the dog. And if you don't get up that hill, you white-livered river rat—"

"Yes, sir. Yes, sir—"

Heavy footsteps sounded, coming nearer, nearer the willows. This was more than Shal could endure. With a deep rumbling roar which seemed to pass through her whole body, she broke from Rush's hold and sprang clear of the willows in one long swift leap. In another moment, the tall thin man in the black hat, screaming with terror, lay face downward, pinned to the earth by her weight.

15

SHAL IN DANGER

It did not take Rush long to follow Shal. With a swift toss upward he landed Lily in the top branches of the willows while he squeezed himself through the green wall of leaves below. By the time Burton arrived, Rush had Shal in a half sitting position, tugging at her collar.

"Get that dog off—or I'll shoot!" came Burton's voice in a cold measured tone. "Quick!" and something flashed in one of his hands. It was a revolver, bright and new.

"Up, Shal, up! Let go!"

Reluctantly Shal's jaws relinquished their hold on the man's shirt and she stood on her feet. The dog was in an ugly mood, her lips in a fixed snarl, her back fur bristling.

"You hurt, Joe?" asked Burton casually as the man struggled to his feet.

"Oh, Lor' Mr. Burton—I don't know, I don't know—"

"Well, get hold of yourself. Stop babbling. I've got the dog covered. What do you mean sicking your dog on us—spying, weren't you?" and Burton turned on Rush. There was something venomous in his swift attack.

For a moment Rush found it difficult to speak. As far back as he could remember, his entire life had been shadowed by his stepuncle, Samuel Burton. His own father had suffered in many ways. And now, for the first time in ten years, he was gazing at the man, face to face, in a mixed state of fear and repugnance. It was evident that his uncle had not heard of his disappearance from Eau Claire, nor did he recognize him. Of medium height, with gray eyes beneath iron gray hair and dressed in a black cloth suit with expensive gold watch chain across the front, Burton made a good appearance. The eyes, however, held a cold glittering light and a sneer drew down the corners of his mouth. This was the man who sought the acres of timber he had inherited from his grandfather, the man who was suspected too of selling worthless stock to innocent people, swindling them of their money over an imaginary city called Rollingstone—

"What's the matter with you? Understand English? I asked you a question—"

Blood surged into Rush's face and he felt his cheeks burn. At the sharpness in Burton's voice, Shal began to growl and Rush realized he must keep his voice calm or she might spring again. The dog mirrored his own emotions and one shot from the revolver would end all for Shal. When he spoke, his voice had such a strained thick quality that he hardly recognized it himself.

"It's the dog's job to guard the Circus Boat—and she was protecting me, too. Any dog would do the same."

"They would, would they? Well, let that dog jump again and it will be her last!" Burton's hand moved the revolver a little. "And remember this—when you speak to me, keep a civil tongue in your head. Address me as 'sir.' What are you doing on Whipple's boat anyway?"

"I help train the animals. Captain Whipple hired me."

"Sir!"

"Sir."

"Shoot now, Mr. Burton," sniveled Joe, who had taken refuge behind Burton. "You've got two shots left. She's a wolf—she ain't a dog. Oh, Lor'," and Joe's lower jaw dropped and his eyes rolled upward. Lily, with her hat askew, sat on an upper branch, a frightened look on her small face as she stared at the scene below.

"What in all get-out is that?" asked Burton, catching sight of her.

"A monkey. She belongs to the boat. Here, Lily—" Rush held out a hand.

"Never mind the monkey. You keep a good hold on that dog," ordered Burton. "None of these animals interest me but the elephant—and the horse, of course. Where is the elephant?"

"He's run away—sir."

Burton stared back in silent contempt.

"You will learn—in time—never to lie to me. Where is the elephant?" repeated Burton, taking a step nearer. A soft growl sang in Shal's throat and Rush felt her quiver beneath his hand. Reaching down, he took hold of her collar with both hands and it was like taking a firmer hold of himself. When he spoke his voice was steady—quiet.

"I am telling you the truth—sir." To avoid the strange glittering light in the gray eyes, Rush focused his gaze on the little scar at the corner of Burton's mouth. Delos had spoken of the scar. . . .

"In case you don't know, young man," and Burton's voice was slow and measured, "this boat and these animals belong to me. Dan Whipple has owed me money for some time and I'm taking over this property right now. The elephant is valuable—worth a lot of money—I plan to start a Circus Boat myself. Now naturally I want a report of *my* animals. Where is the elephant?" And Burton came another step closer.

"Mr. Burton—" began Rush as he took a tighter hold on Shal. How long would he be able to control her? He must use his wits—keep his voice civil. "Mr. Burton, you'll have to believe me. I've just come back from walking around the island, searching for the elephant. I can't find him—there's no place for him to hide in. The boat leaked—I took him outside and tied him to a tree. He got away—I tell you I can't find him."

"So you didn't go rabbit hunting?" Burton's eyes sought the rabbits fastened at Rush's belt. "I'd have said you were out on a lark of your own—"

"Oh, no. I took Shal with me to track down the elephant. She caught the rabbits on the way. We need meat, sir. The lion has to have meat or he'll starve. It's important to keep them well fed."

"They all look fat—too fat to me. Anyway I'm only

interested in the elephant—and the horse. And if the elephant is dead through your carelessness, you will owe me, Sam Burton, quite a sum of money. You might have to work ten years for me to repay it. Maybe this will make you remember where the elephant is—"

"You'll have to believe me, sir—"

"But I don't."

Sam Burton was beginning to show his anger. In the gathering twilight his face had paled, his eyes grown darker. The hand grasping the revolver tightened its grip and his voice had a rasping sound.

"So you still stick to your story? Maybe this will persuade you. . . . I want you to tie up that dog. Keep her in in the boat day and night. No more running around. And listen closely—if you do not produce that elephant in twenty-four hours, I shall shoot her. Shoot your dog. Fair exchange, eh? A dog for an elephant."

There was a roaring sound in Rush's ears, and skies, trees and Sam Burton spun about him in a wild whirl. Nausea pounded at the pit of his stomach. The whirling gradually ceased, leaving him weak and shaken and through a haze he began to see Burton's face. It was smiling, the mouth pulled down at the corners . . . a smile of triumph and amusement. Fortunately Rush had managed to keep on his feet, still holding Shal's collar. But for the revolver, still pointed at them both, he would have let the dog spring, glad to see the man before him torn to shreds. But there was nothing he could do—nothing he could say. Shal could not be sacrificed for his own revenge. The fury and shock in his face must have pleased Burton for he gave a faint chuckle.

"I thought that might bring you to terms. Careful—no

back talk," he warned, as Rush drew a breath to speak.
"Don't ever argue with me when I give orders. No one ever
does—twice. Now—tie up that white brute first. Then come
back and catch the ape. I don't like monkeys. Keep her out
of my sight from now on. Get going! Get going! Don't just
stand there. Joe! Where are you?"

"Right here, Mr. Burton." Joe, cringing in the background, slowly limped forward, rubbing the small of his
back with one hand.

"Stop being so spleeny, Joe. You aren't hurt. I want you
to climb that hill—I've told you four times already—and
bring down the signal before Whipple passes by and sees
it. Then I'll give you a list of things to get from the *Elsie*.
We're going to stay here awhile, sleep in the old pilot house,
until the elephant comes back. It's a long time since I've had
a vacation and I can do some fishing. You'll have to move
fast before that trash shifts around and cuts off the way to
row through—" and the rest was lost as Rush entered the
Circus Boat with Shal.

It took Rush a moment or two to hang the rabbits in the
feed room and then find a rope to tie Shal to a post. His
hands fumbled with the knots and there was a feeling of
numbness in his body. Sam Burton had meant what he said
—Tom must be brought back in twenty-four hours or Shal
would pay the price—with her life. Even now she was
lapping his cheek with her soft warm tongue, feeling his
distress, although her brown eyes were perplexed at being
tied. How could he make her understand? In only two
other instances had she ever been tied before. Since a
puppy, she had followed at his heels, her devotion filling
the cruel gap caused by his father's death. Something must

be done soon, to save her. To bank his hope upon finding Tom within the next twenty-four hours was folly. There must be some way of escape.

"It's only for a little while, Shal," he whispered. "I've got to catch Lily—we're leaving here soon, somehow."

Just to hear his own words comforted him. It was lack of food, exhaustion, and terrible anger at Burton that had made his head swirl. But there was no time for food or rest now—Lily was wandering about somewhere out in the gathering dusk, probably terrified to be alone. Seizing an apple for her from the feed room, he left hurriedly, swaying a little as he walked and conscious that Shal tugged at her rope to follow. Burton sat on the bank just ahead, busily writing on a piece of paper and did not look up as Rush passed. Where was Lily? It was quiet along the tops of the willows. Was she hiding in the dense growth beneath? Frightened, she might have run some distance away. Perhaps if he walked in a circle, encompassing her, she might hear him call . . . softly, so as not to annoy Burton.

Stumbling through the dense undergrowth, Rush made his way, sometimes standing motionless in one spot as he called. Only night birds rustled in the leaves overhead and once he saw something run the length of a limb. However, it proved to be a squirrel scurrying home for the night.

"Lily—Lily—"

First Tom lost—now Lily. A hawk might attack her, a snake might poison her. . . .

"Lily—Lily—"

In the distance Rush could see Burton's back as he still worked over his list. And suddenly Burton's head turned.

"You still hunting for that ape?" he called irritably.

"Yes, sir."

"Well, she just ran into the boat. A fine trainer you are," and Burton settled down to his work once more, straining to see in the dim light.

Lily had entered her own cage and even pulled the door shut after her. Beneath her little blanket she peered out at Rush and reached out one hand for a piece of apple.

"You're a smart girl, Lily. If only Tom would come home like that—"

Exhausted but relieved beyond words, Rush sank down beside Shal and wound one arm about her neck. And as he lay there, it seemed to him that all the animals watched, quietly and wonderingly, seeming to sense that a change of some sort had taken place. Of them all, Shal came first and now she was in great danger. Escape by rowboat was his only hope, provided the channel of water through the debris had not closed. He would know when Joe returned from the *Elsie*. Once he and Shal escaped to the main shore and located Captain Whipple, his responsibilities would be over. Or would they? Sitting up a little straighter, Rush turned and surveyed the animals in their cages.

Burton had said that they were "all too fat, if you ask me." Neither he nor Joe cared how they fared. Tom was of value because of the money he represented and Dazzle was safe—Burton liked horses. And what of the others? Burton did not like monkeys, so Lily, left alone, would pine away. The two cubs, Twist and Turn, had already lost their molasses and Dignity, old and failing, would have no meat. Unwanted, uncared for, they would languish in their cages, watching the doorway, watching for him. . . . Was it right to leave them here—desert them—when he was not certain of finding Captain Whipple? Yet Shal would be shot in twenty-four hours if he did not find Tom!

Voices broke the silence. Joe had returned with the red-lined cape and Burton could be heard giving further directions. The voice gradually grew fainter as the two walked toward the pilot house.

"Tell Simp . . . go immediately. Travel by night. Have that steam pump mended and get a load of wood . . . return as soon as possible . . . three days at the most . . . my list will cover all we'll need. . . . Another lantern, more bullets, blankets . . . coffee, bacon. And . . . my fish pole . . . if . . . the channel closes, find another way to come in," and then the voice stopped altogether.

There would be no escape for Shal or himself if the channel closed—in the night. The boat bumping against the logs would be heard. His only other alternative was to gain possession of Burton's revolver, difficult as it seemed. Joe had spoken of two remaining shots and Burton was sending for more bullets. Only two shots left in the bright new revolver, carried in Burton's right-hand coat pocket!

Forcing himself into action, Rush built a small fire and cooked some grain on the stove. The water was slow in boiling and he waited impatiently, his mind seething with conflicting emotions, wondering what he should do. Only half cooked, the mush stuck in his throat and was flavorless, but it relieved the faint feeling in his stomach. He had consumed most of it when he heard Shal give warning.

"Here, you," called Burton's voice impatiently.

"Yes—sir." Rush went to the doorway. Like the mush, the word "sir" seemed to stick in his throat and always came with an effort.

"Got that dog tied?" The moon was rising and Rush could see Burton fifty feet away on the shore.

"Yes, sir."

"Got a broom?"

"Why, I think so—"

"Sweep out the pilot house. And bring a load of hay for my bed. Got anything to eat?"

"I cooked some mush. There's not much else." Tom's hay for Burton's bed! Just the thought of it riled him!

"Humph—" Burton was evidently hungry and mush hardly appealed. "No mush for me. And ease up on that molasses. I shall be needing it. Move smart now. You can pack the hay in the cape I'm leaving here on the rock. Bring plenty—I like a soft bed."

There was no disputing that Burton was efficient and thought things through. He was a born manager—of the wrong sort, his own welfare always coming first. The cubs' molasses and Tom's hay were now at stake.

It was the revolver that occupied his mind the most, as Rush walked along the shore, carrying the hay packed in the cape and a broom over his shoulder. Only two shots left in the new revolver. . . . And if he were able to steal and hide the new supply of bullets which Joe was bringing from the towboat *Elsie*, the revolver would lose its deadly power —Shal would have a fighting chance. Burton would naturally conserve his two bullets for his own preservation, if left on an uninhabited island three days. He would not waste one on a dog—if that dog gave no trouble. And in that three day wait, Tom might be located. Meanwhile the other animals would be fed and watered under his care—he would not have deserted them. Did he dare take the risk?

It was a narrow margin of chance. A quick vision of Gramp Tolman flashed before him. Gramp, with his blue eyes blazing beneath the old black hat and his words, "An' blast his cheatin' hide! You keep a jump ahead of that stepuncle. . . . The ol' weasel. . . ." Yes, Gramp would take the chance and, if caught, endure the punishment without a word.

A light shone in the pilot house and Burton sat in the doorway, smoking his pipe and polishing his revolver, evidently his latest toy. Depositing the hay outside, Rush stepped through the unboarded window and began to sweep.

"Do a good job or you'll have to do it all over," ordered Burton. "And don't raise too much dust. There's some mice under the floor. Kill them with your broom."

Rush made no reply but continued sweeping. Unseen by Burton, the mice escaped into the deep grass and Rush felt a certain exuberance in their good fortune. If the mice could escape, so could he and Shal. . . . How many bullets did the revolver hold altogether? Probably six. There were more pistols than revolvers in Eau Claire. The leaves and dry twigs swept into a pile, he was about to brush them through the window when Burton spoke.

"What's your name?" Burton had half turned in the doorway and was staring at him.

"Jamieson."

"Sir!"

"Sir."

"Seems as if I'd seen you somewhere before," and the gray eyes passed searchingly over Rush. "Where's your home?"

"The Circus Boat, I guess. I haven't any home, sir."

"Stop stalling. Where'd you come from?"

"My folks came from Illinois, years ago."

"Humph, you look like someone I used to know. From Wisconsin."

Of course it was his father. Delos had said there was a strong resemblance and others had told him, too. There was a long silence during which Burton continued to polish his revolver. Possibly he was thinking back on the days when he was a stepbrother of Charles Taylor. . . . The pile of refuse swept clear, Rush began to brush down the cobwebs from the ceiling.

"Did you say Jamieson, young man?" Burton had again turned to look at him from the doorway.

"Yes, sir."

There was another pause as Burton continued to stare. "By the way—" the man's mouth gave a short cynical smile and there was a taunting note in his voice—"how did the Circus Boat happen to get loose from the towboat?"

"It didn't get loose, sir. Someone cut her lines and the hawser."

"Cut them? Why, who would do a thing like that?" Burton was enjoying himself now, pretending to be shocked.

"Just a low-down river rat, I imagine," replied Rush quickly.

The smile on Burton's face disappeared instantly and Rush was glad a moment later to hear a faint whistle from the water. His control was wearing thin and he was wondering how much longer he could keep his voice normal. Joe had come just in time—

"That's Joe," announced Burton, getting to his feet. "Help him carry that load up here."

A moment later the bow of the rowboat grated on the pebbly shore below. It was evident that Joe had managed to bring quite a load. A large pile of bedding formed a dark mound on the stern seat.

"That dog tied up fast?" asked Joe upon seeing Rush. "If t'aint, I ain't goin' to come ashore."

"Dog's tied," called Burton.

"I brung a lot of blankets," explained Joe, stepping over the side, " 'cause I ain't over my malaria yet. Say, the trash is movin'—nigh closed me in back there."

"Here's hoping it all moves off," returned Burton. "Simp leaving right away?"

"Yes, sir. Right now," came Joe's voice as he bent over some boxes. "Says he'll be back day after tomorrer. He's goin' to get the engines leveled an' lined, too."

"Why, the muttonhead ought to know how himself. What do I pay him for?" There was a moment as Burton thought this over. "What else?"

"Nothin', sir, nothin'. Only yer crew is fussin' some. They wanter go to St. Louis. They don't wanter go north."

"That's just too bad," and there was biting sarcasm in Burton's voice. "Did you bring everything on the list?"

"Yes, sir. Yes, sir. Here's yer pole—I wouldn't forgit that." Joe handed Burton a fish pole. "The rest is in the boxes."

"Get busy, boy—take this up to the house," ordered Burton brusquely, pointing at a good-sized box. "Put the things on the shelves and then fill the kettle with water. Joe will

184

RIVER CIRCUS

build the fire. Did you remember to bring extra line and hooks, Joe?"

" 'Course, Mr. Burton. I got 'em. Lor' but ain't I hungry! I got to thinkin' of that 'lasses and how good it would be a-drippin' on some hush puppies—"

"Stop your noise and give me that lantern."

The wooden box was heavy and twice Rush was forced to stop and rest on the walk to the pilot house. The moon, however, lighted his way and showed him where to place his feet and not stumble. Arrived at the house, he dragged the box across the floor and commenced to unpack. Every moment was precious. With the channel of water closing, all hope of escape in the boat was gone. Destroying the bullets was the only way now and he hoped, desperately, that they were among the groceries.

Bags and boxes of tea, coffee, sugar, and flour were hurriedly dumped on the floor. Surely the second layer would contain the bullets generally packed in a gray-blue box. Salt, pepper, tobacco—ah, there it was, the gray-blue box. How often he had seen the same box among Delos' hunting supplies! The top was loose and he lifted it with trembling fingers. Twenty-four leaden tips with metal cases—twenty-four bullets standing in even upright rows! Voices sounded outside so he opened his pocket and emptied the contents of the box into it. Then moving swiftly he began to place the groceries on the shelf above, the empty gray-blue box between the two cans of tobacco. Burton would see the box there. Otherwise its absence might cause questions and an investigation. Eventually someone would be blamed for sending an empty box instead of a full one. He hoped it would be Simp . . . far away and out of reach. Joe had now entered with a second load, and just behind was Burton. Seizing the iron kettle from the stove, Rush started to leave through the unboarded window, hoping the bullets would not rattle in his pocket.

"Here, you," called Burton, "get clean water from the rocks out front. Don't bring back any mud."

"No, sir," and Rush was gone.

Once clear of the house, Rush began to run. Nothing could stop him now. Yes, he would gladly fill the kettle from the rocks out in front although he had to wade in water up to his knees to reach them. From the farthermost rock he would rid himself of the bullets. From now on no one would suffer from them—or ever see them again.

Wet, his breath coming in short gasps, Rush finally climbed the side of the most distant rock. Was he being watched? He must run that chance. . . . Bracing his feet, he emptied his pocket, throwing little handfuls of bullets as far as possible and listening as they made small splashing sounds—like fish jumping. Then, certain that his pocket was empty, he filled the kettle and waded back to shore, a little excited and a little frightened at what he had done.

Burton was seated at the table in the pilot house sorting out fishhooks by the light of the lantern when Rush returned. It was evident that the man was unusually fond of fishing and meant to devote himself to it the next few days. Although he could not be sure, Rush felt he had not been seen disposing of the bullets. A few moments later Burton rose and, taking his pipe, wandered out and sat beneath the cottonwood tree. It was then that Joe, preparing supper, whined out his troubles to Rush. Whatever grudge he held against him because of Shal's attack was lost in the desire to unload his troubles to a fresh ear.

"My feet—they're the worst," he half whispered, turning to make sure Burton was out under the cottonwood tree. "An' by Jupiter, how my back aches. Seems like I work, work, work—all the time. Never a letup. I'm a slave, I am."

Remembering Burton's threat to enslave him for the next ten years, Rush felt a little compassion. What had Joe done to entangle himself with Burton?

"Sometimes I think I'll find me a nice island an' live there." Joe pushed the coffee pot to the back of the stove. "An' sleep—Lor', how I'll sleep! Git me some wood, boy. You don't ketch me goin' out inter the dark with all them beasts of yours in that boat. No, sir! Say, what you done with that el'phant anyway?" and he leaned close confidentially. "You can tell ol' Joe—"

"I told Mr. Burton the truth," replied Rush, looking straight into Joe's eyes.

"Sure, sure—blime me if I ain't beginnin' to believe you. The man who seen you on the river in the winder tole us you was a good boy—tried to help him an' the kids. We might not have found you but for him. Here, turn this bacon while I take off my boots. By Jupiter, ain't I tired this night. I'm plumb sick of livin' this way anyhow. A rollin' stone don't gather no moss, I says—" Joe suddenly stopped short, a frightened expression on his face. "The boss," and he pointed out toward the cottonwood tree, "don't like to hear me say that. An' I'm always forgittin'. . . ."

Later Joe fed himself little scraps of bacon as he stood

over the stove, and in the lantern's light the grease made his lips shine. But he offered none to Rush, who found it difficult not to watch the meat as it moved about in the hot pan, curling in crisp ribbons when finished.

It had been six days since he had eaten a regular meal but somehow the pangs of hunger mattered less than they might have. Deep within him, there was a strange contentment. He had only to raise his eyes to the shelf and note the gray-blue box resting between the tobacco cans. The box was empty and twenty-four bullets lay at the bottom of the Mississippi. Come what may—even though he paid the price of severe punishment—Shal had a better chance to live. And he was now determined not to desert the animals in the Circus Boat.

16

A WANDERER RETURNS

It was difficult for Rush to leave Shal the next morning and begin his walk around the island in search of Tom. Tied to the post, the dog strained at her rope to follow and twice he was forced to return to quiet her. The experience left him uncertain whether he was wise to leave at all, and the cold breakfast of grain-mush lay like a heavy lump in his stomach as he finally walked along the shore toward the pilot house. It was early—mist lay on the river and seeped through his cotton shirt. No smoke rose from the chimney and there was no sign of life about the house. He was wondering if the empty ammunition box had been discovered, when he spied a hammock slung between the big cottonwood tree and a neighboring maple. A head, still wearing a hat, protruded from a mound of blankets and, taking a few steps closer, he saw that it was Joe, snoring in noisy enjoyment.

"Joe," he called softly and then decided to let the man sleep. Poor Joe, always so weary and used by Burton as a slave. A perfect example of river boss and underling. . . . However, there was a kind streak in Joe. Free of Burton, the man might be an entirely different person.

If only he could leave feeling that Shal was safe. Burton was a man of uncertain temper. If exasperated by any untoward behavior on Shal's part, he would not hesitate to shoot. As she was now, tied to a post and unable to free herself, Burton might even kill her with a blow on the head. It was difficult to push back the wave of fear which assailed him, and for a few moments Rush stood still wondering if he heard Shal bark. Had he tied the rope securely enough? Then realizing that the sooner he made the trip and returned, the better, he plunged into the nearest thicket, following the same route Tom had taken the day before. By the time he had reached the river and halted on the bank, he was wet with mist and perspiration. It was useless to try to see the opposite shore, but for a little while he called and listened. There was no response of any kind and now in his mind there was a leaden conviction that Tom was dead. Drowned in spite of the fact that elephants could swim. Faced with such a swift current, any small elephant would be swept away. No, Tom was dead—but he knew he must circle the island just as he had planned. Later, he would always remember that he had searched thoroughly and left no stone unturned. With an effort he commenced to walk, his feet heavy.

A few moments later he imagined he heard Tom call and he turned back a short way. However, all the time he knew it was his imagination. Now and then it seemed as if Tom walked just ahead of him, his gray legs plodding and lumbering along in their funny gait, the skinny little tail swinging. The instant he stood still the vision cleared and there was no more Tom—only rocks, trees, and the river. It was the sun which had risen in hot fury that befuddled him, he told himself. The sun, worry over Shal, the scant breakfast, and the grief which racked and pulled at him whenever he thought of Tom. To clear away the torturing pictures, he lay flat on a rock and held his head under water a few seconds. He would have liked to remain there to rest but a greater urge started him on his way again.

With his journey half completed, realizing that he was at the farthermost point distant from the Circus Boat, Rush was seized with sudden terror. Shal might be in danger and he could not reach her. She was tied to a post and helpless to defend herself. If Burton had found the empty box, he might avenge himself on Shal. Why had he not thought of this before? He began to hurry, crossing the swamp at random, sometimes knee-deep in mud, not even attempting to find the path he had hewn through the wall of briars the day before. His clothes torn, his face scratched and bleeding, he at length reached firmer land and hastened along the shore. The journey had seemed endless, even with a beautiful day overhead and a chorus of birds singing from every tree. On past the hill with its empty flagpole, on past the wall of willows. . . . He now ran and his breath made a rasping sound and there was a sharp pain in his side. Up the earthern ramp and a sharp bark welcomed him. Through a haze, there was Shal waving her plumed tail vigorously, and then he felt her softness and her warmth. Safe—she was safe—and nothing else mattered.

"I thought I'd never get here. If he had hurt you, I'd— I'd—" and then a smooth tongue washed his scratches and seemed to take away the terror. Shal, with her softness and her warmth. . . .

It was good to be back in the Circus Boat once more. But after a while, when he had become rested, Rush had the feeling he had not done a thorough job that morning. The last half of his journey had not been spent searching for Tom but running in great anxiety to reach Shal. Should he go over the same ground again, retrace his steps? Or should he climb the hill to the flagpole and look carefully about? Even though he believed Tom dead, something within him would not let him give up the hunt. The man Simp was arriving "day after tomorrer" according to Joe last night. Time was precious. . . .

At the foot of the hill Rush suddenly remembered there had been a telescope brought back by Joe the night before. If Burton was out fishing perhaps Joe would lend it to him for a short time. From the top of the hill the magnifying glass would bring the shore much closer and he would be able to see if anything moved among the gray rocks below. His courage rising, Rush turned toward the pilot house. Smoke spiraled from the chimney, but before he went too close he planned to watch and listen. He had no desire to encounter Burton and answer his many questions.

The smoke continued to curl upward in a thin spiral but there was no clatter of pans or sound to show that Joe was within. Following the hedge, Rush approached the unboarded window, careful to make sure his feet did not snap a twig or crunch upon the small stones. A fire still burned in the stove and a coffee pot simmered at the back. Unwashed dishes littered the table and Burton's black suit with its watch chain dangling from a buttonhole of his vest hung on the opposite wall. The rod and tackle were gone and, his courage mounting, Rush leaned forward to see the bed. It was empty and now he was certain that Burton had gone fishing. Had the box of bullets been touched? No, it lay where he had placed it—between the two cans of tobacco.

He now felt more free to search for the spyglass. Had Burton taken it with him and had Joe gone also, to do the rowing? A quick glance through an opposite window told the story. In Burton's absence, Joe had gone back to his hammock and it was evident that he did not expect Burton to return for some time. What would he do—waken Joe and ask for the spyglass? It could do no harm—

"Joe, wake up, will you? Just a minute—"

Even the removal of Joe's hat failed to waken him. The snores continued their regular explosions in Joe's throat and his mouth hung open loosely. Wondering what he should do, Rush glanced toward the river in search of Burton. To his surprise he discovered the rowboat only a little way off shore opposite the extreme point of the island. Burton sat on the stern seat with pole in his hands, his head forward as if dozing. Rush seated himself on a nearby rock for a moment to watch, curious to see if Burton was an expert fisherman. Delos would have said he did not hold his pole correctly and the boat was not properly anchored.

A red-winged blackbird swooped low and Rush turned to watch him. When his attention returned to the rowboat once more, he was surprised to see that Burton had changed his position. He was sitting upright as he stared intently at the opposite mainland. Following his gaze, Rush decided that the man was not looking at the distant shore but at something closer . . . something small and dark, which swam through the water and was headed directly for the rowboat. Was it a large water snake? The head advanced rapidly and broke the calmer surface of the river, causing little ripples to flow behind at either side. Not a pleasant sight, and whatever the creature was, it was not to Burton's liking for he now stood on his feet with an oar in his hands.

"Joe!" called Burton's voice. "Joe!" and this time the voice of the river boss had lost its measured calmness.

There was no response from Joe. The blankets in the hammock rose and fell with each heavy snore. Forgetting his own desire not to be seen, Rush rose and walked forward, a little awed himself by the approaching snake. There was little he could do to help so he stood quietly on the shore to watch. By this time, Burton had dropped the oar and now had his pistol held in readiness. Apparently he had a great dislike of snakes. Scarcely breathing, Rush waited —if Burton fired, there would be one less bullet in the revolver. But if the snake swerved in its course, Burton might not fire. How long would he wait—

A shot rang out and splashed at the side of the strange head. Burton had missed! A second shot sounded and the bullet struck home for the head immediately sank out of sight. An instant later it rose again and turned toward shore. And then to Rush's anxious ears came the most welcome of sounds—the clicking noise as when a trigger is pulled and the barrels of a weapon are empty. Burton had fired his last shot!

"Get a stick and kill that snake!" yelled Burton, suddenly discovering Rush. "Call Joe to help!"

Before Rush could reply, the approaching head reared itself a foot high from the water, in a most menacing manner, showing a powerful neck. There was a splash and something round, solid, and gray appeared and Rush wondered if he imagined that he saw pink splotches—pink freckles—against the gray. Even as he stood staring, unable to move or speak, the plump shoulders and forelegs of a young elephant emerged—Tom! Yes, it was Tom, trumpeting shrilly in pain and anger, his injured trunk curled tightly in a roll as though to protect it from further injury.

Rush could hardly remember what followed—except that he ran to meet Tom. Knee-deep in water Tom stopped short and, oblivious of his pain, roared out his joy at seeing him, even squeezing him with the injured trunk as they stood close together. Somewhere in the background, Rush was conscious of Burton watching from the rowboat and Joe's white terrified face as he fled to the woods for shelter.

"You came back. . . . Oh, Tom, you came back!" was all Rush could seem to say as he hugged the wet gray body with both arms. "I might have known you'd come— Oh, Tom!"

This, then, was what Cy had meant when he said elephants were fine swimmers. Tom had apparently been swimming deep beneath the water, homeward bound, breathing through the end of his trunk. A very fat, wet, lovable river serpent—the first of its kind in the Mississippi waters.

With Burton silent and staring from the rowboat, Rush marched the small elephant to the Circus Boat. Tom climbed the earthern ramp with unusual alacrity, making little squeaks of joy at being home once more. Despite his annoying pranks, he had been greatly missed and every animal watched his entrance with interest, each in his own way contributing a welcome. Added to Shal's barking there were Lily's chatter and Dazzle's whinnying, and for a few moments the two cubs stopped their wrestling. Even Dignity shifted his position for a better view. Although Tom made an effort to enter his own cage, Rush tied him to an outer post and proceeded to examine the injured trunk. The second bullet had grazed the outer edge of the very tip and caused it to bleed a little. Greased with tallow and bound in a clean bandage, Tom fed himself as usual a moment later, stuffing hay into his mouth as fast as he could swallow. Hunger, more than homesickness, had driven the small elephant home for it was apparent that he had missed his brand of hay. He was noticeably thinner and the cuticle around his toenails was ragged and torn in places. Meanwhile apples disappeared at an astonishing rate.

"That's enough," decided Rush as he caught sight of the other animals staring in envy. "The apples are getting scarce. I wish I knew where you went. . . . And to think you crossed the river!" Rush kept repeating, still finding it hard to realize Tom had returned. "When I saw those pink spots come up through the water—I couldn't make a sound. Wait til' Cy hears about it. No, you can't go in your cage yet. The leak hasn't been mended. Where'd you hide, Tom? Didn't you hear me call? What are you growling at, Shal?"

"That dog tied up?" called Burton's voice suddenly.

"Yes, sir," and Rush turned, a bit startled. However, remembering that the revolver was now empty, he felt less fear.

Burton entered, dressed in a plaid fishing shirt and baggy trousers. Joe followed, big-eyed and uncertain in his manner. A nervous giggle escaped him upon seeing Tom's trunk, bandaged with the two loose ends fluttering whenever the elephant moved. As Burton drew near, Tom turned sideways, a truculent glare in his one eye. Although he had no way of knowing who injured him, the first stranger who crossed his path naturally fell under suspicion. Moreover, Burton was not one to attract any animal. His voice and manner seemed to arouse instant antagonism.

"So this is the great prize," remarked Burton, surveying Tom up and down. "Not much to look at." This last observation held a biting scorn and there was increased fire in Tom's eye. "I've heard that he was smart, could do a few tricks, and draw a good crowd. But I wonder— Must say I'm disappointed."

Rush, however, felt that the man was secretly pleased and blustering to offset his humiliation in mistaking an elephant's trunk for a snake's head.

"Well, what are you waiting for? Why isn't he back in his cage? Want to give him a chance to run away again?" Burton turned sharply on Rush.

"There's a leak in the cubs' cage. Tom balances the boat better if he stays here."

"A leak? Haven't you mended it yet?"

"No, sir."

"It's a good thing I'm taking over, I guess. Everything going to pot around here. Joe, get busy on that leak. But put some planks down on the roof first in case it rains. The logs out front are beginning to move and Simp will be here tomorrow to pull us off. Boy, you've made a mess of this boat. Where's the pilot house gone to?"

"It blew off in the storm."

"It will be up to you to pay for these damages. What are you laughing at, you idiot?" Burton addressed Joe.

"The crittur, with his nose tied up. Oh, Lor', I ain't seen anything like it—his comin' right up outer the water. I was skeered," and Joe turned to Rush, "skeered as a loon. Mr. Burton, he don't like snakes, mice, an' things. He was skeered, too—"

"That's enough. Stop your babbling and get to work," interrupted Burton in a harsh voice. "And boy, exercise that horse. I don't want an extra pound on him. Mind what I say. As soon as the leak is mended, put the elephant inside. From now on, he's going to stay put!" Then Burton left, Tom's eye following him with a baleful gleam until he was out of sight.

With the cubs removed from their cage and chained to a second post, Joe commenced to work on the leak. He had finished the roof in an amazingly short time and was an able man in spite of his simple ways. Some years ago he had been trained as a boat builder in Cincinnati, Ohio. Bit by bit, the story of his life came out, Joe talking as he worked, and Rush found that he rather enjoyed hearing him.

"It's a great trade—this boat buildin'," and Joe shook

his head longingly. "There's many a boat floatin' by what's got my nails in 'em," he added. "Kinder like ol' friends."

"Aren't you ever going back?" asked Rush. "Don't you have a family somewhere?"

"Me? Nope. I jus' lived along the docks—til' I met him." Joe pointed a thumb in Burton's direction. "Once a man like him gets a-holt of you, it's hard breakin' loose," and he nodded his head meaningly at Rush through the bars of the cage. "Some day, mebbe, I'll slip away. Me, now, I'd like to sleep an' get over my malaria. Jes' eat an' sleep. Jupiter, but these critturs," he said, pointing at the cubs, "have a cinch. Jes' play all day, eat an' sleep on this nice bed of straw. Why, I could be happy right here—no work to do—nothin' "—and the rest was drowned by the blows of his hammer as he knelt on his knees over the leak.

But for Shal's warning, Rush would not have seen or heard Burton re-enter the Circus Boat. He came through the door hurriedly, his face flushed with anger, the empty ammunition box in one hand. Flinging himself into the cubs' cage, he towered over the unsuspecting Joe. Startled, Joe looked up, roused by a sudden kick.

"You blithering numbskull!" shouted Burton as he shook the box furiously in Joe's bewildered face. "What do you mean by bringing me an empty box! Why, you brainless horntoad—I'd like to kick you right into the river! AN EMPTY BOX—when you knew I was running short of bullets. Not a shot left, I tell you! And you brought an empty box—"

Clinging to the bars, Joe managed to get to his feet in spite of Burton's hard, swift kicks. However, he made no attempt to fight back but merely covered his face with both hands.

A WANDERER RETURNS

"Mr. Burton—I didn't pack—"

"That's right—blame someone else!" and the fist blows now began to rain unmercifully on Joe's stooped shoulders.

The sound of the blows and Joe's cries were sickening and Shal's bark added to the confusion. Close to the cage, Rush paused, his mind whirling. Burton's revolver was empty. The left front door was locked . . . the right front door stood ajar. He had only to shut the one door, turn the key, slip it into his pocket for safekeeping, then pull the chain down when he was sure the two men were separated. Did he dare? Almost automatically he obeyed. The door closed quietly, the key turned easily, and in one fleeting moment he had made the two men prisoners, the key safe in the depths of his pocket.

"Mr. Burton—Simp—Simp—he did it—" Joe was again on his knees.

"Mr. Burton! Mr. Burton!" By pounding on the front bars, Rush finally got the enraged man's attention. Burton turned and glared at him.

"You keep out of this—hear?" Burton was scarcely listening.

"Joe's not to blame!" Rush shouted. "I emptied the box! I threw the bullets in the river last night!"

Burton was beginning to comprehend now. He left Joe crouched against the farther wall and walked toward the right front door as if to come outside.

"You? You threw the bullets in the river? Why, you little—"

Words failed Burton as he charged for the door and seized the short inner handle. It failed to move and he stared stupidly through the bars at Rush. The two prisoners were now on opposite sides of the cage.

"Open this door—open it, I say!" As Burton's hand tugged again at the handle, Rush reached up and pulled hard at the chain which released the partition in the center. There was a loud rumbling noise overhead and a wall of heavy iron bars descended with incredible speed, landing at the bottom with a crash. Taken by surprise, both Joe and Burton remained where they were, motionless and staring.

"Why—why—" and then Burton reached for his revolver. He remembered it was empty and his hand dropped to his side. By now rage and hatred had distorted his face almost beyond recognition as he realized that he was penned in a long narrow compartment alone, Joe beyond his reach.

"If I ever get my hands on you—"

"You'll have to stay in there a few days—until Captain Whipple comes—"

Speechless, Burton stood with both arms limp at his sides.

"And, Joe—he can't hurt you any more. Your door's locked, too, for a while. Maybe you can rest a little—the straw's clean."

Joe did not seem to be greatly disturbed by this change of events. Holding his injured jaw in one hand, he seated himself comfortably on his pile of straw and, leaning back against the bars, gave Rush a slow one-sided smile.

"T'aint bad," he finally agreed, squinting up at the iron partition which separated him from Burton.

17

SO LITTLE TIME—

With eager fingers Rush untied Shal's rope and released her
from the post. And then, beyond Burton's angry watchful
eyes, he went outside and leaned against the Circus Boat to
collect his thoughts. Locking Burton and Joe inside the cubs'
cage had been wholly unplanned. He had acted on the impulse of the moment, and now that the deed was accomplished he felt fearful and a little dazed. True, pulling
down the grilled partition was little short of an inspiration
and spared further beating for Joe. With one door already
locked, it had been easy to lock the second door. But what
of the consequences—what had he to gain? How could he

hope to save the Circus Boat and all the animals from Burton when in twenty-four hours, maybe less, Simp would be returning with Burton's towboat *Elsie?* What chance had he, alone, against the man Simp and the rest of Burton's crew? Twenty-four hours at the most—and every moment counted!

Above his confused and unhappy thinking, however, one immediate need stood out above all others. The red-lined cape must be returned to the flagpole on the hill, for Captain Whipple and his searching party might be passing by that very afternoon. Unfortunately, the signal had served to attract Burton—it could attract others as well. It was his one and only contact with the outer world.

"Shal!"

The dog, chasing a squirrel through the brush and enjoying her freedom once more, ran obediently to him.

"You're to stay in the doorway, Shal. On guard! I won't be long. Here, lie in the sun."

On his climb up the hill, carrying the cape on one arm, Rush found himself turning hopefully to Joe. As a carpenter employed in the shipyards, Joe knew boats and had lived on the Mississippi long enough to know how to meet emergencies. Could he count on Joe for help? The man appeared to be dominated by Burton. Even before he gave Joe the slightest bit of freedom, Rush knew he must be sure of the man's trustworthiness. If released from the cage too soon, Joe might remain subservient to his river boss, even to the point of unlocking Burton's door. Could Joe withstand threats and promises of reward from a smooth-tongued villain like Samuel Burton? Gramp Tolman had told him to keep a jump ahead of his uncle. . . . He had taken the step in this instance—perhaps too hastily. The cage door had been so easy to close—just one push of the hand. And now how was he to keep another jump ahead?

"I was an idiot—a fool. There might have been a better way."

It took only a moment to fasten the cape to the pole and then he waited, watching the river below. There were all kinds of boats traveling up and down, big excursion steamers, freight boats, barges, and flatboats—all hurrying to make up lost time caused by the storm. If only he might see the red *Flora Belle* come chugging upstream, jaunty despite her blunt shape, with the black smoke pouring from her funnels. And what he'd have given to see her slow down and Cy put out in a small boat, rowing toward him as he stood there. . . . But no *Flora Belle* passed by. Strange boats, all of them strange, hurried on their separate ways.

The thought of Cy in a rowboat, however, reminded Rush of Burton's small fishing boat, pulled up on the shore just beyond the pilot house. Where was it now and was there any chance of his rowing it to the main riverway to call for help? Because of the tips of green trees it was impossible to see. He would have to walk in that direction to make sure it was there. Half running, Rush descended the hill, passed the Circus Boat with Shal guarding the door, and hurried on to the old pilot house beyond. To his great disappointment, even before he reached the shore, Rush saw there was no boat. What could have happened to it? Burton had planned to fish that very morning—and then his eyes, swiftly searching the debris to the left, suddenly spied it. The boat was afloat, moving along a narrow channel of water and now out of his reach. In his anger at finding the empty bullet box, Burton must have leaped ashore and left the boat untied. And as if to confirm his suspicions, Rush then saw the torn cover of the empty gray-blue box on the sand at his feet.

This hope of escape so quickly blighted left Rush with a feeling of forlorn despair. Undoubtedly, from now on he would be blamed for the loss of Burton's boat—just as he was held responsible for the loss of the pilot house on the Circus Boat. Burton would never admit his carelessness— Rush could not count on any sense of justice in the man. The rowboat was gone. . . . Had he time to build a raft? If only he could scoop out a white pine tree—an Indian dugout.

The rowboat, following a narrow open current, was making good headway, and watching it, Rush realized that the entire mass of lumber and driftwood showed unsteadiness. The old cottonwood snag seemed more submerged, and once it gave way the whole mass of debris would lunge forward, powerful because of its own weight. What a pity the Circus Boat could not accompany. . . . However, properly hitched with ropes to the moving mass, possibly the Circus Boat could be pulled free of the muddy shore. This idea came with such force and surprised him so much that Rush sat down on a rock and, hugging his knees, tried to visualize the whole proceeding.

First, the Circus Boat must be properly balanced—Tom returned to his cage. Was there enough rope? Yes, huge coils of it lay in a closet off the amphitheater. With the water once cleared of the debris, how would he guide the Circus Boat between the islands to the main river? Both sweep-oars had been lost. Get Joe to make one. Joe—Joe—

everything hinged on Joe. He must win Joe's interest, confidence, and good will. Time was short and the debris was moving away.

Back in the Circus Boat Rush found Joe still lounging on his bed of straw. Burton was carefully inspecting the wall of his cage. Shal had not left the doorway and her attention was riveted on her two new charges. For some reason the cubs did not resume their wrestling but stood together tied to their post, staring curiously at the two strangers now occupying their home. The constant scrutiny of their small sharp eyes was more than Burton could bear.

"Here, boy," called Burton, "can't you hitch those two beasts somewhere else? They want to come back here to their own cage and I'll tell you now—I won't have them in here with me. Tie them to another post. And bring us some water. Do you expect us to drink the bears' water? I say— how long do you think you're going to keep us in these filthy cages?"

"I don't know. It all depends upon Captain Whipple. He'll have to decide everything."

"Whipple!" The thought of Dan Whipple finding him in this plight sent the blood rushing into Burton's face. It was like adding salt to a wound.

"See here, boy." Burton's voice suddenly became conciliatory, almost friendly, although his gray eyes illy concealed his inward anger. "I don't think you know what you're up against and maybe I'd better warn you. My man Simp is a pretty rough character and if he finds me here in this cage—why, I don't know what he'll do to you. Of course you know he's on his way here—right now. He'll be here tomorrow. What can you do against him and my whole crew? They'll shoot your dog and anything else that stands in their way. That crowd will be so mad they will probably string you up by your thumbs—throw you in the river. A lot of things could happen. And who's going to know but what you were accidentally drowned? Only Joe here would know and if he opened his mouth the same thing would happen to him. Now, get wise, use your head before it's too late. If you will open this door, maybe I can forget the whole thing."

Little beads of perspiration stood out on Burton's forehead and the knuckles of his clenched hands showed white. Rush knew, as if he had been told, that Burton was filled with horror at the thought of his own men finding him locked in a cage once inhabited by bears. He might lose his prestige as boss and become the joke of the river front. It was bad enough to be found by Captain Whipple—but his own men—the thought was agonizing. Perhaps in all his life, Burton had never suffered so much mentally. But Rush felt no pity. Joe's swollen jaw and frightened eyes were a sad testimony of Burton's brutality. "Maybe I can forget the whole thing" were meaningless words. However, the black pictures of what Simp and the crew might inflict upon Shal and himself were unnerving and he turned away from Burton shaking his head, hoping the man would see no change in his expression.

"Is the leak mended?" he asked the dozing Joe.

"Good 'nough," answered Joe, slowly opening his eyes. "I was jest finishin' when—" The rest of the sentence remained unfinished but the look which Joe gave Rush was eloquent enough.

"I'm going to put the elephant back in his cage—so if it

isn't right, the floor in your place will get pretty wet. Want to make sure?"

Joe rose languidly, one hand clutching his jaw, the other his back. A few blows of the hammer, a little extra oakum packed in, and he nodded at Rush.

"Safe now," he offered and returned to his bed of straw with a deep sigh.

Both Burton and Joe were silent as Rush led Tom inside his own cage, filled his drinking tank, and removed the breast strap. A few moments later he changed the cubs to a farther post.

"You gonna give us some dinner?" asked Joe suddenly. "I left some water an' a ham bilin' on the stove. You could throw in a few taters an' t'wouldn't be much work."

"All right." And despite the granite-faced Burton, the two exchanged smiles. "I'm sort of hungry myself."

"See here, boy," and Burton suddenly spoke, his voice sounding as though he were reasoning with a child, "never mind the leak—never mind the food. Let's get this thing settled. Do you really mean to keep us here until Whipple comes? How do you expect him to find you?"

"I put up the flag again," replied Rush. "He'll see it from the river just like you did."

"So you put the flag back," repeated Burton slowly. "I rather thought that was where you went. But don't you realize it may be four or five days before Dan Whipple comes along? Meanwhile Simp will be here. You're not thinking this through at all. Just keeping me cooped up in here is piling up trouble for you. Now what do you say— open the door and we'll call it quits. I give you my word as a gentleman, neither you or the dog will be hurt—nor the animals—" Burton was almost pleading now and kept running his hand through his hair.

"I just don't believe you, Mr. Burton," declared Rush, shaking his head positively. "I don't think you'd keep your promise and then I'd be a lot worse off. You aren't Captain Whipple's friend or you wouldn't try to steal his boat. Everyone on the river knows you don't like him. It was you —or one of your men—who cut the lines and separated the Circus Boat from the *Flora Belle*."

"The little boy's smart, isn't he?" It was amazing the way Burton could change his tactics, voice, and facial expressions in a moment's time. "So you think I had the lines cut! Well, what if I did—what if I did! Whipple owed me money and I have my ways of collecting what's owed me. So you don't trust me," and Burton gave a short laugh. "Boy, you're a trader. You want higher stakes. All right, I'll give you a present if you'll open that door. I'll push it through the bars to you now if you say. It's brand new and cost me plenty. Not many boys your age own a revolver like this—" All the time Burton talked, he was pulling the revolver from his pocket, breathing on it and polishing it with his shirt sleeve to make his offer attractive.

"I don't want your revolver, Mr. Burton. I couldn't use it. And I don't want to talk about it any more. I was left in charge of this boat and the animals and I mean to take care of them."

For the moment Rush's courage had mounted again and his fear diminished. His own words gave him strength. Memories of the unhappiness both he and Delos had suffered that past year from Burton and his lawyer, Gramp Tolman's tales of his grandfather's bitter fight and pluck to possess the Jamieson timber passed before him, and he wished at that moment that Gramp Tolman were standing there beside him. How the old man would have enjoyed it all!

"The kid's got a mind of his own, ain't he?" exclaimed Joe, sitting up suddenly, and there was a note of praise in his voice.

"Keep that trap of yours closed or I'll close it for you!" And forgetting the partition, Burton swung toward Joe and kicked the iron bars. The blow must have hurt for he winced in spite of himself. "All right, young fellow," he threatened, glowering at Rush, "you've sealed your doom, I'm through. Don't bellyache to me a few days from now. It's too bad—I could have done a lot for a boy like you." Burton put on a pitying expression. "You speak well, look decent enough. Yes, I've seen you before—somewhere. Why, I could take you into business with me on the river and you'd never want for anything again! But look at yourself—see what Dan Whipple did for you—just look at those clothes you're wearing! Just look at them!"

Rush looked down at his clothes. They were torn, the wool trousers had been caught and snagged by briars on his trips around the island in search of Tom. Both the trousers and shirt had been the best that Eau Claire stores offered and Delos, knowing his need of money, had paid for them himself. The contempt in Burton's voice seemed to be aimed at Delos, the best friend he had ever had. The old trapper might be humble and unworldly in his ways but he was utterly honest and kind at heart. Rush felt his temper rise but had sense enough to know that it would please Burton to upset him.

"The clothes are all right," replied Rush in a level voice. "A friend bought them for me and paid—honest money. I'm going now and look after the ham, Joe. And I'll bring back your watch and chain, Mr. Burton. Maybe you'd like your clothes—"

"Don't bring my clothes to this dirty place. But I want my watch and chain. And I wish that elephant would stop staring at me, and stop piling dirt and stuff on his back. First he looks at me with the right eye and then he turns and stares with his left. What's the matter—of all the addlepated creatures—"

Over in the pilot house, the wood in the stove had burned low. By the time Rush restored the fire, added the potatoes to the ham, and boiled them together, an hour slipped by. Meanwhile he ate generously of the different delicacies half opened and strewn about on the table—strawberry jam on thick slices of bread, molasses cookies and long strips of yellow cheese. It was evident that Burton liked his food and bought the best of everything. When the ham and potatoes were tender, Rush ate until satisfied, finishing with a long deep sigh of contentment. With nourishing food in his stomach, he could work harder and think faster. Then, carrying the kettle of ham and potatoes on one arm, a loaf of bread under the other, and the watch and chain in his pocket, Rush made his way back to the Circus Boat, wondering in what manner he should feed his two prisoners. After some thought he finally decided that slices of ham and potatoes cut in halves could be squeezed through, likewise bread, wrapped in paper. By no means did he intend to unbolt a door. Also he decided to give the watch and chain first to Joe and then let him pass it to Burton. In that way there would be no sudden trickery.

Shal greeted him at the doorway of the Circus Boat, wagging her tail with an air that somehow she had been enjoying herself. Once inside, however, Rush stopped short. Burton was very wet, his hair plastered to his forehead as he sat on the floor of his cage, mopping his face with a handkerchief. Joe, in the farther cage, was not so wet and in quite a happy frame of mind as he dried his hands on the front tail of his shirt. Across, in an opposite cage, Tom with his bandage gone was occupied in sucking dry the last of the drinking water in his tank. Upon seeing Rush, he hastily emptied his trunk into his mouth and swallowed noisily. A few wisps of hay in a distant corner then claimed his attention.

"Well, are you satisfied now?" called Burton, his voice shaking with anger. "No one can tell me you didn't purposely fill that tank with water before you left. You knew that one-eyed beast would squirt it all over us! We're soaked—it's an outrage! I'll have you and that animal skinned alive when Simp gets here—"

"Took three duckin's to empty the tank," observed Joe cheerfully, winking his right eye at Rush. "Your dawg seemed to enjoy watchin'. . . One good thing 'bout it, I won't have to wash my shirt this week and—"

"No more talk from you—"

To complete his sentence Joe winked his left eye. There was no doubt now in Rush's mind that progress had been made, for Joe's winks were decidedly friendly.

18

JOE MAKES A
DECISION

Despite his swollen jaw, Joe showed marked appreciation of his dinner pushed through the bars of his cage and wrapped in paper. Two thick slices of ham, four potatoes, bread and butter topped with jelly were eagerly and noisily devoured. It was apparent to Rush that the partition of iron bars had already served to strengthen Joe's morale. Safe from the punishment of Burton's boot, he was beginning to talk more freely.

"You're a good cook, boy," he said happily between smacks. "Blamed if you ain't. I could do a better job chewin', though, if I had some Perry Davis Pain Killer.

You ain't got any, have you? One of my teeth seems loose."

"That stuff!" and Burton snorted in disgust.

"Cy keeps all his medicines in a closet off the feed room. I'll go and look," replied Rush, glad to favor Joe in any possible way.

Cy's supply of medicine did not appear to include the Perry Davis Pain Killer although Rush searched thoroughly. The only substitute was a large bottle of brown liquid which smelled strongly of wintergreen and was marked "FOR TOM'S SORE TUSKS—Apply freely."

"It's the next best thing." Rushed pushed the bottle through the bars. "Tom had his tusks taken out—so use all you want. It can't hurt you—"

"Lor's sakes," and Joe gave a twisted smile of appreciation, "I hope it don't grow a trunk an' tusks on me. Thanks, boy. It smells good."

Meanwhile Burton made no attempt to eat but watched Joe in silent contempt as the fumes of wintergreen filled the zoo. To Rush, the smoldering glow in the man's eyes brooded unspeakable evil, and to uphold his courage he did not glance at him any more than it seemed necessary. Once free of his cage, Burton would be merciless in his revenge. With his hands performing their tasks mechanically, Rush prepared the animals' dinner. Despite all, Dignity must have his meal of fresh rabbit meat sprinkled with oil, the bears their molasses, Shal some scraps of ham. Lily, Tom, and Dazzle had their usual portions but he noticed that the apples in the barrel appeared withered and he wondered what he would do when they were gone. Bananas seemed more remote than ever. And always the same questions turned over and over in his mind: When should he approach Joe and ask for help? Would the logs move out in time? Suppose Joe refused to assist . . . how could he force the man to work?

The animals fed, Rush climbed the stairs to the amphitheater and looked out over the islands toward the river. As yet, there was no sign of Simp and the *Elsie* and he gave a tremulous sigh of relief. Perhaps Simp would be delayed by some unforeseen trouble . . . the discontented crew might have left him. Almost anything could happen on the Mississippi. Was not he himself finding it true?

The clock in the feed room below twanged twelve wheezy notes. One half of the day was gone. Hurrying to the supply closet, Rush dragged several coils of rope across the floor to the window. He then dropped them over the sill to the ground. They fell with heavy dull thuds, and at the sound Shal barked from her post in the doorway. Three moments later he approached the cubs' cage with Shal at his heels. Burton, with his dinner still untouched, was testing the strength of the bars surrounding him, hopeful of finding a loosened one. Joe was relaxed on his bed of straw, chuckling at Lily. Glad of an audience, she was trying on her hat at different angles.

"Joe, I need some help. Will you come outside?" asked Rush, and he unlocked the door.

"Lor'." Joe's eyes grew round with surprise and he sat up straight with a start. "I ain't askin' to come out, boy. This is the first easy spell I've had in a long time," and his glance rested fearfully on Shal. "I'm safe in here. . . . How'm I goin' to know that dawg won't finish me off?"

"You keep your hands off Joe," ordered Burton, walking to the front of the cage. "What right have you asking him for help? I pay him—"

"There's nothing to be afraid of, Joe," continued Rush, ignoring Burton. "I'll hold her by the collar if you like—"

"Joe—you stay where you are!" rasped Burton. "Don't be a fool. Why, that brute can tear you in pieces in a second! Didn't you get enough the other day? Look at her—she's more wolf than dog—"

Not wishing to be confined alone, Burton was using every argument to keep Joe caged and sharing his disgrace. The gift of liniment had made Joe friendly to Rush but Burton still held the upper dominating hand. How long would it take for Joe to overcome his fear? There was so little time—

"Would you feel safer if I put the dog in the feed room and closed the door?" asked Rush after a pause.

"He'd only have to call or whistle and the dog would break down the door," warned Burton. "Don't listen, Joe."

"I wouldn't do anything to hurt you, Joe. I gave you a good dinner and some liniment, didn't I? I need help and I don't want to talk about it here. Of course, if I had to, I could send Shal in after you. But I don't want to do that—" Again Rush felt the pressure of time as the clock in the feed room struck the half hour.

"You ain't playin' no joke, boy?" Joe's voice was a little hoarse and his eyes pleading as he looked up at Rush. "You'd put that dawg in the feed room an' shet the door sure enough?"

"I'll keep my word and there'll be no jokes," Rush answered indignantly. Calling Shal, he crossed the floor with her, commanded her to enter the feed room, and closed the door after her. She obeyed quietly and made no whimper of protest.

"If you go out there," Burton was saying as Rush drew

near, "you're the biggest numbskull I ever knew. You're walking right into trouble—"

"I don't want that dawg in here after me," wailed Joe. "I've gotter go, Mr. Burton. There ain't nothin' else to do. I'm safe if he keeps that door shet—"

"Come on, Joe. Shal will stay there unless I call and I won't call if you don't play any tricks on me. Come outside —I want to talk with you."

"You blasted fool—you idiot—he'll work you to death. Remember your malaria—"

"Don't listen," encouraged Rush quietly. "Just hurry, we haven't much time. We'll go down on the rocks and talk."

Clutching his bottle of liniment in one hand and clinging to his jaw with the other, Joe reluctantly stumbled out of the cage, glancing fearfully at the closed door of the feed room as he passed and then back to Burton glowering through the bars.

"You see how t'is, Mr. Burton," Joe called as he walked down the earthen ramp. "I ain't got no choice but to go."

Away from Burton and unmolested by Shal, Joe heaved a deep sigh and leaned against the side of the boat. "An' you're sure this ain't no trick? Lor', but it seems good to be out here."

"Keep your voice low and come over here, Joe. Sit down and lean against this rock if you want to. Look at the old cottonwood snag now. She's moved, hasn't she?"

"Yup. Is that why you got me out here, boy? Jest to look at an ol' stump?"

"No—no—it's more than that. Here, put some more of that liniment on. Don't get it in your eyes. Now listen to me. I've got some ideas and I need your help." Rush in a low voice then unfolded his plan, his gaze first on Joe and then on the black snag which had lowered considerably since morning. "Once we get outside of these islands—we can find Captain Whipple and he'll protect you. If you help save the Circus Boat and animals, he might be able to find work for you in the shipyard again. You'd be free of Burton."

At the word "shipyard," Joe's face brightened and then he shivered and backed against the rock as if for support. "But—Mr. Burton, he has ways of reachin' me—an' he'll be awful mad. *I know*. He's a hard 'un, boy—"

"The law has ways of reaching him, Joe. You'll have to trust Captain Whipple. He's a fine man and very fair. You've been made to do things you wouldn't do yourself. If you want to, make Mr. Burton think you have to help me or I'll call Shal. It's true that the dog would break down the door if I called . . . but I don't want to do that. Joe, it's your chance to get free—you've nothing to lose—"

"Mebbe you're right," and Joe nodded thoughtfully, battling between hope and fear, "but, boy, you ain't allowin' much time for so much work. It's close connectin'. Simp might get here tonight. He's a smart 'un, Simp is, an' Burton pays him plenty. They work hand in glove together. He might come an hour from now—"

"That's the chance I'm taking. You won't be blamed because you are helping me under protest. I'll keep threatening you with the dog and Burton will hear it inside. That will be your protection. Don't you see how it will work, Joe? There's lots of rope—more of it on the second floor. Once we get the boat harnessed to the logs, we'll move with them. But we've got to hurry and get ready. Remember you'll be working with the law from now on. Please, Joe, these animals in the zoo mustn't suffer. They'll need their regular food—that's why I try to save the molasses—"

"Sure. I understan' now—"

"If Captain Whipple owes Mr. Burton money, let the law settle it." Rush hoped that little by little he was beating down Joe's resistance.

"Oh, Lor'—Cap'n Whipple don't owe Mr. Burton any money," and Joe's frankness gave Rush his first encouragement. "It's one of his tricks—making money on the river. He's got other captains worried the same way. Rams 'em in the night, blames the other fellar an' keeps houndin' 'em for damages. But Cap'n Whipple, he's not weak-kneed like most. He paid onc't an' no more."

"Captain Whipple's right. How much time do you think we have before the snag gives way?"

"There's no tellin'." Joe shaded his eyes against the sun and then looked beyond to the island where the *Elsie* had anchored. " 'Course, while I'm here, you might as well order me to swim out an' look at it. I'll bellow some about the cold water but you keep on orderin'. . . . An' long's I'm goin' out, I might just as well take along the rope an' hitch up. I know the best way to tie them logs . . . special knots."

"Will you, Joe? That's great. You won't be sorry—I promise you!"

"Like you say, I ain't got nothin' to lose—an' it might work. I've got my own way of tyin' the rope to the boat though," and Joe began to remove his boots, trousers, and shirt. "Wonder if he knows Mr. Robinson," he muttered as he took his first step into the water.

"Mr. Robinson?"

"Yup. He's the big boss at the shipyard. . . . Now start yellin' at me, boy. I'll make some back talk 'bout my malaria—but don't you worry none. I ain't as del'cate as I look. . . . Lor', how I'd like to get my ol' job back again!"

During the next fifteen minutes, Rush lived up to his promise, ordering Joe to swim to the right, then to the left, or he'd call the dog. Joe's wailing of his aching back and the chills which were bound to follow must have sounded realistic enough to the listening Burton inside the Circus Boat.

"This ain't no way to treat a human! Jest wait til' Simp comes—" yelled Joe over a wet shoulder. "You won't feel so smart orderin' me around then!"

Bearing the two ends of rope attached to his waist, Joe finally leashed the logs securely, his naked skinny body shining in the early afternoon sunshine. Twice he paused to look out toward the island where the *Elsie* had formerly anchored, and Rush knew that the man was laboring under intense fear and he determined to keep Joe outside if possible, away from Burton's questioning and influence. Two long lengths of rope stretched through the water to the opposite ends of the raft when Joe returned to the shore, a little spent and breathless.

"You don't see no sign of Simp?" he asked even before he could turn and look back.

"No—I've been watching."

"The snag is shaky," announced Joe. "I give her a shove an' she moved a mite. Them logs will go out by mornin' an' mebbe sooner. You think we're foolin' 'im in there?" he asked, pointing a worried finger toward the Circus Boat.

"You sounded awful mad—and sick," Rush told him

and was pleased to see a smile move Joe's swollen mouth. "Here, put on more liniment. How do you plan to fasten ropes to the boat? Keep your voice low—"

"I don't think the rings'll hold. They might pull out. An' onc't we start, someone's got to cut them ropes—quick! You can't reach them rings 'less you hang by your feet. Now I'm plannin' to put an end of rope through each winder an' tie 'em together inside. One stroke of a sharp knife an' we're free of the logs. You can't pull the whole side of a buildin' out an' it's easy to pull out the rings."

"You're right, Joe. You're a real help—"

"What we goin' to use for a sweep?"

"There are some long boards at the base of Dazzle's stall." Joe's use of the pronoun "we" fell like music on Rush's ears. Joe was actually planning, taking part!

"That's good," and Joe rose to pull on his clothing. "Seems like I see an' ol' ladder in the pilot house. I'll bring it here an' climb it with the rope ends. You stand in the winders waitin' an' tie the two ends together. When them logs start it'll be like takin' a ride—the logs like hosses an' us hangin' on behind. But you'll have to talk real mean when we go in there with Mr. Burton watchin'. The dawg, she's mindin' good. She won't come through the door 'cause you talk so loud?"

"She won't leave the feed room unless I call her name. Honest, Joe."

"I kinder wish there was a lock on the door."

"Even if I locked it, she'd break the window and jump to the ground. Someday, you'll be friends. I don't think she'd hurt you, even now."

"I never had a dawg of my own. . . . You keepin' 'er in there til' I'm through?"

"Just as you want. Remember, if Simp comes, you won't be blamed for anything—you've been forced to obey orders."

"It'll go hard with you, if Simp comes." Joe's eyes regarded Rush sorrowfully. "Mr. Burton—he's got no heart. Humans is like so many flies to 'im. He just swats 'em around. He messed up my life—like I tole you. 'Rollin' stones don't gather no moss.'. . . Seems kinder good to be able to say it out here."

Because of his many ailments, Joe objected pitifully to climbing the ladder and Burton, listening within, must have been considerably surprised at Rush's heartlessness. With the two ends of rope drawn through the windows and tied together just above Burton's cage, Rush felt much had been accomplished, however, and tried to hide the joy he felt. It was a jump ahead, as Gramp Tolman would have said. Joe, rubbing his back and appealing to Burton for sympathy, managed his part with unusual skill.

"Serves you right," scolded Burton. "Why didn't you stay in your cage?"

" 'Cause the dawg would fetch me out," whined Joe. "You don't understan', Mr. Burton. I've got to do what he says or I'll be tore to pieces."

Later Rush overheard a conversation between the two and was pleased with Joe's replies.

"He ain't talkin' much, Mr. Burton. He's got me guessin', too. You heard him orderin' me, cross-like an' sharp. . . . No, I ain't seen the *Elsie* yet. I'm watchin'. . . . Yup, if Simp comes roun' the island in a rowboat, I'll tell you. . . . Why did I swim out to them logs? To see if they was loose. Lor', the water was cold. I'll be laid up tomorrer. . . . Wish I knew what he was doin' . . . soon's I find out

I'll let you know. . . . No, I can't open the door, Mr. Burton. If I try to get the key from 'im, he'll holler for the dawg. We're in a bad fix all right. The kid's kinder smart. . . . He's callin'—I've got to go!" and Joe dashed off at an imaginary call, beginning to enjoy, somewhat, the role he was playing.

"Ain't had so much fun in a long time," confessed Joe after the third quizzing and realizing that Rush had overheard beneath the window. "He's awful worried. Seems like it hurts his dignity to be found in that cage. Any sign of the *Elsie?*" he whispered fearfully, noting the telescope in Rush's hand.

"No." Rush shook his head and drew Joe out of Burton's hearing. He was beginning to feel weary and every reference to Simp or the *Elsie* quickened his pulse and left him more exhausted than before. "I think we'll get off before they come, don't you, Joe?"

"All depends on that ol' snag. You think we're foolin' 'im?" Joe nodded in Burton's direction and Rush realized that each was seeking reinforcement from the other.

"Best acting I ever saw," replied Rush stoutly. "You want some help now?" he asked, seeing a hammer in Joe's hand.

"Yup. I'm takin' off the plank from the stall. The boat's all set to go now an' I'm startin' the sweep. Them kitchen knives sharp?"

"Very—"

"I'll keep one handy 'tween the winders to cut the ropes when we're afloat an' I'll leave a box nearby for you to step on an' reach up."

Yes, Joe was now taking hold in true riverman style!

He might even know their present location on the Mississippi—

"Joe—where are we? The map in the feed room doesn't tell me much. It doesn't show the islands."

"Lor', boy, it's hard tellin'. We're below Cassville, I think. Some of these lil' islands appear an' then, by Jupiter, they're gone again. The ol' river changes fast an' the pilots have to change their maps fast, too."

Hurrying against time, Rush and Joe worked feverishly to finish the long sweep-oar. Shadows from the sinking sun streaked the wooden floor of the zoo and there was a hushed expectancy in the air. If Burton surmised the plan by now, he said little as he stalked back and forth pulling at his shrunken trousers. In Rush's mind, there was little doubt of Joe's loyalty though he continued to watch him carefully. However, Joe had apparently reached the point of revolt after years of suffering in Burton's employ and was about to remove the heavy yoke.

Meanwhile Lily, released from her cage for exercise, made the most of the occasion, running along the thirty-foot stretch of rope over Burton's cage. At first she spent some time peering down at the new inmate, as if wondering what new species could be occupying the cubs' cage. At last, deciding that the rope along the wall had been arranged for her own benefit, she entertained Burton below in joyous abandonment, her hat askew as she jumped and twisted. For her last act she consumed an apple as she dangled by her tail, finally throwing the apple core below. By this time Burton, with his dinner still uneaten, most unhappy and worn out with much speculation, napped soundly on his bed of straw and the core, as if expertly aimed, landed directly in the palm of his outstretched hand.

19

IN THE FOG

Under Joe's swift and capable hands the sweep-oar was finished that evening beneath the light of a lantern hanging from the ceiling of the zoo. In anticipation of the snag's giving way at any moment, a sharp knife was placed near the stretch of rope between the two windows and everything of value brought aboard the boat, including the red-lined cape from the hill. Shal was now stationed in the outer doorway to give warning if she heard Simp arrive. To Rush's relief, Joe did not demand that the dog be tied.

"Give her a little time and she'll be coming up to you to

be petted," Rush encouraged. "She knows that you are helping me and my friends are her friends. I'd like to send her hunting for a rabbit but I'm afraid the boat might go out before she came back. Tom—stop that noise!"

"He keeps thumpin' his nose on the water tank," explained Joe from the rear window where he was setting up two tholepins for the sweep-oar. "Seems like it ain't sore no more."

"He's just plain mad because I made him drink out of a pail," explained Rush. "It would suit him fine if I'd fill the tank and he could do a little more spraying. We're about ready now, aren't we, Joe?"

"Are we ready for the moonlight row?" gibed Burton, who joined into the conversation whenever possible. "Joe, that oar doesn't look very strong. Just one push and I'm afraid it'll snap in two. Of all the crazy notions. . . . Seems to me you've given up complaining and are working with the boy tooth and nail. Not afraid of the dog either. When Simp gets here, I guess we'll have a thorough investigation. Simp won't like all this . . . not a bit of it. Thought I heard the *Elsie* whistle just then—" Suave, cool in outward appearance, Burton, with talk of this sort, always gave Joe a battle to maintain his courage. However, after such outbursts, Joe only worked the faster.

"She'll give a jerk," he warned Rush in a whisper, "a hard 'un. Then I think it's best for you to run an' cut the ropes. I'll make for the oar. Ain't much chance of me goin' back to Mr. Burton now, I guess. If Simp comes before we go, well, I guess they'll kill me a-tween 'em."

"Don't think about it any more than you can help," comforted Rush. "And, Joe—I think there's a fog on the river or there wouldn't be so many whistles. Simp wouldn't row here in a fog, would he?"

"No tellin' about Simp."

"When the snag gives way—we won't be able to see—"

"That's right, boy. I'll have to feel with the oar—float with the current. Mebbe you'd better go above an' hark a bit. Look for lights."

From an upper window Rush leaned out, straining to hear and see. Fog, as he had suspected, was sifting in, cutting off the entire world outside. After a while, even the whistles ceased to blow and the only sound which came to his ears was the lap of water against the logs. In a little while, if all went well, Joe would be guiding the Circus Boat between two islands with a single oar managed from a stern window—a heavy responsibility on his thin shoulders. Would the man be able to endure the pressure and the risk involved? If the Circus Boat became grounded, sprang a leak, and filled, she would immediately sink. But before she sank Burton and the animals would have to be released, given a chance to swim and save their lives. Would Joe help him in opening the cages or would he be forced to work alone? The entire day had been full of distorted fears and misgivings. His whole body ached and his feet moved slowly as he descended the stairs to the zoo.

"No lights, Joe. The fog's pretty thick and getting worse."

"Fog, eh?" asked Burton. "I suppose you think that's in your favor. Well, I've never seen a fog yet that could stop Simp—"

"Mebbe you'd best get a wink or two," offered Joe

kindly, turning away. "You ain't used to all this. I'll set by the oar in case she moves."

"If you'll call me in an hour, then I can let you have your turn, Joe," and Rush hesitated for lack of words. "You'll never change your mind, will you?" he asked, nodding in Burton's direction. "You won't let him scare you—"

"Never you fear, boy," and Joe looked Rush squarely in the eyes, "I'm puttin' my eggs in your basket now. Rollin' stones don't gather no moss." Joe raised his voice defiantly as he faced Burton. "An' from now on I ain't no rollin' stone. You heerd me that time, didn't you, Mr. Burton?"

Burton made no reply but shrank back a little into the shadows of his cage. And as he watched him, Rush found himself wondering why Burton disliked the old saying which Joe quoted so often. Rolling stones . . . Rolling-stone . . . why, that was the name of the imaginary city in Illinois, which Len Slocum had spoken of only a short time ago. It had been a cruel, dishonest scheme, robbing people of their money and finally their lives, and his half uncle was said to have been involved in the trickery. This was why Burton hated the saying! Undoubtedly the words "Rolling stones" sent cold chills of apprehension down his back even though it had happened two years ago. Joe had been innocent enough in the repetition, little suspecting the discomfiture it caused Burton. Later he would talk more with Joe about Rollingstone, but now, overcome with weariness, Rush stretched himself out on the zoo floor, the cape rolled under his head as a pillow.

It seemed only a lapse of seconds before Rush heard Joe

call, Shal bark, and felt his body roll to one side. Staggering to his feet, he ran to cut the rope between the windows as Joe shoved the oar between the tholepins, ready to steer. Beneath him was the grinding sound of wood drawn over rocks and the suction of resisting mud. The lantern swung back and forth from the ceiling as pans rattled in the feed room, and above all sounded the loud wail of the frightened animals.

"Get me out of here! Get me out of here!" yelled Burton, pulling at the door of his cage.

There was no time to calm Burton. With Shal at his heels, Rush joined Joe at the big oar as the sound of grinding ceased. However, in another moment the Circus Boat began to turn in circles.

"We're loose, boy! I'll right her soon with the oar!" Joe, his face shining in the lantern's light, was jubilant with joy. "The fog's thick but we're goin' with the current. I'm thinkin' it will take us between the islands all right if the logs don't block us again. If so—" Joe did not finish his sentence. "I can handle the oar an' t'would help if you'd go above an' listen. Tell me what you hear an' see. Rushin' water may mean a rock. I can't tell any of the sounds from here. Be sharp, boy—"

Fog—suffocating, milk-white fog. Leaning far out, Rush could see nothing because of the white film which seemed to blind his eyes. Not even a dark shadow to tell the line of shore. In the distance a little bell kept ringing—some ship anchored in the fog. The only other sound was the swirl of water as the Circus Boat followed the current.

"Can't see a thing, Joe—I'm listening!" Rush called after a pause.

"Be sharp, boy!" came Joe's voice from the floor below.

Shal was beside him now, leaning out, and he could hear her pant, feel her warmth. In time of trial she never failed . . . and he put one arm around her and drew her close.

"Keep listening, Shal," he whispered. "Bark, if you hear rough water . . . bark."

The tension in his voice made her lift her head inquiringly, and as if in answer he felt her tongue against his cheek. As he started to speak again, the branch of a tree scraped across the roof overhead and the green leaves brushed his face. Ducking back, he pulled Shal with him.

"We've just passed a tree—close to the shore, Joe!"

"I'm watchin'!" came Joe's voice.

What else lay ahead? If only he could see, warn Joe and help to end this perilous voyage, the blind following of an unknown channel. . . . How wide was the space between the two islands? If the logs jammed, what would happen to the Circus Boat? If the impact was violent and she sprang a leak—again came the old pictures of fear as he clung to the sill, his arm once more about the dog's neck.

"What now, boy? Hear anythin'?" and Joe sounded as though he was short of breath.

"Just fog—no lights—I don't hear anything."

After his first outcry, Burton had become silent. Now and then Dazzle whinnied and once Rush heard Tom pound the floor with his trunk. How long would this blind ride go on? If only they could anchor until the fog passed. But there were no anchors. And it was impossible to lasso a tree or stump in this fog—and Rush gripped the sill with both hands until his fingers cramped. He must stay at his post as Joe had asked. Joe was an old riverman and knew what he was doing. If the Circus Boat came through safely, there would be nothing too good for Joe. Captain Whipple should be told the whole story and find work for him in the ship-yard at Cincinnati. Joe was a hero, straining every muscle over the big oar, steering for safety, saving the Circus Boat and animals. Tiny Tom had cost a lot of money. Without Tom the parade would not be a success. . . . Images of people and animals passed before his eyes and swirled through his mind as he clung to the sill. And then came the ear-splitting shriek of a whistle—close, too close—and bells right overhead.

"Joe! Joe!"

There was no answer from Joe. A loud crash and Rush was hurled backwards, a row of benches crowding him against the foot of the stage. Somewhere in between Shal became caught and he could hear her crying as she strug-gled to reach him. Then came the call of voices and the sound of bells. Almost at the same time he felt Shal's hot breath on his face, the grip of her jaws on his sleeve.

"I'm all right, Shal. Here, let me up."

At the bow of the Circus Boat there was a flash of light. A rope ladder was being lowered through a hole high up on a side wall. Feet began to descend, and because of Shal's angry barking a man paused halfway down, swinging a lantern as he tried to see below.

"Hey, you! Call off that dog. I'm coming down."

"Come ahead, sir. Quiet, Shal. . . . What happened?" Rush reached the bottom of the ladder just as the man reached the floor. Dressed in a blue suit with brass buttons, the stranger held the lantern high in order to see Rush.

"For the love of Mike—it's a boy!" he called to other people somewhere outside. "See here, who are you?" he demanded of Rush. "Where's the Captain of this—this boat? Where are your lights? Don't you know that the law requires a person to tie up or anchor in a fog like this?"

Before Rush could answer, Joe appeared, running to him across the floor, his face anxious, worn. "Boy, you're safe! I didn't know—"

"We're safe, Joe. We must have hit another boat. . . . There's a hole in the wall. This man—"

"Who are you? What kind of a boat is this, anyway?" A second man had reached the floor and was staring about. "Is it a showboat?"

"No, sir—it's Captain Whipple's Circus Boat. The Captain's not here—"

"Captain Whipple! You mean Dan Whipple?" asked the first man, who was young and sandy-haired.

"Yes, sir." At that moment Tiny Tom trumpeted and the rest of the animals joined in with their cries.

"Caesar's ghost! You got animals below?"

Rush nodded. "I'm the assistant trainer. We got separated from the towboat in the last storm and drifted to an island. We were just coming through a narrow channel in the fog. I'm sorry, sir, we had no anchors. Is there much damage to your boat?" and Rush addressed the second stranger, who was older and appeared to have more authority.

"Ripped into our paddle box—but it's not too serious. You've suffered more damage, I think," replied the man. "I'm the mate, Mr. Burns. I guess you'd better go aboard and explain a few things to our Captain, young man. Jim," said Mr. Burns, turning to the sandy-haired youth, "take him up. I'll go below and see how things are."

"Yes, sir. Come on, boy. Maybe you'd better do something about that dog though before he bites someone."

"She won't hurt anybody. Shal, go below with Joe. And don't worry," Rush consoled Joe, whose eyes were round with fright, "I'll be right back. You take care of everything."

"Yes, yes—be sure an' come back, boy—"

As Rush mounted the rope ladder and came through the torn wall, he was conscious of many people staring at him . . . figures unreal and indistinct in the white fog which still hung over all. Dawn had just begun to lighten the east and it was evident that the passengers aboard the boat had been routed from their beds by the loud crash. Many were hastily dressed, wrapped in shawls and coats. They were, however, in good humor, no doubt relieved to find the damage not serious. Several lanterns flashed in his face as he came over the rail, the sandy-haired young man leading the way.

"For the land's sakes!" shrilled a lady in shawl and curlers, carrying a bird cage. "It's a boy. Where's your father—is he the Captain?"

"What kind of a boat is it?" several questioned. "Is she leaking?"

Unable to stop, Rush hurried on for fear of losing sight of the young man with sandy hair. It was a long boat and a long walk, as he followed the fancy rail of white trimmed with gold scrolls to an upper deck and then went forward to the Captain's cabin in the texas. By now his knees had begun to feel weak. Down below in the gray haze he could just make out the boxlike shape of the Circus Boat, insignificantly small compared to this huge ark of white and gold. It was impossible to see the name of the boat and he felt himself in a strange world and very much alone. What would the Captain of such a boat say to him? Roused from his sleep, would the man be in a fit of temper? Should he speak of Samuel Burton and tell what had happened? . . .

"Captain Harris, sir," and the young man was tapping on the Captain's door.

"Come in," called a deep voice.

"This is the—er—boy in charge of the boat which we just hit, sir." The young man pushed open the cabin door. Lights from wall lamps streamed out and reached Rush as he hesitated on the threshold.

"Come in, come in," repeated the deep voice.

Inside, the brilliance of the lights made Rush blink for an instant and then he became conscious of two people in the room. The older man, presumably Captain Harris, bearded, with keen brown eyes and hair brushed straight back, sat at his desk while a younger man, tall and with strikingly blue eyes, stood by a window just behind him. Both men wore the stamp of wind and weather. The Captain was the first to speak and there was surprise in his deep voice.

"Well! So you're the young man in charge—where's your Captain?"

"We became separated, sir," and Rush realized that his voice faltered.

"Separated? Speak up, boy. Don't you know it's against the law to be afloat in weather like this? What's your Captain's name?"

"We had no anchors. It's Captain Whipple's Circus Boat, sir—and I've got all the animals aboard. The Circus Boat got adrift from the towboat. I'm trying to find Captain Whipple—"

"Dan Whipple!" Captain Harris sat up straight in his chair and then turned to look at the man behind him. "Steve! It's Dan Whipple's boat that hit us. Great Scott, this *is* a surprise! So you're the boy who got adrift—" and, somewhat speechless, Captain Harris turned to stare once more at Rush.

"Yes, sir. I'm the assistant trainer. I was hired for two weeks."

"How many animals have you got aboard?"

"Six, sir. And a man—"

At this point the door burst open suddenly and the mate, Mr. Burns, appeared. He was breathing fast as though he had hurried and was the bearer of important news.

"Captain Harris—I beg pardon, sir—but I must speak to you—immediately!"

"Go ahead, Mr. Burns."

"There are cages of animals on the first floor of this Circus Boat. But in one cage there is a man—I can hardly believe it, sir—"

"A man?"

"Yes, sir. He's Mr. Samuel Burton of Eau Claire. He's locked in there. The attendant called Joe says the boy here has the key in his pocket. Even if I had the key I wouldn't be able to open the door. There's a big white dog guarding it. She's pretty ugly, sir, and she might spring—" Mr. Burns paused for lack of breath.

"Sam Burton!" Captain Harris had risen to his feet in astonishment, his mouth open, when the tall man by the window gave a shout of amusement, as though unable to restrain himself.

"And what," asked Captain Harris in spite of the outburst behind him, "are you doing with Samuel Burton locked in a cage? Is this a prank?"

"Oh, no, Captain Harris—it isn't a prank," replied Rush earnestly. "I was just about to tell you about him. You see, Mr. Burton was trying to steal the Circus Boat and all the animals from Captain Whipple. I was alone in the zoo when the lines were cut and I drifted away from the towboat. Mr. Burton searched and found me on an island. I got a chance to lock him in one of the cages—and I did. I wasn't playing a prank. I don't like him—he's my step-uncle—"

By this time there was a choking sound and a second shout of laughter from the tall man by the window. In another moment Captain Harris joined him, shaking helplessly in his chair, as the first mate looked from one to the other in bewilderment.

"Perhaps I should explain," and after a moment or so, Captain Harris dried his eyes with a handkerchief, "that Pilot Hanks," and he motioned toward the tall blue-eyed man, "and I are both familiar with this trouble between Captain Whipple and Sam Burton. Dan Whipple is one of my oldest friends and I talked with him briefly only two days ago at Bellevue. He was very much worried about losing you and the Circus Boat and thought that Burton must be the blackguard. And to discover you in this dense fog with Burton caged in your zoo—well, it's unbelievable, although strange things happen on the Mississippi," and Captain Harris dried his eyes again.

"And Sam Burton is your stepuncle?" asked the pilot, coming forward and pushing a chair toward Rush. "Here, boy, sit down—you look a little done in."

"He's no blood kin, sir. It's nothing I can help." Rush seated himself.

"What's your name?" asked Captain Harris.

"Rush Jamieson Taylor, sir. I come from Eau Claire, Wisconsin. I'm using my mother's name. My stepuncle is trying to get hold of the timber my grandfather left me— it's a long story—"

"This all sounds very familiar," nodded Pilot Hanks. "Very typical of Samuel Burton. I suggest we let Sam simmer in his cage a little while longer and let the boy talk, Captain Harris. You know my cousin Abe Lincoln in Springfield has been searching for Burton this past month. There's an inquiry being made in the Rollingstone swindle and Abe thinks that Burton was one of the accomplices. Burton worked on this end while others managed the New York angle."

"By all means, let Burton simmer awhile. Mr. Burns, keep him in the cage and tell him nothing! Later I'll lock him in one of our cabins. Don't let anyone down there—not a single person, until we get this young man's story."

"Yes, sir," and Mr. Burns was gone, his face expressionless but his eyes staring at Rush as he closed the door.

"Do you happen to know, young man," asked the Captain, turning to Rush suddenly, "the name of this boat?"

"No, sir. I couldn't see in the fog. I wanted to ask. And I've heard of you both before but so much has happened, I can't seem to remember—"

"Well, this is the packet *Doctor Franklin Number Two*—"

"The *Doctor Franklin!* Captain Harris, she's the first big boat I ever saw on the Mississippi—she's beautiful!"

"Yes, she's a fine boat," acknowledged the Captain smiling a little, "but there's more to my story. The *Doctor Franklin Number Two*, commanded at that time by Captain Blakely, is the very boat which carried a hundred passengers upriver to those prairie wastes called Rollingstone City two years ago. Most of those people starved to death or were frozen. I have always felt it was a sort of stigma placed on the *Doctor Franklin*. . . . It's just a fancy of my own but we Captains get very sentimental and superstitious about our boats, I guess. However, your delivering one of the miscreants—and I firmly believe Burton is a miscreant—back to the very boat which carried his victims to their doom, somehow lessens the stigma. Now, I've made quite a speech, but you understand?"

"Yes, sir—I'd feel that way, too."

"I'm sure you would. Now, boy—talk freely. We are your friends as well as Captain Whipple's. Maybe at last, we are about to see some justice done on the Mississippi River. . . . A scourge by the name of Samuel Burton is in high danger of being removed!"

20

THE SHOW GOES ON!

Within the hour Joe was summoned to Captain Harris' cabin aboard the *Doctor Franklin Number Two*. He came, stumbling up the stairs, his face blanched a peculiar white, and he gave an audible sigh of relief as he caught sight of Rush.

"The animals are all hollerin'—an' Mr. Burton's hollerin', too!"

"I'll be going down soon," replied Rush as he rose and stood beside Joe. "Captain Harris and Pilot Hanks want to see you for a few minutes. They're our friends, Joe. They don't like Mr. Burton very well—"

THE SHOW GOES ON!

"We don't like him at all," interrupted Captain Harris with some vigor. "Come, sit down, Joe. The boy's right—you're with friends and feel free to talk. We'll help you all we can. Have you lived on the river all your life?"

"Off'n on," and Joe sank his lean frame into a chair. "But I like the shipyard best. In Cincinnati." Joe gave a loud gulp of embarrassment and stared at his feet.

"Was the big boss named Robinson?"

"Yes, sir—yes, sir—that's the one."

"Humph, I know him well. I understand that you've been working for Sam Burton for quite a while." There was a look of compassion on Captain Harris' face as he noted Joe's bruised jaw.

"Too long, I reckon. I ain't drawed a free breath since I knowed 'im."

"I imagine once Burton gets his claws on a man, it's hard to get away," offered the pilot.

"That's it, sir. He kinder saps you dry one way or 'nother. I didn't dast to try boltin' til' the boy," and Joe nodded his head at Rush, "talked to me."

"And now, Joe, I want to ask you a pretty important question." Captain Harris leaned forward and looked at Joe earnestly. "As long as you've decided to break from Burton and go along with the law, you must help us all you can. And we'll protect you. Think back a moment before you try to answer this question. Did you ever happen to hear Mr. Burton speak of Rollingstone City?"

For a long moment Joe's dark eyes showed his bewilderment and effort to remember. And then he finally shook his head and gulped again in his nervousness.

"No, sir. . . . 'Course I heard of the Rollin'stone

swindle two years ago. But Mr. Burton, he never said nothin'. He came an' went a lot those days an' there's a good many thing I don't know about."

"But he never liked to hear you say 'Rolling stones gather no moss,' Joe," encouraged Rush. "I thought that maybe the words 'Rolling stones' bothered him—"

"Mebbe," and Joe looked up, a little surprised. "I never thought of that. Seems like he hated that sayin'—started in two year ago—"

"He didn't mind your quoting it before then?"

"Naw—but I'm wonderin'—" began Joe, scratching his head thoughtfully.

"What?" asked Pilot Hanks intently, and he edged his chair nearer. "Keep thinking, Joe."

"One day I was alone in Mr. Burton's office an' I see some pitchers on the desk."

"Pitchers?" asked Captain Harris, perplexed.

"Yes, sir—you know, the kind you hang on the wall. Well, I was waitin' for him so I looked at 'em. Mr. Burton come in an' put 'em in a drawer quick-like an' he tole me if I ever looked at things on his desk again, he'd whale me. They was pitchers of buildin's an' streets. Then I see them same pitchers on some posters he sent to New York and they was marked 'Rollin'stone.' I jest happened to think of it—"

"Humph," and Captain Harris nodded at Pilot Hanks, "we're getting warmer. If we could get hold of some of those old prints in Burton's possession, we'd have some proof of his guilt. Where does he keep letters and papers like that, Joe? In a safe?"

"Yes, sir," answered Joe with a faint chuckle. "But you'd never guess where."

"Will you tell us?" asked Pilot Hanks.

"Sure, I ain't got nothin' to lose," and Joe rubbed his sore jaw ruefully. "Mr. Burton's got an ol' boiler on the *Elsie* that ain't workin'. The door's rusted together—he ain't looked inside for some time. There's a safe in there an' it's plumb full of papers an' stuff. I'm bettin' he ain't throwed out a paper—he saves everythin' like that."

"Good! You won't be sorry, Joe, for helping us. Does anybody else know about that safe?" asked Captain Harris.

"Naw—folks jest think it's an ol' boiler. An' even if they did know, everybody's skeered of Mr. Burton an' wouldn't dast open that safe even if they could."

"If we can prove that Sam Burton was involved in the Rollingstone racket, we'll be free of him for a long time." Captain Harris clenched both fists. "For a long time," he repeated. "Now just one more question—you know that he hated Captain Whipple?"

"Yes, sir—I heerd plenty."

"What, for instance—"

"Well, he said Cap'n Whipple owed him money—a lot of money."

"Same old racket," muttered Pilot Hanks.

"An' the only way he could get paid was to grab the Circus Boat. He said the el'phant was worth somethin' an' he might start a Circus Boat himself some time."

"How do you think the Circus Boat got separated from the Whipple towboat? Do you know anything about that, Joe?" pursued Captain Harris.

A peculiar expression crept over Joe's face and he lowered his eyes to his feet again. It was a minute before he spoke and his voice was so low that it was difficult to hear.

"Sure, I've got an idea. . . . You see," and he looked appealingly at the two men and Rush, "I had somethin' to do with it—"

"You had to obey Burton's orders of course," encouraged Pilot Hanks.

"Yes, sir. Me an' a fellar named Pete—we cut the lines an' hawser. I didn't know the boy then—or I wouldn't ha' done it. Mr. Burton had a mean way of makin' you do things. If you did somethin' onc't he'd hold it over your head an' threaten to tell. After a while you got in so deep, you couldn't get out. I wanter go back to the shipyard," and Joe began to twist his hands. "I don't want no more of Mr. Burton. I don't want to see him again, long's I live—"

"That's the way we feel, too," Pilot Hanks agreed. "And now, Captain Harris, I've another idea. I'm due in Springfield next week to see Abe. Why don't I take Joe with me and let him tell his story? His evidence is very important and he'll need a lawyer to protect him—"

"Splendid," replied Captain Harris with enthusiasm. "There's no better lawyer in the whole United States than Abe Lincoln. Nor a more honest one. I'd place my life in his hands any day. It's a great idea, Steve."

A few hours later Samuel Burton was removed from the zoo on the Circus Boat and locked securely in a cabin on the *Doctor Franklin Number Two*. In the minds of all who saw him, Burton was a very unhappy and worried man.

THE SHOW GOES ON!

Captain Harris listened courteously enough to his protests of innocence but was firm in his orders that Burton remain a prisoner until the law proved he was not guilty. And while Shal stood guard over the zoo and two burly roustabouts from the *Doctor Franklin* resisted all intruders, Rush and Joe enjoyed a full-course dinner at a small separate table in the elaborate dining room of the packet. Dazzled by the array of food, neither Rush nor Joe knew where to begin and when to finish. Golden fried chicken, thick pink slices of roast beef, fresh vegetables, custards, jellies, pies, puddings, and ice cream, with smiling waiters in white coats ready to replenish a plate or sauce dish the moment it was empty!

"I never et like this before," whispered Joe between swallows. "Sometimes we got leavin's from the boats at the shipyards but not like this—"

"Joe!" and Joe's reminiscences were interrupted by a sharp exclamation from Rush, "I just saw a waiter come through the door with a lot of fruit. And on the top were bananas! Ask for fruit, Joe—ask for fruit! We'll each take a banana to Lily. I just can't believe my eyes! I never ate one myself but I've seen pictures—"

"Sure, sure," nodded Joe, somewhat startled by Rush's excitement, "we'll take her some bananas. I wonder now, if she'll stop long enough from tryin' that bonnet on to eat!"

A short time later, with the sun shining brightly and the band playing, the gold and white *Doctor Franklin Number Two* steamed her way up the Mississippi River pulling the boxlike Circus Boat behind her. Whistles of passing boats tooted in recognition and passengers leaned over rails to watch.

"Mebbe they think the *Doctor Franklin's* gone into the Circus business!" Joe grinned happily from a forward window where he and Rush stood together. "Look at that paddle wheel—ain't she purty?"

The churn of the big wheel of the packet ahead, the splash of white water, and the steady pound of engines gave Rush a surge of happiness and exhilaration every time he looked out. There was nothing to fear or dread on the Big River now and in a few hours they would be meeting Captain Whipple at Cassville, for word had come that the *Flora Belle* was tied there for repairs. Never had the river looked so beautiful and the water singing beneath the floor at his feet held a gurgling sound of joy. Every animal had been fed. Lily had grasped her piece of banana with both hands and devoured it with strange little sighs of contentment, showing she had eaten such fruit before, and Joe had fed Shal bits of roast beef from his pocket, his face a study as the dog licked the palm of his hand. If only he could be certain that all this happiness could last!

According to the calendar on the back of the feed-room door, it was exactly two weeks ago to the day that Rush had entered Captain Whipple's employ. Although Captain Harris and Pilot Hanks had complimented him on his efforts to preserve the Circus Boat, how was Captain Whipple feeling about the whole affair? And what had happened in his absence? Were he and the Circus Boat given up as lost, even though they were found again, would he be held in utter disgrace, with the pilot house gone and a hole in the boat's side? And how did Bertie feel now about riding Tom—had he experienced a change of heart? Even now

perhaps Bertie had not told Captain Whipple of how much
he, Rush, longed to head the parade. Never could he forget
that morning outside of Lansing as he rode Tom with Shal
leading the way, her white head up, her plumed tail waving.
In spite of all he had suffered, would he be dismissed from
the Circus Boat as incompetent—.

"Gosh-a-mighty!" exclaimed Joe suddenly, "look over
there—clos't to shore! It's the *Elsie*, boy, goin' downriver
to fetch Mr. Burton from the island! See! There's Simp
hisself out on the bow windin' rope. . . . Lor', what'll
Simp say when he finds the camp empty an' Mr. Burton
gone? Look! He's turnin' an' starin' at the Circus Boat. Oh,
Lor', he knows somethin's diffrunt now. Honest, I ain't had
such a good time in all my life! He can't believe his eyes
an' he's callin' Pete to come!"

"And you're sure he doesn't know about the papers and
things in the safe—"

"Naw, naw, Simp don't know a thing. He only came to
work a year ago. Nobody knows but me. If Simp knew Mr.
Burton was locked up in the *Doctor Franklin*, he'd bust a
trace an' throw ten fits! Oh me, Oh my! I wish't we warn't
goin' so fast—I'd like to yell—" and Joe fairly danced in
his excitement.

"We got away just about in time, Joe," said Rush
soberly. "I hate to think of what would have happened to
us if Simp found Mr. Burton in the cage. The fog did us a
good turn after all. We wouldn't have bumped into Captain
Harris and Pilot Hanks."

"That's right," agreed Joe, nodding his head vigorously.
"An' to think I'm goin' to take a trip with Pilot Hanks!

Why, boy, he's famous on the river—a lightnin' pilot. You know I feel kinder important, havin' a lawyer an' everythin'."

"From what Captain Harris said, I guess Mr. Lincoln is even more important than Pilot Hanks. They're cousins, you know," and Rush smiled at the look of awe on Joe's face.

"If I can get my head to workin', mebbe I can remember more to tell 'im. You know, I reckon Mr. Burton'll be awful glad to leave the *Doctor Franklin*. All them dead folks must be hantin' 'im by now. Wonder if he got a dinner good as ours. You know, boy, I'm sorry 'bout somethin' that happened—"

"What, Joe?"

"Well, you was hungry that first night in the ol' pilot house. Your mouth was waterin' when I cooked the bacon an' I didn't give you none. I could-a slipped you a piece. Livin' with Mr. Burton was makin' me mean—like him."

"I guess we're quits, Joe. You took a bad beating because I threw out the bullets. Don't worry. How's your jaw?"

"Clean forgot it!" exclaimed Joe and he felt of his face. "It's almost well! Seems like what's good for el'phants is good for me. Look at that crittur now. Happy as a clam, daubin' up his back with dirt an' hay. He's a queer 'un. All of 'em seem like children when you get to know 'em."

In some way, grapevine fashion, word must have reached Captain Whipple that his Circus Boat was safe and about to join him at Cassville. As the Circus Boat, towed by the *Doctor Franklin Number Two*, rounded the bend and hove in sight of Cassville, Rush could see several boats lying at the levee but the gayest and brightest among them was the red *Flora Belle,* aflutter with ribbons and flags. And as the packet and Circus Boat drew closer, whistles high and low blew long blasts and a group of people gathered on the wharf waved and cheered.

"Lor', boy, they seem right glad to see you back!" exclaimed Joe, not a little impressed. "An' just wait til' they know about the prize package you're bringin' home in the *Doctor Franklin!"*

Rush, unable to reply, only stared over Joe's shoulder. All doubt and fear of having failed was now lifted from him like a cloak as he gradually recognized familiar figures and heard their voices. There was Madame Whipple in a window of the texas, her white curls shining in the sun as she leaned upon the Captain's arm. And there was Cy getting ready to cross the plank to the levee. Out on the bow stood Effie in her best dress and close beside her was Bertie. All were smiling and talking while Mr. Baker paced back and forth across the deck in true theatrical style. There were other people whom Rush scarcely knew but all appeared happy—jubilant—ready to welcome him back! And suddenly there rose a general laugh of released emotion as Shal appeared in one of the upper windows of the Circus Boat and barked joyously.

"Good girl, Shal!" Cy's voice came ringing over the water.

The first to come aboard the Circus Boat was Madame Whipple, like a small winged bird, holding out her arms to Rush.

"I knew you'd do it!" she whispered as she kissed him on both cheeks. "I knew it!"

"Well," boomed Captain Whipple's voice close by, and

then a big hand gripped his shoulder. "I'm proud of you, my boy. You didn't desert the ship! I see that all of the animals are here—Bless you, boy. Cy, take over for me now. Dan Harris wants to see me on the *Doctor Franklin*. Something very urgent, he says. I'll be back soon—"

And while Cy threw an arm around Rush and the others clustered about, there was a loud noise from Tom, who thumped the end of his trunk on the floor of his cage in a most vigorous manner.

"Same old Tom," laughed Cy. "Wants the center of the stage!"

"Joe!" exclaimed Rush suddenly. "Where's Joe—has anyone seen Joe?"

"There's someone in the feed room," replied Ellie, looking very pretty as she stood beside her leading man, Leslie Wood. "He looked as though he was getting ready to climb into one of those big grain boxes. Is that Joe?"

"That's Joe!" yelled Rush as he ran to pull forward the bashful Joe. "We wouldn't be here now but for Joe. He steered us from the island to the river," Rush patted Joe's arm in his enthusiasm. "He knows all about shipyards—boats—"

"But where'd you find him?" asked Cy, who suddenly approached with Lily and placed her in Madame Whipple's arms.

"He was one of Mr. Burton's men," replied Rush to his mystified listeners. "But he's our friend now. I guess Captain Harris is telling Captain Whipple all about it now. Joe, these are the people I've told you about—we all live together—just like home—"

"Lily! Lily!" exclaimed Madame Whipple, "your hat's

on backwards! And I smell bananas—you've been eating a banana, Lily!"

"We missed you a lot," and Bertie clutched Rush's hand in a tight squeeze. "And there's news—big news—when I can see you alone!"

"Of course we knew Sam Burton must be back of it all," said Captain Whipple, reaching up to smooth Blackie, perched on his shoulder. Supper was finished and Rush, Shal, Joe, Cy, and Captain Whipple were gathered together in the privacy of the texas. "We found the cut lines and hawser and knew it wasn't an accident. No one, except my mother, thought you'd weather the gale, Rush. And it got so we didn't dare express a single doubt in front of her. She said you'd come back with every animal, safe and sound, and that I shouldn't cancel the big-top I ordered a month ago. She's my mother—God bless her—so I did everything she asked. I had to. So the show goes on!"

"Did Captain Harris speak of Joe's going to work at the shipyard?" asked Rush anxiously.

"Yes, he did. It seems that he knows Mr. Robinson well and will make arrangements as soon as Joe returns from Springfield. And Joe, he has every confidence that Mr. Lincoln will clear you of your difficulties and has sent word to authorities south of here to arrest Simp on the towboat *Elsie*. The law will open the safe."

"Yes, sir," uttered Joe, unable to say more.

"As you all know, Sam Burton is in the Cassville calaboose. He will stand trial later. There has been more and more evidence coming in, confirming his guilt in the Rollingstone matter, and he has practically confessed. The hours spent in a zoo cage must have broken some of his spirit. Meanwhile, Rush, your timberlands are safe. Captain Harris repeated your story to me and I know most of the picture. And now, what are your plans?"

"Why, I haven't any plans, Captain Whipple. I was hoping to stay aboard the Circus Boat. Of course my time is up—the two weeks probation are finished. . . . You might not want me after all. . . . The Circus Boat is damaged, the pilot house gone—"

"Not want you! Of course we want you! Never mind the damages—you brought the boat and animals through a terrific storm—brought them back to me. Not only that but Captain Harris and I both believe you have rendered the whole Mississippi Valley a service in apprehending Sam Burton. And now that Sam Burton is out of our way, I supposed you would return to your home in Eau Claire. Why, we had forgotten all about the probation, hadn't we, Cy?"

"As far as I was concerned, there never was any," and Cy's dark eyes smiled at Rush.

"And now that you will stay, we'd better decide some other matters. Have you talked with Bertie since your return?"

"No, sir. All he said was that he had good news for me."

"Bertie and I had a long talk three days ago. It seems that he and Tiny Tom don't get along very well together. Tom stands him on his head and pulls off his buttons." Captain Whipple's mouth twitched at the corners. "Bertie thinks you are the one to ride Tom and head the parade. What do you think?"

"I'd like it a lot. . . . I'd like it very much . . . but the handbills—"

"I never did get around to having those handbills printed. So if you want the job, it's all right with me. Now where does Shal fit in?"

"She'll be in the tableau. But the other morning when we trained outside of Lansing, she just naturally marched ahead of Tom, all by herself. It would take very little training to teach her that it's her place—"

"No more said. Tom, you, and Shal head the parade. What about school during the winter, Rush? If you work summers, you should study winters—"

"Yes, sir. I'd go to school in Galena."

"Why Galena?"

"My schoolteacher Mr. Slocum will be teaching there from now on. And I made some friends on a flatboat coming down the Chippewa. They might let Delos and me live with them. Their name is Tolman and old Gramp Tolman knew my grandfather. But of course if Delos won't come, I'll go back to Eau Claire."

"Who's Delos? The guide?"

"Yes, sir. I lived with him after my father died."

"Perhaps between us all, we can persuade him to come. Of course, Captain Harris told me that Sam Burton was your stepuncle. If you like, we shall never mention him again as your uncle. You can forget the whole relationship. And you must go to college, Rush. Sell some of your timber if you have to—but go to college."

"Yes, sir."

"You like the river?"

"Better than any place I have ever known, sir."

And to hide the tears of joy in his eyes, Rush leaned forward, wound his arm about Shal's neck, and hid his face in her deep ruff. No one spoke . . . and the sound of the Great River outside filled the little room.

The zoo was cool, quiet, and dim. Through the open window Rush could still see the waning light of a torch basket as it flickered at the end of the levee in the night wind. All were asleep but Shal, who took her usual post by the door and Tiny Tom, who turned slowly as Rush opened his cage.

"Tom—" and Rush could hardly keep the tremble out of his voice, "I want to tell you something—"

This time Tom did not search about for an apple but remained very still, listening—as Rush leaned against him.

"We start training in the morning," Rush continued. "There's a big field nearby and we'll practice marching. Captain Whipple says I am to ride you from now on. We three are to lead the parade, Tom—you, Shal and I—up and down the streets of all the towns along the Mississippi!" And the last words came out breathlessly.

Tom stirred. . . . Gently, very gently, the small elephant wrapped his trunk about Rush's waist, lifted him from the floor with a soft purring sound, and set him down again.